THE OTHER SIDE

AJ WYNN

Also by AJ Wynn

Willowbrooke

First paperback edition 2024

Cover designed by: Rachel McEwan Designs

Edited by: Sam Willow

Proofread by: EF Watson

Campus map design by: Shepengul

Author illustration by: Bugdrawstuff

Ebook ISBN: 979-8-9895960-2-7

Paperback ISBN: 979-8-9895960-3-4

www.AJWynn.com

For Caitlin.

I never knew what it was like to have a sister until I met you. The kindness, support, and understanding you have shown me in the fifteen plus years we've known each other has changed my life.

Love you. ❤

TRIGGER WARNINGS

This novel contains mentions of grooming and an off-page suicide.

If these are sensitive topics for you, please take care and prioritize your mental health and well-being while reading.

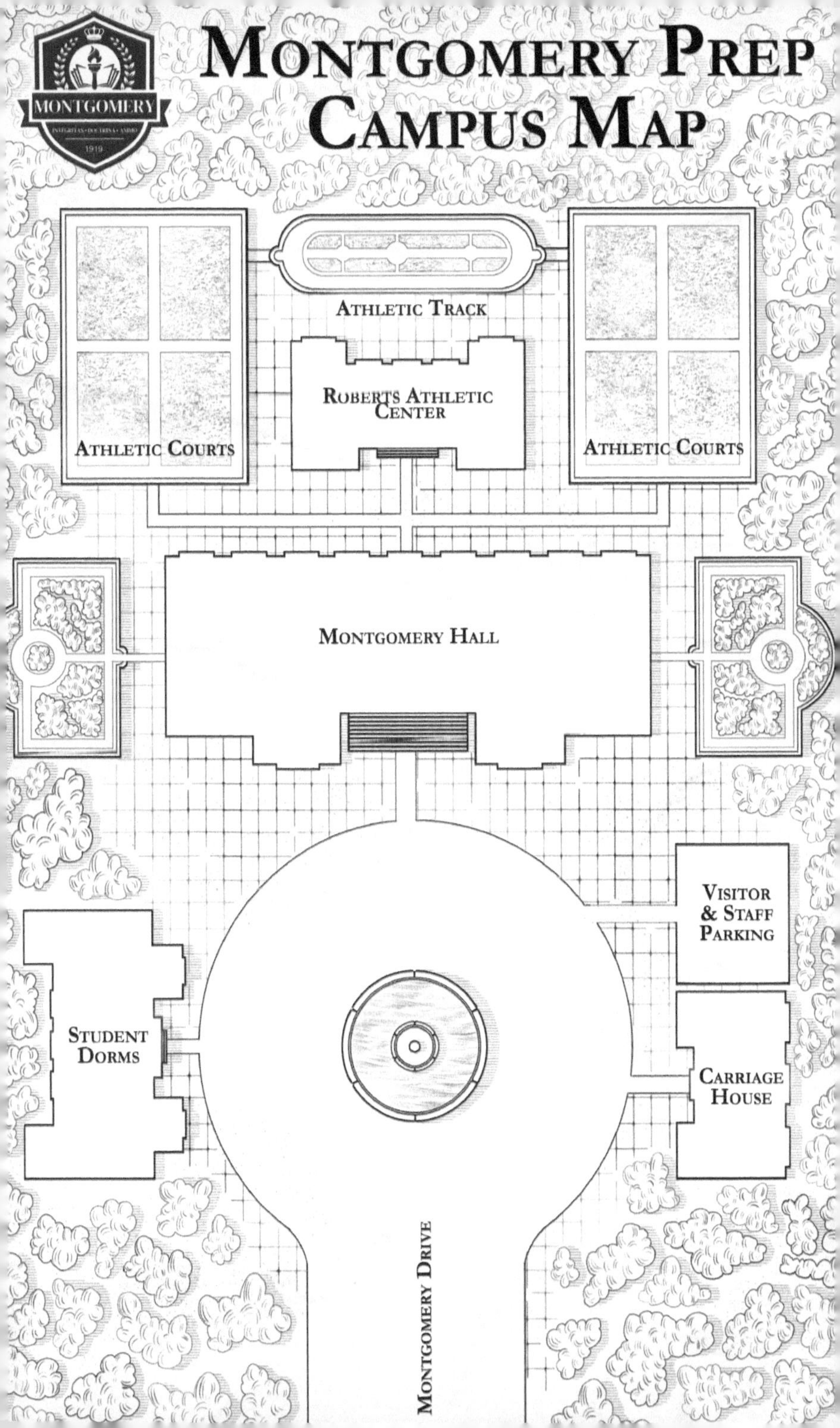
Montgomery Prep
Campus Map
MONTGOMERY
1919
Athletic Track
Roberts Athletic Center
Athletic Courts
Athletic Courts
Montgomery Hall
Visitor & Staff Parking
Student Dorms
Carriage House
Montgomery Drive

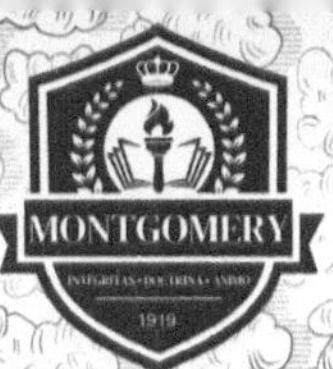

THE OTHER SIDE

AJ WYNN

PROLOGUE

"What are the police doing here?" I tried not to look too obvious as I stared down the hall toward the headmaster's office where one officer was casually leaning against the doorframe. It wasn't every day...or any day really, that the police came all the way out to Montgomery Prep.

"Just routine procedure." Jolene didn't even bother to glance up from her data entry. Blonde frizzy hair pulled into a bun at the top of her head, and her lime green chunky sweater made her cherubic cheeks look pinker in contrast.

I set down the two containers of food, with our lunch, on her desk, hazarding another curious glance at the officer. I could hear murmuring coming from Headmaster Winston's office, indicating another officer was inside. But whatever they were discussing didn't seem important enough for any of them to have decided to close the door and conduct the conversation in private.

"What routine procedure?" I questioned, my gaze still on the officer, who was oblivious to my attention.

"When students run off." She continued to type away on the keyboard.

"Run off?" I turned my wide eyes to Jolene. "Who ran off?"

Finally, she glanced up at me, sighing, perhaps annoyed with my questioning. I knew she was inundated with work at the end of the school year, trying to get grades updated, and helping students submit last-minute transcripts to finalize their college admissions. "I think his name was Daniel Grant."

I blanched. If he was who I was thinking of, that wasn't possible.

"You mean Daniel Graham, the junior, on scholarship?" I tried to clarify.

Jolene nodded, eyes fixed on the spreadsheet in front of her.

"There must be a mistake. He wouldn't run away."

"Well, that's what the police and headmaster said." Jolene shrugged, her fingers continuing to glide across her keyboard.

"But he's—" I paused. It didn't make any sense. "He wouldn't have. He just took my Classics final yesterday."

To be fair, I didn't know him that well. I didn't know any of my students very well. They liked it that way, and so did the school. But he was a good kid and smart as a whip. He knew how lucky he was to be at Montgomery Prep and took advantage as much as he could to set himself up for what would come next.

I could sense the same drive in Daniel as I saw in myself. He came from nothing and would do anything to find his own path to success, despite a low-income upbringing. I couldn't see any reason he'd leave without telling a single person, and certainly not two days before the semester ended.

"There must be a mistake," I whispered, repeating myself.

The voices grew louder as the headmaster escorted both police officers back into the lobby of the administration offices. "Sorry to make you drive all the way out," Winston apologized half-heartedly.

"It's no bother." The one who had been in the office, taller than the other, waved him off.

I felt my pulse spike.

I had to say something.

They were wrong.

But I was nervous to speak up in front of the headmaster. So instead, I waited until he shook both their hands and retreated into his office.

Following the officers up the stairs, I called out to them just before they made it back into the main entrance hall, where there were likely students milling about. "Excuse me."

The officers spun around.

"Did I hear you're investigating a missing student?" I could feel my cheeks burning.

"A *runaway*—not missing," the officer who had listened from the doorway replied.

"Daniel Graham?" I questioned, hoping they wouldn't ask me how I knew. But then again, at a school as small as Montgomery, nothing stayed secret for long.

The taller officer narrowed his gaze on me.

"He's in one of my classes," I added hastily, hoping that would suffice for how I'd known, and tell them that I was familiar with Daniel. "He wouldn't have run away. He's very bright. If he's really gone, then he's missing. Should I file a missing person report? He's very responsible. He would have told someone he was leaving."

"No need to file anything," the shorter officer replied. "We'll handle the investigation from here."

"He didn't run away," I repeated more firmly, sensing they disagreed. He didn't have the money, resources, or family clout that the rest of the students at the school had. If they considered him a runaway, I was certain nobody would look for him.

"Thank you, Miss..."

"Violet Price," I told them. "I teach history. I'll be staying on campus over the summer. I can answer any questions you have about him. But I'm telling you, he didn't run away."

The taller officer gave me a dismissive smile that came off as more of a sneer than I assumed he had intended. "Thank you, Miss Price. We'll let you know if we need anything."

Without another word, they both continued up the stairs.

I knew I wouldn't be hearing from them.

And I never did.

1

ANTICIPATORY ANXIETY

In twenty-four hours, Montgomery Prep would be swarming with students.

In twenty-four hours, my summer break would be over.

While staunchly an anti-morning person, the last day of summer was perhaps a rare occasion where those precious extra moments of sleep weren't worth it. I didn't want to waste a moment of my last day on campus with the waning solitude of summer.

Other than a few support staff, I was the only faculty member who had chosen to stay at Montgomery Prep during the school break.

When I had made the request to Headmaster Winston, in the spring, his wooly grey eyebrows had furrowed, as if he couldn't imagine what I would do for three months all by myself.

What he should have been asking was "What wouldn't I do?"

Like a lazy college student, I slept in most days and took hikes in the vast forest surrounding the picturesque, yet isolated, prestigious preparatory school, nestled in the Maine countryside.

The only thing that had disrupted what would have been a perfect summer was a shadow cast by the as-yet unsolved disappearance of Daniel Graham.

Bitterly I thought the school board and donors would be so proud of the headmaster for how he had been able to completely sweep a missing student under the rug.

I'd tried following up with the police multiple times, only to be told upon my last visit that if I brought it up again, they would start investigating me. The smug look on the officer's face as I'd paled at the threat still made my chest tight with anger.

They wanted everyone to forget he even existed.

But I wasn't everyone else.

I was Violet Price.

Like a dog without a bone, or perhaps a cat without someone to terrorize, I was usually too curious for my own good. It had been difficult to rein in my blunt attitude and lack of filter during my first year at Montgomery. But the challenging effort had been worth it.

Still firmly believing that Daniel was missing, not a runaway, I couldn't accept that he'd abandon everything he had worked so hard for on the precipice of his senior year. With my arguments falling on deaf ears and having no family to speak of, other than some absentee guardian, there was no one looking for him.

There was no one to fight for him.

But I was only one person; there was only so much I could do to look for him on my own. And as both the newest teacher and the youngest by over a decade, at Montgomery Prep, nobody would listen to me. They had been well trained to keep their heads down, pander to the board and donors, and ignore any suspicious activity. And without any help, I'd been spinning my wheels since the police refused to talk to me about the case and wasn't sure what more I could do to try and figure out what had happened to him.

Montgomery was an elite institution, and the families who paid handsomely for their children to attend didn't want to deal with a scandal. Neither did the board or the headmaster. If I wanted to keep my job, still tenuous after the first year, I would have been wise to keep my head down too.

But I knew in my gut I wasn't done. I just wasn't sure what my next move was…yet.

Slipping on some comfortable workout pants, a well-worn tee, and sneakers, I took a moment to relish the soft, stretchy fabric that would soon make way for my simple but boring teaching uniform of slacks and button-ups. Grabbing my coffee mug and a granola bar, I threw a blanket over my shoulder on my way out the door, almost forgetting my tattered and dog-eared copy of *The Odyssey*.

Built by William Montgomery in the eighteenth century, what was once Montgomery House became Montgomery Prep sometime during the Second World War. The campus was comprised of three main buildings that surrounded a grand courtyard, complete with a fountain.

From stone and mortar, the main school building looked like a mix between a foreboding castle and a sprawling manor home that belonged in the English countryside, rather than the backwoods of New England.

While decades of renovations had provided the addition of modern convenience and structural adaptations that allowed for the conversion to a school, the main building provided dreary classrooms, dungeon-like administration offices in the basement, and a grand dining hall with neat rows of long tables.

A generously sized guesthouse for Montgomery's extended family had been converted into student dorms, and the carriage house was where half the faculty, including myself, resided. All in all, there were close to four hundred students and thirty or so faculty, not including the additional facility staff and student monitors.

Hiking out across the vast lawn that spanned behind Montgomery, I spread my blanket out just at the edge of the forest, where the trees would provide enough shade to keep me from sitting in the heat and humidity that so often lay like a heavy blanket over late August days.

I immersed myself for a few hours in the Homeric epic, having long ago lost track of how many times I'd re-read the classic. But I still managed to find something new, notice a previously missed line, or make note of some new compelling piece every time I revisited it.

The sun's warmth having set in, I closed my eyes, thinking of the day when my mountain of student loans would be paid off and I could save up for a trip to Greece and walk through the streets where ancient history had been born.

I was lucky to have gotten a job at Montgomery, and it had been an accident, really. The history teacher I replaced had suffered a heart attack in front of his class two months into the fall semester last year. The school had scrambled to find a replacement so far into the term.

My master's advisor was a Montgomery alumna, and I was her fourth call, as the first three already had teaching jobs or were busy with their own academic research projects. At the time, I'd been working retail to stay afloat and crashing on an acquaintance's couch while I desperately looked for a decent position where I could apply my degrees. The stress of counting pennies and knowing I was days away from requesting a temporary forbearance on my loans, after a series of unfortunate events that I'd prefer to forget, was heavy and overwhelming.

When my old advisor reached out, I was on the verge of admitting defeat and dragging my sorry ass back home to Michigan to regroup. I didn't have much to go back to. While I loved my mother, our relationship was delicate, and when I first moved away, it had broken her heart. I didn't want to put her through that again because Michigan would only ever be a pit stop for me, on the way to somewhere else...anywhere else, really.

And anywhere else just happened to be Montgomery Prep.

2

JOLENE'S RETURN

I stirred on the blanket, eyes fluttering open as I realized just how warm I'd become, a sheen of sweat covering most of my skin.

"Ahh fuck," I cursed. Not only had I slept the morning away, but I had a feeling I'd have a sunburn manifesting by the end of the day. I should have known better than to not bring sunscreen with me. Tanning my pale ass skin had never been possible, despite my best efforts.

Gathering up my things, I marched back across the lawn, noting the handful of cars in the side parking lot. I hadn't realized I had been *that* tired. Even the sounds of some of the administrative staff arriving hadn't roused me from my midday nap.

Guess I should have slept in anyway.

I smiled as I spotted a bright red VW Bug with cat bumper stickers in the lot. Jolene was back from break!

I hustled over to the carriage house to drop my stuff back in my room, which was a quaint little space. All one large room, with a kitchenette to the right of the door, and the bathroom in the far right corner. There was a generous fireplace, which I put to good use, on the left-hand side of the room, and I had arranged my bed to sit between the fireplace and a lovely window seat built into the bay window.

Setting my things down, I ticked off my to-do list in my head. I needed to iron all my shirts and slacks, tidy the kitchen, and I still had to finalize my syllabus and get prints at the admin office the next day, but I was too excited to reconnect with one of the few people who had welcomed me to Montgomery.

Jolene had argued that I could just reuse the same curriculum the last history teacher had used for decades, but I disagreed. As the youngest faculty member Montgomery had ever employed (and probably the poorest), I had something to prove.

The other faculty looked at me with pity, thinking me naive and green, but although that may have been true, it didn't mean that I wanted to ascribe to their same level of work ethic. This job mattered to me more than they could ever know because they weren't saddled with crippling debt. Most of them had families to go home to and lives they cherished, but I was still trying to figure things out.

You're only twenty-eight, I had to remind myself, *you have plenty of time.*

Swapping my old T-shirt for a Montgomery Prep polo, lest anyone give me shit for dressing too casually, I scurried off to the admin building to greet Jolene before returning to my lesson planning, cringing at the mere thought of the mess of documents needed for the process strewn across the floor of the lounge above my room.

Surprisingly, the chill of the usually dank main building was a welcome relief from the oppressive humidity outside. I braced my hand against the stone wall as I descended the main staircase to the administration offices in the bowels of the castle.

My first year at Montgomery had been kind of miserable. The faculty ostracized me, the students tried to take advantage of my new position at every turn, and I was constantly aware of what I was to them: an outsider.

But Jolene's infectious cheer and unwavering encouragement were some of the reasons I had made it through. The others were the free room and board, and the salary, much heftier than public schools, which allowed me to send money home to my mom to help with the mortgage and make more aggressive student loan payments.

"Jolene?" I called out when I reached the bottom of the steps, surprised to find the offices mostly empty.

I shivered at the thought of being alone down there, as the lower level had always given off an ominous vibe reminiscent of something out of a horror movie. Curiously, the offices didn't bother me as much during the summer, perhaps because of the sunny atmosphere outside or the longer, brighter days, but even so, I didn't want to linger.

Jolene Reynolds was Headmaster Winston's executive assistant and school receptionist. In her forties and a little more than kooky, she commuted to Montgomery because they didn't allow animals on campus.

I wasn't sure what Jolene's current cat count was, but she fostered occasionally, so the number was always fluctuating.

While she was the butt of many spinster jokes on campus—she handmade seasonal and themed sweaters for herself, after all—Jolene was very sweet, just a bit of an odd duck.

"Jolene?" I called again.

Her head popped out of the headmaster's office down the hall. A smile brightened her face as she realized it was me calling for her.

"Violet!" she cheered as she barreled down the dim hallway toward me. The force of her almost knocked me back. "I missed you so much!"

"Me too." I grinned, returning the embrace.

"I wasn't sure if you were around today; you missed lunch." She righted the hot pink, hand-knit cardigan around her shoulders. A felt cat on one side of the sweater was just out of reach of the ball of yarn on the other.

"I fell asleep reading on the lawn." I pouted, still a bit put out by the lost time.

"I've got so much to tell you!" She paused, taking a look around to make sure we were alone before continuing. "Did you hear that Mr. Jennings decided to suddenly retire!?"

"Really?" I leaned against the front reception desk. "I assumed he'd die here, like my predecessor." The thought was morbid, but so many of the school's teachers were absolutely ancient and had no plans of going anywhere, so it wouldn't have been a long shot.

Jennings was one of two English teachers employed at Montgomery, quite well tenured, and a good friend to Headmaster Winston. "Do you know why?" I wondered aloud.

"Nope!" Jolene's eyes lit up with delight at the gossip. She was such a wealth of information, but I was the only one privileged enough to be privy to most of it. "The headmaster called me over break to help him with the retirement paperwork. He was pissed!"

"But they got a replacement?"

"Yep, I processed the hiring paperwork at the same time, so I'm sure it was someone the headmaster knows. Harper, I think, was his name," Jolene offered.

"Well at least I won't be the newest teacher anymore." I smiled at the thought of a little heat being taken off me. But if the new English teacher was connected to the headmaster, it wouldn't be much of a reprieve. Still I was adamant about making this year better than my first, working on my confidence with both students and colleagues, and trying to work through the anxiety of job insecurity.

"Did the headmaster mention anything about Daniel Graham?" I asked, too curious not to.

"Who?" Jolene asked, her nose buried in a stack of papers she was collating for the welcome events in the coming week.

"The student who went missing at the end of the school year." I was surprised she didn't remember.

"I thought he ran away?" She looked up at me, confusion etched on her face.

"Well, that's what the police said, but he had too much to lose—his scholarship, running the student newspaper, his senior year." I could have gone on, but I refrained.

Jolene gave me a pitying glance. "Sometimes it's the brightest stars that burn out the quickest, Violet. Maybe he was under too much pressure. I've seen it before," she offered sympathetically.

Sure she had been working at the school for almost twenty years, so I believed her about having seen similar things happen before, but she hadn't taught Daniel; she hadn't seen the light and determination in his eyes.

And maybe I was reaching, having seen something of myself in Daniel. If I had been given the opportunity to attend a place like Montgomery, I would have been just as steadfast in my development, itching to milk every drop of advantage out of the stuffy and antiquated institution.

Am I too close?

"Any chance you'll come grab some drinks with me in town tonight?" Jolene changed the subject. "We need to catch up and enjoy our last moments before the chaos of move-in day."

"I'm not sure." I bit the inside of my cheek. "I'm not a big drinker."

"That's okay," she replied hastily. "Just one—on me. And I'll drive too."

When I hesitated she added, "Please, it's our last night before the campus is overrun with rich brats." Jolene's big round eyes pleaded with me.

Jolene, with her permed bleach-blonde hair, round pink cheeks, and endless supply of homemade, themed sweaters, was impossible to refuse.

So I didn't.

3

AMOROUS INTENTIONS

No matter how hard I tried, I couldn't focus on what Jolene was saying while a hot blonde guy across the bar continued to eye fuck me every time I glanced up, refusing to drop his lascivious gaze from mine.

The dive bar she had chosen was dim and heavy with conversation and laughter. The bartender on my side of the bar flitted back and forth, filling orders and collecting payment, his focus solely on the tasks in front of him. Despite being a random weeknight, the place was full, likely due to a game that was playing on the handful of monitors scattered around the bar. Occasionally an excited or disappointed roar would envelop the space, drawing my admirer's attention from me briefly, before locking back on me once more.

I rarely drank, and the quick buzz and warmth in my cheeks confirmed as much. One of the main reasons I tried not to imbibe was because I tended to become rather amorous with some liquid courage in my system. It had gotten me into trouble in the past, and I had a feeling it might get me into more trouble that night. But would it be the good kind of trouble that ended with me spent and satisfied, or the bad kind with regrets and a hangover?

I had barely taken a sip of my second drink, and was considering what a one-night stand might be like, as I had never been daring enough to try one before. But it had been just long enough since I'd been with anyone, and I'd had just enough to drink that the thought of going home with a stranger, to feel desired, even for a few minutes, felt like it might not be so bad.

I hadn't intended to get a second drink, but Jolene was so entertaining, while regaling me with stories from her time in Florida visiting family, that it had felt like the right thing to do.

"Oh no." Jolene frowned, looking down at her cell phone. The bells attached to the cat's collar on her cardigan jingled as she turned to the bartender to get his attention to close her tab.

"Everything okay?" I tore my attention from my admirer.

Jolene chewed on her lip as she re-read the text.

"Kitty emergency?" I guessed.

Her big brown eyes flitted up to mine, guilt laced in her expression.

"You should go," I gave her permission.

"But I'm your ride." She frowned.

I smiled gently, giving her arm a reassuring squeeze. "I'll get a cab back to campus. It's okay. Go take care of your babies," I encouraged her.

I'd have to put the ride on a credit card to afford it while I waited for the first paycheck of the school year, but I knew she'd only be stressed if she stayed. And I was curious to see where things would lead with the stranger across the bar, so maybe it was better this way.

"If you're sure, I'll close out the tab." She nodded to the bartender as she spoke, signaling for the bill.

"Don't worry about it." I waved a hand at her, sneaking a glance at the mystery man across the bar.

His brow was raised in interest as he watched Jolene hop off the stool and sling her purse over her shoulder.

"Lunch tomorrow?" Jolene asked hopefully.

"I'll bring it to your desk, like usual." I reached out, giving her a firm hug, holding my breath so I didn't suffocate on her cloying perfume, before she hurried out of the bar.

It took the handsome stranger all of two seconds to sidle up next to me. "Can I get you another?" He leaned in, his breath heavy with the scent of whatever brown liquor was in his rocks glass. My stomach turned, the fantasy of a one-night stand dying a quick death.

Why is the thought of men always so tempting, but in reality, it's never quite as I had imagined it would be?

"I'm not sure," my voice wavered as my eyes met his, deep choco-late and hooded with lust.

What were the implications of accepting a drink? I'd typically had unpleasant experiences with things that had initially been presented as gifts or tokens of affection from men, only for them to be turned into something that could be used against me later.

"Another round for..." The man peered down at me, expecting my name.

"Violet," I offered instinctually, wincing slightly at the admission.

"Another round for the lovely Violet," he confirmed.

I turned to call after the bartender, "Can I just get water?" I was unsure if he heard me or not.

"I haven't seen you here before; you live close?" The stranger swirled his glass, his eyes still laser-focused on me. His intensity made me uncomfortable.

"I teach at Montgomery Prep." Even the small amount of alcohol turned me into quite the open book, it would seem.

"There you are," a smooth voice called out, dropping a heavy arm around my shoulder.

I looked up in alarm to meet an unfamiliar pair of striking blue-grey eyes, framed by dark hair.

The new stranger flashed me a brilliant smile, while my brow furrowed. As he dropped his mouth to place a soft kiss at my temple, he whispered, "I think he slipped something in your drink when you were trying to get the bartender's attention."

I felt the breath whoosh out of me.

I was immediately overwhelmed with a barrage of emotions all at once. My stomach roiled with the dark and devastating thoughts of what could have happened to me. I'd been taken advantage of before, by more than one man who I'd thought had loved me and who I had trusted with my life, until I hadn't, but this kind of betrayal stung in quite a different way, deep and sharp.

My eyes connected with the newcomer's once more, my throat bobbing as I swallowed the bile at the back of my throat.

"Thanks for keeping my girl company." He clapped a hand on the blonde's shoulder, a little too roughly, wordlessly communicating for him to fuck off.

The blonde's jaw set, as if he was gauging whether or not to argue, but after a moment, his shoulders dropped. His eyes, no longer tempting, but lethal, dropped to my half-full drink, likely confirming the accusation that had been secretly levied against him.

"Sorry." I shrugged, feigning an apologetic smirk at his poor luck.

Without a word, he stormed off, slamming the bar door behind him.

My rescuer released me, reaching over to dump my drink into the grate at the edge of the bar.

"I don't—I don't know how to thank you," I stuttered, still in shock from the close call. "He would have—"

"It's okay." The stranger was sympathetic, ruffling his hand nervously through his hair. "I'm just glad I saw him."

"Can I, umm, get you a drink?" I managed. "I don't even know your name." He was handsome, devastatingly so, but I inwardly winced at the thought. I had just evaded potentially being assaulted and was already entertaining the idea of being attracted to someone else.

Simultaneously I thought, *What is wrong with me?* and *This is why I have a one drink max.*

"I'm good." He held up a bottle of beer, still mostly full.

"Will you sit with me?" I nodded to Jolene's empty stool, my chest still tight with anxiety over the possibility of being drugged by a stranger.

"I don't think he'll come back." The man glanced over his shoulder at the door before sliding onto the barstool.

"Maybe..." I trailed off. I was struck by him. He wore his dark brown hair short, but I could still see a slight wave to it in the dim bar light. He was dressed casually in distressed jeans and a polo shirt, but I couldn't quite get more of a read on him.

"I'm Violet." I stuck my hand out. The situation was so awkward, it was the only thing I could think to do. He had saved me from...god, I needed to stop my mind from wondering about all the awful things that could have transpired.

"Chance." He smiled, returning the handshake.

His skin was soft and warm; his touch had an instant calming effect, so much so that I found myself shaking it for longer than socially acceptable as I got lost in the feel of him. "Sorry." I dropped his hand, feeling my skin heat even more as a full-body blush engulfed me.

My eyes lingered on the lithe muscles of his tanned forearm as he pulled back from the exchange. His shoulders were broad, but his waist tapered, leaving me wondering if perhaps he was an athlete.

His outfit would have me thinking he was a yuppie, but the clientele of the dive bar was decidedly more blue-collar, and most snobby rich guys I knew, and I knew a few, wouldn't have intercepted a spiked drink. They would have watched on, curious to see the event unfolding, perhaps even offering to assist.

There had to be something more to the man before me, who was a growing list of contradictions.

"It's okay," he chuckled, taking a swig of his beer. "Did I overhear that you teach at Montgomery Prep?"

"Yeah." I nodded. "History."

"And how do you like teaching?" Chance leaned his elbow casually against the bar, his attention fully on me and quite overwhelming.

"It's good—I mean, it's not exactly what I thought I'd be doing," I hedged.

He cocked his head. "No? What did you think you'd be doing?"

"Not teaching." I shrugged. "But I have a lot of student loans to pay, so it is what it is."

"How many degrees?" He leaned forward slightly, a curious curve to the corners of his lips.

I could get lost in those lips.

"Three." I took a grateful sip of the water the bartender finally slid over to me.

"Gorgeous and brilliant." Chance smiled. "An excellent combination."

My stomach flipped at the compliment.

"Are you going to tell me what they're in?"

"Classical history, European history, and a masters in ancient history." I took another sip, "Oh, and my teaching certificate."

"What got you into such archaic studies?"

"I probably watched Indiana Jones one too many times as a kid," I replied honestly. "But I can't afford to study or do field work abroad, so I'm here instead."

"If money wasn't an issue, what would you do?"

His ardency continued to crackle under my skin. I was both unnerved and delighted by feeling so drawn to him. I hadn't felt that kind of pull in a very long time...maybe ever, really.

Whatever he asked, I wanted to answer without thinking. "Move to Europe—probably Greece," I clarified. "Write some kind of magnum opus about Euripides or Homer."

"How do you like teaching at Montgomery?" Chance savored a pull from his bottle.

I gave a nervous laugh. "Do you want the professional answer or the real one?"

Chance smirked at me. "I think you know which one, Violet."

The way my name rolled off his tongue was like velvet. I resisted the impulse to shiver.

I shook my head. The magnetic pull toward Chance persisted in its disconcerting splendor, but still I found myself leaning toward him, wetting my lips as I tried not to stare at his.

"It's difficult working there," I finally responded.

"Why?"

"The students are entitled. The faculty are just as elitist. And they cover shit up, which doesn't make for the safest environment. I always feel like I'm one breath away from being discarded." He'd said he wanted the truth.

"What do they cover up?" His tone was more concerned than curious that time.

"A student went missing in May." I probably shouldn't have told him that. "Are you a reporter?" I asked, suddenly fearful.

"No," Chance chuckled, shaking his head. "Your secrets are safe with me." He reached his hand across, giving my knee a reassuring squeeze, the muscles in his forearm flexing with the motion.

And then he let it rest there.

I tried to ignore my heart, hammering in my chest. I didn't think I'd ever wanted to kiss someone so badly in my entire life. He was so handsome and kind, I didn't even care that it was probably only because of the alcohol that the impulse felt so strong.

"What happened to the student?"

"I don't know," I relayed. "He went missing two days before the end of the semester. The police insist he ran away and won't take it seriously."

"Why not?"

"Daniel was a scholarship kid, not like most of the super rich kids who go to Montgomery. They want it to go away, I think. Don't want to spook parents or donors. But I had him in one of my classes, and he wasn't the kind of kid to take off like that." I took another sip of my water, feeling the weight of his disappearance so very heavily in that moment.

Chance was the first person I'd talked to about it who seemed to be taking me seriously, or even cared about it at all. Maybe I should have gone to the media, but I had so much to lose.

"So you knew him?" Chance asked.

"He worked on the school newspaper. It's a small school. Everyone knew him." I shook my head. "He wouldn't have run away. He knew how lucky he was to be there and what kind of opportunities would come out of the alumni network."

"Hmm," Chance hummed.

"And the headmaster, don't get me started. If he didn't have to allow scholarship students in through alumni gifted grants, he'd be happy to keep the doors closed to anyone in a tax bracket under a billion dollars." I snorted.

"Sounds like an asshole."

"And a misogynist," I added.

"Typical," Chance offered. "Are the students really that bad?" he asked after a moment. "They can't exactly control the circumstances into which they were born." Chance winced, realizing how it sounded as it left his mouth.

"But they *can* control how they treat people—that's the difference," I asserted.

"Cheers to that." He lifted his almost empty bottle, draining the last of the beer after clinking it against my almost empty water glass.

"I should probably head back there." Reluctance was laced through the sentiment as I pulled out my phone, opening a rideshare app.

"Of course." He flashed me another brilliant but understanding smile.

I looked down at the app, sighing at what I was seeing. No cars available.

I bit my lip nervously.

Chance glanced down at the screen.

"I can give you a ride to Montgomery," he offered. "I'm heading that way anyway."

"You are? You're sure?" I met his eyes again. "You've already done more than enough for me—I don't want to inconvenience you."

While I would have felt bad if he had to go out of his way for me, I couldn't ignore the warmth flooding my core at the thought of spending more time with him, in confined quarters.

"It's no problem, I promise." He grabbed my hand and led me out of the bar.

4

A KISS GOODNIGHT FOR THE AGES

"Why do you stay at Montgomery if you don't like it?" Chance asked after a bout of companionable silence on the drive back to campus.

"Do you want the professional answer or the real one?" I giggled softly, repeating myself from earlier. The buzz from my second drink had given way to a mixture of drowsiness and deep-seated lust as the darkness enveloped us both, driving alone, in the middle of nowhere.

I couldn't say what it was about him that put me at ease; surely his intervention at the bar was a major factor, but there was a gentleness about him that made me feel safe. It also made me that much more attracted to him.

Chance laughed as he took the exit for Montgomery, off the county highway. "Go on," he goaded me.

I sighed. This wasn't the kind of story you just shared with a stranger. But Chance didn't quite feel like a stranger, despite the truth of the matter. "I was dating someone who preferred to take care of things, so all I had to do was worry about my student loan payments. I was still working." I felt it necessary to add, "But I had a hard time finding a job in my field, and I couldn't contribute much. So when things started going south, I found his dick in someone else and myself out of a place to live, with barely a penny to my name."

Chance pulled in a breath through his teeth.

"I'm not originally from the East Coast and didn't know any-one—"

"Where are you from?" Chance interrupted me.

"Michigan," I offered.

Chance nodded his head in acknowledgement.

"So I started calling around to any contacts I had for a lead on any kind of job that would make me enough to get by. As luck would have it, my master's advisor was a Montgomery alumna, and when she heard I was looking, she called about a sudden vacancy in the history department that they were having trouble filling. I guess they have really high expectations, but like most places, don't want to pay for them." I wondered if he could see me rolling my eyes in the darkness.

"Anyway," I continued, "I fit the bill. Decently educated. But young and a woman, so they can justify underpaying me." I leaned my head against the cold glass window. "But it's not all bad. I get free room and board, and when I'm not teaching, I have plenty of time to myself. Even have a secret cozy little space that's my own."

I glanced over at Chance. A dreamy smile softly settled along his face.

"That does sound nice," he agreed.

"I've spent all this time talking about myself and you've told me nothing about you," I suddenly realized. "What do you do?"

"In between jobs," Chance said. "But I like photography."

"What kind of photography?" I asked, allowing my eyes to trace the sharp contours of his face and jaw as he drove. I couldn't help but let them settle on his perfect lips.

"Old school—I've got an antique camera that takes gorgeous shots. It's a nightmare to have to set up a darkroom for development, because I don't trust modern places with my prints—too easy for the negatives to get ruined or lost, but the results are worth it." His passion and enthusiasm for the hobby was apparent.

"What kinds of things do you like to shoot?"

"Mostly nature, but occasionally portraits." Chance's lips again lifted into a smile. "Maybe you can be my muse."

"I'd like that." I smiled to myself in the darkness. Butterflies swarmed in my stomach at the thought of seeing him again...of being more than his muse. I couldn't remember the last time I'd felt a connection like this with someone, almost as if I'd known him for a long time. Kindred souls, perhaps?

But all too soon, we arrived at the Montgomery campus, the trees of the surrounding forest receding to reveal menacing stonework in the clearing that held the campus grounds.

"You can park just over there." I pointed to the lot on the side of the carriage house.

Fidgeting in my seat as he pulled into a parking spot, I gathered every ounce of courage I could muster to ask, "Would you mind walking me up?"

Chance put the car in park. "I'd love to."

"I'm on the fourth floor. There's only stairs." I wanted to be honest about the trek. Thankfully most of the faculty that stayed on campus had not yet returned, and I had always been the only resident on the fourth floor, so we wouldn't have to deal with anyone seeing us.

"I'll survive." He chuckled, getting out of the car and making it to my door just before I could open it myself.

"Thanks." I took his offered hand as I exited. My mind was racing a million miles a minute, trying to figure out what I was going to do as we walked toward the carriage house.

What do I want to happen here?

What am I willing *to let happen?*

Chance kept my hand in his as we ascended the three sets of stone stairs to the fourth floor, where I was the sole occupant.

"This is me..." I stopped in front of my door; my nerves were on overdrive.

With my back to the door, I peered up at Chance through my lashes. He seemed to be waiting for me to make a move, maybe not wanting to be disrespectful after the close call in the bar.

"I don't think I'll ever be able to repay you for what you did tonight," I started, raising my finger to trace the buttons on the front of his polo shirt. "What may have been a small act on your part may have completely altered the trajectory of my entire life." The sentiment was perhaps a bit hyperbolic, but I felt it was the truth.

"I'm glad I was there." Chance's eyes darkened slightly as he decreased the space between us by millimeters. "I'm glad I met you, Violet." His voice was low and husky.

"I'm glad I met you too, Chance." I closed the distance, leaning in for a hug. "Thank you." I took a moment to breathe him in, the musk of his aftershave, the fresh soap scent of his shirt and hair. I reveled in the feel of his arms constricting around me and the warmth of his body permeating through the layers of clothes that separated us.

I glanced up at him, which was my undoing.

Unable to continue denying myself, I wrapped one hand around the base of his neck and whispered, "I really want you to kiss me," before his lips descended on mine, having received permission.

Chance was gentle at first, taking his time with me, pulling me closer while simultaneously pressing me against the door.

My stomach flipped as he explored my mouth; my heart was beating out of my chest. I knew the drinks were softening the edges of the experience, but I didn't think I'd ever been so physically attracted to someone before. I felt as though my entire body was vibrating with need for him—an entirely new, but exciting experience.

My first love (and first soul-crushing heartbreak) had been my high school sweetheart and the love had been young, but friendly and comfortable. My most recent relationship had burned fast and bright, but lacked a lot of emotional depth.

I cleared my head, trying to focus on the gorgeous man I was happily drowning in. I didn't want to think about anyone else, certainly not anyone from before. I only wanted to think about Chance.

Moaning into his mouth at the feeling of his desire settled just below my stomach gave him the incentive he needed to let his tongue slip past my lips, exploring my mouth with both expert skill and ease.

I could taste the faint crispness of his citrusy beer on his tongue, along with an essence that just felt so quintessentially him. I let one hand keep him close, still resting at the base of his neck, while the other slowly descended down his chest, gently squeezing his hardness.

Chance pulled away, a groan escaping as he rested his forehead against mine. Our panting breaths were the only sounds in the dim hallway.

"Come inside," I whispered, aware only after the words had escaped my lips of the double meaning they may have indicated.

"You're making it very hard for me to be a gentleman." Chance chuckled against me, leaning in to suck my bottom lip between his before releasing it abruptly. "You've been drinking." He traced a finger along my jaw.

"I'm not drunk." My beseeching tone undermined the attempted assertion. And while I could still feel the buzz of the liquor humming through my veins, I felt I was present enough to consent. "You don't have to be a gentleman," I teased, hoping he understood what I was implying. Heat pooled between my legs, and the thought of having him inside me made me squeeze my thighs together to alleviate the building pressure.

"You're killing me, Violet." His eyes were closed, his brow knitted together, as if he was in pain.

"Please..." I didn't mean to sound so desperate, but frankly, I was. It had been over a year since I'd been with anyone, and I hadn't realized how much I needed to feel something until Chance happened along.

"I shouldn't—I can't," Chance corrected himself, taking a slow step back from me, his hands still around my waist. "Could I get your number?"

"Only if you're coming in." I raised an eyebrow in challenge—one last-ditch effort to get what I wanted.

Chance cocked his head, letting his eyes rake over me. I was still catching my breath; my lips already felt swollen, and I was sure my cheeks were pink from both the kiss and the lingering effects of the alcohol in my system.

He took another step back.

I frowned up at him.

"Don't worry, I'm certain I'll be running into you again." He smirked.

If he was a townie and thought I'd be back at the bar soon, he'd be mistaken. But the spark of my pride prevented me from continuing to beg or giving him my number anyway.

Maybe it was the alcohol that made his rejection sting a bit more than it should have. Or maybe it was the fact that I had never been more forward with a guy in my life. The physical attraction continued to throb between my legs.

"Open your door," he commanded, taking another step away. "I want to make sure you're safe inside your room."

I dug in my pocket for my keys and was pleased when the deadbolt didn't stick despite the humidity outside. I turned around one last time and found him another few paces back. "Goodbye, Chance," I lamented softly.

"Goodnight, Violet." He smiled before turning to walk away.

I closed the door behind me, sliding down with my back pressed against it. He had gotten me so hot and bothered I knew I wouldn't be able to sleep without touching myself. I was angry with him for leaving me that way, but I smiled at his words: "I'm certain I'll be running into you again."

I sure as hell hoped so.

5

YES, CHEF

I watched the campus buzzing with activity from the attic of the faculty dorms, or what I affectionately referred to as my lounge.

During winter break the previous year, I had discovered the long-abandoned room. I had access through a trapdoor in my bathroom, which could be a bit precarious at times, but was always worth the risk to have such a large, cozy space to myself.

The high vantage point made for an excellent bird's-eye view of the myriad of students being dropped off, some by their parents, some by their staff, and some by nobody at all, to get situated in the dorms.

I had found the students at Montgomery to be such a mixed bag during my first year. Some seemed like normal teenagers, some were quiet and much too mature for their young age, but others were absolute terrors. I shivered at the memory of Claire DeLongpre, one of the queen bees of the school.

And as if summoned by my thoughts, I watched as she marched across the courtyard, her long blonde hair trailing behind her in waves, with two people, likely family staff, struggling to follow in her wake as they carted her belongings toward the dorm building on the west side of campus.

She screamed parental neglect and insecurity, but so many of the teens at the school did, as their wealthy parents shipped them off to boarding school, neatly tucking them away. Out of sight, out of mind.

But the kids knew. They felt it. How could they not? And their character was often showcased by how they projected the disappointment of being abandoned.

I knew all too well how it felt to be discarded by people you thought you loved, even by people who still loved you but didn't know how to do so in the way you needed. I sympathized with so many of the students at Montgomery, but they didn't often make it easy.

My stomach grumbled. The coffee I'd had that morning had worn off, and it was, after all, close to lunchtime, so I knew I'd have to vacate my sanctuary, at least for a little while, to go get something to eat. The ramen noodles I'd survived on over the summer, while the school's kitchens were closed, had more than outworn their welcome. But I hadn't had much of an option, needing to stretch my measly budget as far as I could get.

I donned the same slacks and Montgomery polo I'd worn the day before as I snuck across campus, trying to avoid being pulled in to help the students by one of the dorm monitors. Thankfully, I made it to the administrative offices without incident.

"Jolene?" I called out. I wanted to confirm her lunch order before grabbing food from the kitchen.

But again, I found the offices oddly quiet and empty.

Everyone must be upstairs helping.

I startled as the sound of a door closing caught me off guard.

"Miss Price, can I help you?"

Headmaster Winston's tall and imposing figure made its way down the hallway toward me in the lobby area. With a full head of light grey hair, big bushy eyebrows, and a stern jaw, Winston was easily intimidating, and he knew it. Maybe it was the years of reprimanding students, but anytime he spoke to me, no matter how friendly his tone, I always felt as though I was in trouble for something.

"I was going to bring lunch to Jolene," I squeaked.

"I sent her out on some errands; she won't be back until right before the mixer." He shuffled behind her desk, picking at the messages left for him on the notepad next to her phone. Even in the warm weather, he still donned his signature three-piece suit. His appearance and authority were always the most important things to him, especially when parents and board members were about.

"The mixer?" I swallowed, taking a step back from her desk without realizing what I was doing until his gaze snapped up to meet mine.

"Oh that's right, you weren't here last year at the start of the fall semester." He smiled, but it felt more predatory than genuine. "There's a faculty mixer in the great room."

The great room was a large lounge space just off the main dining hall. During the school year, it was where most students preferred to socialize between classes and on the weekends. Full of comfortable sofas and study tables, it was like my secret lounge, just on a much grander scale.

"I'm sorry nobody told you. It starts at six sharp. We serve drinks and appetizers," he offered. "Cocktail attire," Winston added. "Nothing too short; don't want anyone thinking you're loose."

I pursed my lips, willing every fiber in my body not to react to his obvious sexist bait. I could feel his gaze on me, waiting to argue. But he'd get nothing from me. "Thank you, sir. I'll see you at six then."

"Have a nice afternoon, Miss Price," he called after me as I ascended the stone stairs back to the main level, taking deep breaths to calm me as I went.

"Asshole," I muttered under my breath when I was sure I was well out of earshot.

I wound my way through the maze of service halls to enter the kitchen from the back, hoping I'd be able to grab some food and go undetected. But fate was not on my side.

"Violet Price. I know you aren't planning on taking food out of my kitchen without at least saying hello," a deep voice with an unmistakable Southern accent called across the din of the kitchen staff scurrying around.

I turned toward the voice. "Chef Lenny." I gave him a hard salute, my flat hand perpendicular to my forehead.

The grumpy old school cook and former Navy officer broke his eye contact with me to scold one of his assistants for chopping carrots inefficiently.

We had formed an unlikely bond the year before when he caught me sneaking into the kitchen, hoping to find some nonperishables

I could squirrel away in my room during winter break when the kitchen would be closed.

He had taken one look at me and his face had softened. I hadn't had to tell him why, he just knew. And he showed me through the pantry, talking through the various items that were overstocked and wouldn't be missed, but that would store well and could be easily cooked in the small kitchenette in my room.

Later in the year, he told me I reminded him of his granddaughter. He also confessed I was probably the only faculty member who knew his name or bothered to speak to him like a human being. He was certainly curmudgeonly, but I felt comforted by having a surrogate parent on campus. And my father had been in the service, although I'd never met him, so I felt a kinship with Lenny, leading to my respectful salutations in his presence.

"Any leftovers I can grab for lunch?" I asked sweetly.

Lenny rolled his eyes but tilted his head toward some metal trays covered with tinfoil across the kitchen.

"What do you know about the yearly faculty mixer?" I asked him as I grabbed a to-go box from the stack that never seemed to run out and had appeared shortly after my first run-in with Lenny.

"I cook the food," he answered shortly, walking down the line and inspecting the work of the kitchen staff to make sure they were on track with their assignments.

"Yeah, but what do they do? Do I have to just stand around listening to everyone brag about their summer vacations for hours?" I scooped a pile of mashed potatoes into the box, leaving a divot in the middle for the gravy I knew was in the next metal container.

"Don't know. Donors will be there." His tone was clipped.

They didn't invite him.

"Oh." I frowned. "Lucky you then."

That garnered a laugh, at least.

I plucked a roll from the last tray before closing the box and going to stand next to Lenny. "I'd give you a hug, but I know you'd hate it," I told him. "I'm glad you're back."

"Where else would I be, Violet?" He chortled.

I smiled, watching his aged hands move quickly while chopping next to one of his assistants, his chef's coat still a pristine and crisp white, always perfectly starched.

"I'll see you tomorrow for lunch," he commented, not looking up from his task.

"Yes, chef." I again brought my hand up to my forehead in a respectful and affectionate salute, before turning on my heel and striding out of the kitchen.

Taking the long way back to the carriage house, I passed the empty sports fields behind the main building and the athletics center that had been built years ago, after a generous donation from famous alumni and insanely successful businessman-turned-powerful politician, Thomas Roberts.

I kicked at the perfectly manicured grass, slowing my pace as I approached the rose gardens that were situated between the main building and the carriage house. I always went out of my way to pass through them when they were in bloom.

And although they were nearing the end of their bloom, they were still plush and fragrant.

Sitting on a shaded bench, neatly tucked away at one corner of the rose garden, I tore off pieces of the still-warm roll, dipping it into the mashed potatoes and gravy, indulging myself in the carbohydrates and non-processed food. The tastes were a delight on my tongue, so rich and salty.

Oh how I've missed Chef Lenny's cooking.

I had an ideal, but secluded view of the courtyard in the center of all the buildings on campus.

My eyes gently swept over the exterior of the carriage house. Covered in ivy, it was picture-perfect. It was the smallest building on campus, originally used as stables and housing for coachmen. In the seventies, it had been converted into studio-like apartments for the faculty who chose to reside on campus, as opposed to commuting from one of the small towns that dotted the surrounding area.

I sighed fondly as I found the windows at the top floor of the faculty dorms, planning out what I could get up to in the lounge by myself that evening, before remembering I'd be otherwise occupied with the faculty mixer.

While the sweet floral aroma combined with the heavy lunch left me feeling sleepy and lethargic, I eventually coaxed myself to get up, hoping to finish what was left of my fall lesson planning before the mixer.

When I was almost to the carriage house, I caught a flash of someone walking into the main building. I blinked and they were gone. I thought I must have been going mad. Because the man had looked exactly like Chance.

I shook my head.

Am I that desperate to get laid?

Trudging up the three flights of stairs to the fourth floor, I couldn't help but ruminate on the dalliance from the night before. I was still kicking myself for not giving him my number or just shoving him into my room, but I was also still a bit sour that he had refused my invitation, even though, deep down, I knew it had probably been the right thing to do.

He could have just come in and cuddled.

But I wouldn't have let him just cuddle with me. I wanted much more from him. The rejection smarted; however, it was unlikely I'd ever meet him again, so I tried not to think of his gorgeous blue-grey eyes and how deftly they had followed my every movement, or how good he had tasted and smelled, or how fantastic of a kisser he was, or how well-endowed I imagined he was, given what I had felt straining through his pants.

No, I refused to think about any of those things.

Even if they were *all* I could think about.

6

DEN OF VIPERS

The mixer was even worse than I had imagined it would be.

I should have known after Lenny's tip-off about the donors being on the guest list. Conversation was stilted, and while drinks were being served and consumed en masse, I was far too nervous I would look at the wrong person in the wrong way to do much more than nursing the same flat glass of champagne I'd been served when I'd arrived over an hour earlier.

I adjusted my pantyhose in the knee-length dress I was wearing. It was black, thankfully conservative, despite being form-fitting, and conveniently the only dress I owned. I'd thrifted it during high school, for a funeral, and I was lucky it still fit over ten years later, thanks to the spandex and polyester blend.

I had hoped to lurk in a corner and gossip with Jolene during the event, but Winston continued to find things going awry that he tasked her with handling. Heaven forbid the donors ingest a lukewarm canapé.

I watched Jolene's frizzy, permed, blonde hair bob and weave amongst the guests as she hustled to put out whatever non-existent fire Winston had noticed. I'd offered to help her when I'd first arrived, but she'd refused, saying she'd get in trouble with the headmaster.

I was surprised she had decided to forgo her usual sweaters to wear instead a grape-colored, floor-length velour skirt with matching short-sleeve mock neck top, complete with a very large beaded necklace that I had a sneaking suspicion she had made herself.

I loved her and her quirky, yet dated style. I didn't even bother looking at her shoes, knowing she only owned one hideous pair of black chunky mules. She was a lost cause in the fashion department—not that I wasn't in my own way, but I adored her just as she was.

Watching the room full of elites over the rim of my champagne glass as I feigned another sip was like watching a secret dance in which nobody knew the moves they were supposed to make, only those that others should be making.

The faculty fawned over the donors with overly enthusiastic laughter and suggestive touches. The whole thing felt so pretentious.

I didn't want to be paraded around to impress donors. I wanted to teach and return to my little hovel.

I didn't want to act like Montgomery was some bastion of civility when I could see the tendrils of corruption winding through every piece of the institution.

I didn't want to pretend that a student hadn't gone missing and that everyone in the room was complicit in preventing his disappearance from being properly investigated.

My cheeks strained to maintain the fake smile plastered across my face. It was disingenuous, like everything else at Montgomery.

I felt someone watching me from across the room. My gaze bounced around until I was able to see Milton Cox shift his attention off me the second he realized I had spotted him. He was a combination of all the worst stereotypes of men who worked in IT. Greasy hair, wireframe glasses too large for his face, an unfortunate sense of fashion that rivaled Jolene's, body odor, and socially awkward to the extreme.

Jolene had long harbored a crush on him, and had he not given me the ick immediately upon meeting him, I might have encouraged her to pursue something. Milton gave off "nice guy" vibes in which he did and said all the right things, but they lacked sincerity, as if he was expecting praise or a reward for treating women like they were equals.

"I thought they didn't allow students into the mixer."

Startled from my thoughts, I didn't have to glance up to recognize the low, seductive tone of Montgomery's resident cougar, the art teacher, Serena Lawrence. Once a model in her youth—which she found the most ingenious and obscure ways to bring up in any conversation—as with most women over a certain age, she had been discarded by the men who had previously doted over her and had taken to focusing on a younger set of gentlemen. Or at least that's what she'd told me.

I didn't judge her for wanting to date younger men, being hypersexual (her words), or being very open about her latest conquests. What I did judge her for was the fact that it was painfully obvious she didn't like me. I toyed with the idea that she was threatened by me, but if anything, it was simply my youth, something which neither of us had any control over.

She was gorgeous, despite the sour disposition. Wearing a deep green cocktail dress that snuggly fit every curve of her body, perfectly manicured nails, and a bright red lip that matched the sole of her stilettos, she always looked stunning. If she hadn't made up her mind so quickly to target me so outwardly, I thought there might have been a world in which we could have been friendly. I found her commentary on our chauvinistic male colleagues quite entertaining.

Still, she relied on the same few jabs to try to get under my skin. Her favorite being my small stature. At four foot, eleven inches, I was mistaken for a student more often than I would have liked. My height was a bit of a sore spot for me, admittedly, but there wasn't anything I could do to change it.

"Nice to see you too, Serena." I sighed, not wanting to give her any more ammunition.

"How's my favorite little misanthrope doing this evening?"

I rolled my eyes, not deigning to respond.

"Have you seen the new English teacher? Fucking gorgeous." Serena leaned in closer. "How long do you think it'll take for me to get to know him a little better?"

I scoffed. "You know very well there is a strict non-fraternization policy at Montgomery. If Winston or Jones get a whiff of you fucking him, they'll fire you."

Serena replied with a tinkling laugh, clearly amused by my assertion. "If that were true, I would have been let go a long time ago.

Discretion is the key. As long as the men don't see you as a threat, they won't do anything drastic."

She leaned down further; the wine on her breath was heavy. "Worth it for the fun, don't you think?"

"Do I strike you as someone who has fun?" I deadpanned.

Serena cackled at that.

I'd known that Serena had slept with a fair amount of the male staff. Even if she hadn't regaled me with the stories herself, the suggestive glances they'd throw her way, especially at an event like this, when they were a few drinks deep, made it pretty clear they were considering requesting her company again. I tried not to focus on the fact that all of them were married, Serena included.

But Serena was right. For someone like her, who knew how to play the game, she would never be punished for any impropriety, as long as she kept things under wraps. Me, on the other hand, I constantly felt I was walking on the razor's edge. I was lucky that Winston was too lazy to try and find a more reputable history teacher to replace me over the summer. But I had no doubt that if he'd gotten a whiff of someone more well-esteemed who might be interested, I would have been quickly ousted.

So I did what I'd always done: I kept my head down, did the work, and gave them no reason to look my way.

"Serena, darling!" Winston called to her from across the room. "Come introduce yourself to Doctor Bryant, one of our new donors."

"Duty calls," she preened, giving a dainty wave of her fingers to the well-appointed older gentleman next to the headmaster. "Have *fun*."

I rolled my eyes.

I continued to watch the various groups ebb and flow from the comfort of my solitary corner. I was a bit jealous of the Deputy Headmistress, Marilyn Jones, as she commanded the authority Winston could only hope to achieve, but was relegated to dutifully occupying donor's wives.

Her short silver hair was neatly coiffed, as usual. She opted for impeccably tailored dark-hued pantsuits, with patterned silk blouses, and always wore heels. I didn't know how she managed to walk around in them for the entire school day, but I aspired to be her.

She had been indifferent toward me since I'd joined Montgomery, but it was a pleasant indifference, and the same attitude with which she graced the rest of the faculty, so I didn't mind. Jones was much stricter than Winston, always taking on the difficult tasks that he didn't want to handle. The faculty that wasn't afraid of her resented her, but I only saw her as doing her job.

Idly, I wondered if I could find some sort of angle to weasel my way into her charms. I would have loved to be mentored by someone like her. She was no-nonsense, and saw the school for what it was, but still found a way to tolerate the limitations of the institution. However, Marilyn Jones didn't strike me as someone who had the time or the desire to take on a mentorship.

"Nice to see you, Miss Price. Still skulking around by yourself, as usual."

I looked up to regard the bespectacled English teacher and newspaper advisor, Kenneth Banks. He had always been slightly awkward around me, but I noticed more and more that he was awkward around many of the staff. At some point during the evening, he had lost his sport coat, revealing his signature striped suspenders.

"Did you have a nice summer, Kenneth?" I ignored the jab. I had been open to being friendly with my colleagues when I had first started at Montgomery, but they had quickly shunned me. I wasn't a glutton for punishment and had decided early on to keep to myself instead of trying over and over again to get in their good graces.

They could sense I was different from them, and didn't want me. And I refused to change myself to bend to their petty whims. Besides, the things they would have wanted me to change (my age, my gender, my income level, I could go on), were things I could do nothing about.

"Oh, you know, summers at the Cape can be terribly dull, but I suppose it beats being here." He took a sip of the amber liquid in his lowball glass.

I bit my cheek, trying not to scowl at the thought of how someone like Kenneth Banks had no idea how privileged of a life he led. As I mentally scrolled through the appropriate topics I could divert to in order to change the subject, a thought occurred to me.

"Do you remember Daniel Graham?" I dared not make eye contact, afraid I would give away the depth of my interest.

Still, I could feel Banks raising an eyebrow next to me. "Yes, I remember Daniel," he replied in a low tone, not wanting to chance being overheard.

"Do you know what articles he was working on before the school year ended?"

"I told the police everything I knew. I have nothing to hide." He was immediately defensive.

I couldn't have that.

Peering up at Banks, I waited for him to look down and make eye contact with me. "I'm not implying anything," I stated sincerely.

His shoulders noticeably relaxed at the confession.

"I've been bothered by his disappearance. I don't think he's a runaway like the police have decided." I probably shouldn't have been so open with Banks, but he may have known Daniel the best of anyone on the faculty.

Banks sighed. "I don't believe so either. Daniel was a true journalist. He kept his investigative work very secret. He probably knew that if I found out ahead of time, I would have discouraged him, but when a student comes to you with a well-written exposé, it's much more difficult to ignore."

"How much shit did you get in for publishing the article he wrote last year on the rising use of amphetamines amongst the student body?"

"Enough." Banks snorted.

That was an understatement. Jolene had confided in me that the headmaster had almost fired him, and it was only Banks apologizing to a couple of donors who took particular offense that had turned the tides. I wondered if Banks held any resentment toward Daniel for having to grovel as a result of the article. Then again, he had likely known it would get him into hot water, and he let it go to press anyway.

Realizing that I had already pressed my luck with getting any information out of Banks about Daniel, I decided to move on to another area of interest. "Have you met your new counterpart? I haven't seen him here yet."

Banks nodded. "He said he'd be late. He's young. You'll like him."

"What? Just because he's young?" I snorted at the implication.

"No, because he's almost as curious as you." Banks chuckled. "I still don't know why Jenkins decided to retire so suddenly. He joked about being interred in his office."

"Why do you think he left?"

Banks glared at me. "I couldn't fathom a guess. And he stopped joining me for golf, so I suppose I'll never know."

That was odd. The two English teachers had always been very tight, from what I could observe. But it sounded like Jenkins had dropped off the face of the earth.

"Speak of the devil..." Banks nodded toward the man striding toward us, a determined look set upon his handsome face and a glint of mischief in his piercing blue-grey eyes.

7

A CHANCE ENCOUNTER

"Chance Harper, let me introduce you to Violet Price." Banks swept his hand out, motioning to me, frozen, next to him.

Chance looked even more devastatingly handsome in a well-fitted black suit and crisp white button-up shirt. He had opted not to utilize a tie, which allowed him to leave the top two buttons undone.

This man was like my walking kryptonite.

But then reality sank in.

Chance was the new English teacher.

We'd be working together.

Nothing could transpire between us, or I could lose my job.

Furthermore, he had chosen to omit the part about him working at Montgomery the night before. Had our exchange been meant as some cruel prank? I'd been ostracized by everyone else. I didn't know how much more I could take.

My heart sank.

"Oh, we've already been acquainted." Chance gave me a knowing smirk. "It's nice to see you again, Violet." He ran the back of his knuckles casually down my arm, causing a shiver to run through me.

Instinctively I flinched away from his familiar touch, trying to ignore the fact that I could feel a blush already creeping along my cheeks and a heated coil tensing in my lower half. I didn't want anyone to get any ideas. "It's Miss Price," I sniped.

Chance's eyebrows shot up in surprise; his amused expression remained.

"I forgot to mention she bites." Banks snickered at my reaction.

Chance leaned down to whisper, "You look as good as you tasted last night, in that dress." I couldn't tell if his tone was teasing or sincere. Not that it mattered.

I tensed, my eyes locking with Banks, who was keenly observing our interaction, but from enough of a distance to not have heard Chance's comment.

"I ran into him while I was in town yesterday," I nervously explained to Banks. "He introduced himself when he overheard me mention to someone that I taught at Montgomery."

Banks gave a knowing nod, accepting my watered-down explanation for our initial meeting.

Nobody at Montgomery needed to know about the panty-dropping kiss we had shared in the hallway outside my apartment door, or the butterflies in my stomach that hadn't gotten the message that something was seriously wrong here and they needed to stand down immediately.

Feeling suddenly overheated and sensing the panic rising inside of me, I blurted out, "I need a new drink." Without giving Banks a proper goodbye, or allowing my gaze to land on Chance, I stormed toward the bar at the far side of the room.

"I'll go with you," Chance said from behind me.

"I'm fine," I threw behind me, not bothering to see if he was following me because I could feel him gaining on me.

"I need a fresh drink myself," he replied, letting his hand come to rest at the small of my back once I made it to the bar.

Again, I jerked away from him.

"What the fuck do you think you're doing?" I hissed just under my breath, so only he could hear me. "Are you trying to get me fired!?"

His brow shot up in surprise, but before he could answer me, Headmaster Winston appeared behind him, clapping a hand on Chance's shoulder. "Mr. Harper, I see you've met the lovely Violet Price."

I clenched my jaw at the sound of affection as he spoke the word "lovely" to describe me.

"She's been very accommodating, Headmaster." Chance glanced up at the intimidating older man, who had even a few inches on Chance's already tall frame.

"Please, call me Chuck." He waved a hand at Chance.

My lips parted in a mix of shock and annoyance.

Only the most prestigious donors and tenured faculty were given permission to call the headmaster by his nickname. I knew in my gut then, Chance Harper had to be filthy rich to have immediately garnered such a privilege.

I felt like a fool all over again.

"It must be nice not to be the newest teacher at Montgomery." The headmaster regarded me with a tone suggesting humorous condescension. "But still the youngest." He chuckled. "Chance has three years on your twenty-eight, my dear."

"Does he?" I smiled through gritted teeth.

Winston ignored my indignance. "Since you two seem to be getting on so wonderfully, why don't you introduce Chance?" The headmaster phrased it as a question, but the invitation was clearly compulsory.

Without receiving so much as a nod, he slipped his hand through my elbow, and I found myself being dragged to the podium.

"I couldn't," I attempted to decline, knowing it was too late for me.

"Nonsense, I insist," Winston dismissed me.

Chance's eyes darted back and forth between me and Winston as he followed behind.

I mouthed the words, "Help me."

Chance swallowed, unsure of what to do.

If there was any part of me that thought something salvageable existed between Chance Harper and myself, it died in that moment.

He had made a very big mistake in making an enemy of me.

"Come along, dear." Winston pulled me up the couple of stairs to the raised platform at the far end of the room before releasing me and making his way to the front of the stage.

Cheeks surely crimson from embarrassment, I twisted my fingers nervously in front of me, letting my gaze fall to the floor, not wanting to make eye contact with the myriad of colleagues who no doubt looked on in amusement at my predicament.

Headmaster Winston tapped the microphone harshly with his index finger, testing to make sure it was working. "Turn the music down," he called to someone running the sound system at the back.

A moment later, the classical music that had been playing through the speakers was cut and a hush fell over the crowd.

"Hello esteemed colleagues, faithful board members, and generous donors," Winston began. Center stage, with warmth and brevity filling his voice, he was in his element. All eyes on him. "I want to welcome you to another spectacular school year at the Montgomery Preparatory School."

A polite applause broke out amongst the crowd and I followed suit.

Winston basked in their energy and continued with a twenty-minute keynote speech I hadn't been expecting when I'd been forced to stand at the back of the stage in my uncomfortable heels.

Toward the end, which at the time, I hadn't known was the end, I began teetering on them so precariously, I considered feigning some sort of swoon rather than taking them off in front of everyone. But I didn't want anyone to think I was drunk, so instead I subtly shifted back and forth, trying to evenly distribute my weight and focus on anything other than the pain shooting through the balls of my feet.

I could feel Chance's eyes on me, but refused to acknowledge him.

Finally, I could sense Winston was wrapping up his time in the spotlight and practically lunged for the microphone when he said, "Our young Miss Price would like to introduce our newest addition to the teaching staff."

While trying to ignore the awful tenderness lancing through my feet as Winston spoke, I had come up with a short but sweet introduction I was sure would please the headmaster.

"Last year, I was welcomed with much kindness and open arms when I joined this distinguished institution," I lied. "I would like to extend the same warm welcome to our new English teacher, Chance Harper."

Stepping back as the room erupted in more applause, I motioned for Chance to take the microphone. His heated gaze locked on mine for a split second before he was forced to move past me to the front of the stage.

You lost your chance, buddy.

Taking advantage of the cacophony to make a hasty retreat, I tuned out Chance's deep and melodic voice and instead made for the closest exit, only to be immediately foiled.

8

THWARTED

"Violet!" Jolene exclaimed. Always one to greet me as though she hadn't just seen me quite recently, she pulled me into a tight embrace.

She began venting about all the errands Winston had sent her out on during the day, but I couldn't ignore my throbbing feet, or the fact that Chance Harper had once again spotted me and was making his way through the crowd in my direction.

"Jolene," I interrupted her, placing my hand on her forearm, "I don't feel very well. I'm so sorry. Can we talk tomorrow?"

Her face fell.

"I'll bring you lunch," I offered, glancing quickly over her shoulder. Serena had managed to intercept Chance.

Ha!

"Please tell me it wasn't the canapés. I swear they were all at the regulation temperature."

"No." I shook my head. "Just a migraine coming on. And my feet are killing me."

"Were you over by the sound booth? Because somebody shattered a glass over there. Are you bleeding?" Her brow furrowed in concern.

"I don't think so." I gulped when I realized Chance had managed to evade Serena, but I couldn't see him in the crowd. "I'm sorry. I'll see you tomorrow, okay?" I gave her hand a quick squeeze and turned to leave, only to run right into a brick wall, which turned out to be Chance's impressively muscular chest.

"Woah." Chance's hands darted out to my shoulders to steady me. "Sorry."

"I need to go." I pulled away from him.

"Leaving so soon, Miss Price?" The headmaster once again appeared out of nowhere to scold me.

Is everyone in on this plot against me?

"I'm sick." I glared up at him, just over Chance's shoulder, both infuriatingly blocking my exit.

"I was just offering to escort her back to her room." The corners of Chance's mouth turned up at the opportunity. "Don't want anyone fainting on the front lawn." He chuckled, turning to the headmaster.

Was that asshole mocking me?

"Good man." Winston again clapped an approving hand over Chance's shoulder. "Nice to see chivalry is alive and well."

I stifled a snort at both the sentiment and the person who was delivering it.

"C'mon, let's get you to bed." Chance wrapped his arm around my waist, sending the traitorous butterflies soaring at the intimate contact.

I attempted to step out of his hold, but he only tightened his grip.

His audacity was appalling.

"Jolene, they're out of vermouth at the bar. Be a dear and grab another bottle from the kitchens," Winston instructed her, when I turned to bid them both farewell. The words died on my lips as Jolene quickly scurried to carry out his request.

The moment we were far enough from the party, I ducked out of Chance's grasp.

I slipped my heels off and marched across the front lawn toward the carriage house.

"Hey, wait up!" Chance called out, jogging to catch up with me. "You're fast for such a short little thing." He was easily able to keep a regular stride with me as I was forced to speed walk, not wanting to all out sprint toward the confines of my apartment.

"Fuck off, Chance," I growled.

"Hey." He reached out for my wrist, but his grip was light, so I was able to easily pull it through his fingers.

"Don't touch me," I snapped.

"Violet," he tried to reason with me.

"I hope you've enjoyed yourself, making a fool of me. I don't need your help, so go back to the party," I snarled as I stomped up the front stairs of the carriage house.

"That wasn't my intention, I swear," Chance argued, dodging the door as I swung it wide, missing his pretty face by less than an inch.

Drat.

I'd never made such quick work of the three flights of stairs up to my room than I did that night. I couldn't be out of Chance's company soon enough. I didn't understand why he wouldn't release me to lick my wounds and wallow in self-pity.

"Violet, please let me explain." He was close—too close. I could feel his body behind me as I struggled to unlatch the door lock, which had decided that was the perfect time to stick.

"What!?" I wheeled around, leaving my keys dangling in the lock. "What do you want from me?"

"Last night—I know I didn't dream that kiss. You don't have to pretend you're not interested."

"You rescued me from sexual assault! I thought you were a good guy." I threw my hands in the air. "Or was that some kind of elaborate setup to get me into bed, but then you decided long-term torture would be more fun?"

"Set up? Torture?" he sputtered. "What are you talking about?"

"Just because you're rich doesn't mean you can go around humiliating women for sport," I hissed.

"Humiliating?" He shook his head, trying to keep up.

"Please," I pleaded. "Just go back to the mixer so they don't think I'm sleeping with you."

His eyes widened in response. "Is that what they'll think?"

"You obviously don't need this job," I accused him. "But *I* do." I pointed my index finger into my chest repeatedly to drive the point home. "If they think there is anything going on between us, *I'm* the one who will get fired."

"Why would they fire you?" Chance questioned.

"It's part of the code of conduct. There's a strict non-fraternization policy." I huffed.

Chance's shoulders fell. "I didn't know."

"Well now you do."

"Violet—"

"Why did you lie to me?" I couldn't contain the hurt in my voice. But I had to know.

Chance shook his head again. "I was going to tell you—I planned to, but I just wanted to get to know you first."

"That's a bullshit answer," I called him out. "You knew exactly what you were doing. Admit it."

"You were being so open, and I thought if you knew, you wouldn't have been as honest with me. But I really just wanted to talk to a cute, smart girl I met in a bar. Would you have been so candid if I'd told you I was teaching here?" he argued.

My resolve faltered momentarily at what felt like a genuine compliment and a truthful response. But it didn't change the fact that he had lied to me. Lying was the one thing I couldn't get past.

"Can I come in—just to talk?" he asked softly, but not suggestively.

"NO!" I turned again, tugging at the lock, silently begging for it to open.

My breath hitched as he caged me in from behind, the warmth of his front flush with my back. I tried to ignore the bulge I felt against my backside and his soft breath against my neck. I couldn't help but press back into Chance, relishing our closeness, despite my anger.

Chance's right hand slid down my arm until he had a hold on the key, and his left arm snaked around my waist, coming to rest on the door handle.

My heart might have skipped a beat at our close proximity, my breath coming out in soft pants, my core clenching, being so close to him again. The physiological reactions he elicited from me were becoming a huge problem.

"You have to pull the door toward you, while you turn the key, when it sticks," he whispered as he performed the same motion. My door quietly clicked open, but I stood frozen at the threshold, his arms still around me.

"Mine does the same thing," Chance answered my unspoken question.

"Yours..." I murmured, trying desperately to hang on to any semblance of sense left in me. I still wanted him. Despite everything he'd done, my body still wanted him.

I was on the verge of pulling him into the room with me when he replied, "I'm right next door."

I gulped. Of course he was.

There was no escaping Chance Harper, it seemed. But I wasn't going to give up so easily.

Wordlessly, I retreated into my room, closing the door in his face.

"Goodnight, Violet." He chuckled on the other side of the door before the sound of his footsteps faded back down the hall.

9

THE RUMOR MILL

Chance Harper was trouble.

I was all too familiar with men like him.

It wasn't long ago that someone just like him had shredded what was left of my already fragile heart.

I wasn't about to let it happen all over again.

With men like him, it was all about the thrill of the chase, not what came next or the consequences left in the wake of their conquest. I couldn't deny I was physically attracted to him, but he was a liar. Now that he'd exposed himself, I couldn't unsee him for who he really was.

The entitlement oozed from every pore on his body; every word that slipped from his plush lips was calculated—these were the things I needed to focus on, to save me the hassle of falling for another in a long line of assholes that preceded him.

I had well proven to have terrible taste in men. Chance Harper would be no exception.

With only a few days until the official start of classes, I holed up in my secret lounge, savoring the last precious moments before I'd be swept up in a whirlwind of course prep, test grading, and lecture outlines. I'd put in a lot of work over the summer to prepare, but there were always things that needed to be adjusted on the fly.

Not wanting to leave my sanctuary, I selfishly texted Jolene, asking to raincheck for lunch, remembering that I had told her I'd meet her while trying to escape the mixer. Almost immediately she replied saying she was still running around like a mad woman for the headmaster with all his last-minute whims, so that worked out better for her. I promised I would still be by, food in hand, on the first day of school.

A warm breeze floated through the open windows of the attic lounge, the last wisps of summer fading along with it. A faint smell of the overripe rose garden circled the large space, pulling a dreamy sigh from my lips.

I felt change in the wind.

All my prep was seemingly paying off.

On the first day, I got to class early, only had to threaten two students with expulsion, and felt like a million bucks in my best pencil skirt and a fresh white blouse I'd gotten on clearance from the one department store in town, over the summer.

"Chef Lenny." I saluted him as I came through the kitchen doors just after lunch service began, although he was already busy prepping for dinner.

"Still haven't made any friends your own age?" Lenny grumbled.

"What's wrong with the likes of you?" I beamed.

"I'm not making you any food that isn't already on the menu." He shook his dicing blade at me across the kitchen bench where he worked diligently.

"I ask for salad one time and you never let me forget it." I rolled my eyes.

Lenny huffed.

"Relax—just grabbing two plates to go. I promised Jolene I'd bring her lunch." I scanned the top shelves for the to-go boxes he kept hidden for me.

"I heard you left the mixer with the new English teacher." Lenny side-eyed me. He was such a gossip. Usually I loved it, but today, not so much.

"Trust me, it wasn't by choice." I rolled my eyes.

Someone had moved the boxes to a shelf just out of reach for me, so I grabbed a stepladder and dragged it across the tile floor, creating a dreadful clunking noise in the process.

"Violet!" Lenny scolded.

"Sorry!" I hefted it up on my shoulder and carried it over to the shelves.

"Just be careful. You know if I'm hearing about it—"

"I know, I know." I scowled. "He insisted on walking me to my room in front of the headmaster—who has his head so far up Chance's—"

"Violet!" Lenny admonished.

I teetered on the stepladder to reach the boxes. "The point is, I didn't have a choice." I plucked two containers from behind a stack of Bundt pans. "You don't have to worry about anything happening between us. I think he's atrocious." It wasn't exactly a lie.

Lenny narrowed his gaze, seeing right through me, but amused by my distaste, nonetheless. "Remember, there are eyes and ears everywhere at Montgomery," he warned me solemnly.

I frowned at his comment, knowing he was right. With a quick salute, I headed toward the food staging area to fill the containers up. Jolene wouldn't mind if her food didn't look as meticulous as Lenny instructed his staff, so I dumped the pork belly, fingerling potatoes, and asparagus all together in each container.

The sous chef assembling plates to my right looked horrified, but silently handed me two forks, despite his outraged scowl.

By taking back service hallways, I was able to avoid running into any students or staff. However I had no choice but to pass through the main entrance hall to access the stairwell that led to the administrative offices below.

It was there that Chance Harper stood, his piercing blue-grey eyes alight when he spotted me.

I was ashamed to admit that my heart might have skipped a beat and my eyes, of their own accord, raked down his lean form, clad in black trousers that fit him perfectly and another crisp white shirt, sans tie, that was somehow so much whiter and brighter than my own.

The image and feel of his body pressed against mine, his mouth on me, his hands coiled around my waist, pulling me to him, flashed through my mind, causing a full-body blush.

Why did he have to be so attractive, and even worse, such a good kisser when he was also a liar and a scoundrel?

Anger and desire coursed through me in a simultaneous dance, vying for dominance.

I hated that I'd told him to leave me alone, and yet there he was.

I hated that while we both existed at Montgomery, there was no escaping him.

But most of all, I hated my traitorous mind for still wanting him...for being so very pleased at the thought of him seeking me out despite my earlier attempts to rebuke him.

"I missed you at lunch, Violet." He leaned casually against the banister, careful to keep his voice low, as there were students dotted around the periphery of the large hall.

"It's Miss Price," I reminded him curtly. "And I don't eat in the dining hall." I tried to sidestep him, but he mirrored the action, blocking my access to the stairwell.

"Then where do you eat?"

Somewhere I don't have to see your stupid, handsome face.

"None of your business." I stacked the containers on top of each other so I could hold them with one arm, allowing me to use the other to shove him to the side.

"I'll see you around, Violet." I couldn't tell if his tone was mocking or resigned.

Being that I wanted to dislike him, I decided on the former, muttering words of distaste for him under my breath as I made my descent.

"Jolene?" I called out as I reached the bottom of the steps.

The basement offices were in fine creepy form on the first day of school. With the weather outside being rather overcast, shadows of dubious origin lurched from every nook and cranny, only to disintegrate as they reached the cast of the even more sinister glare from the malicious overhead fluorescent lighting.

Thankfully, I'd never been to a morgue before, but I imagined it would evoke similar dread and depression as the lower level of the main building at Montgomery.

Further adding to the discomfort of the basement, the stone effectively muffled sounds, so you often didn't hear others until they were right upon you, which could be rather disconcerting. Despite the stone enhancing disembodied voices from the offices beyond the corridor, the incessant buzzing from the overhead lights always caused an immediate and slowly increasing throbbing headache to set in.

How all the staff managed to work down here every single day was beyond me. Jolene had once told me, "You get used to it," with a shrug, when I asked. I certainly would never get used to it.

"Violet!" Jolene exclaimed, her saccharine voice bouncing off the walls, producing an odd dissonance. A moment later, her head popped out of the records room door. The hallway light flickered overhead as she locked the door, making it appear as though the bright yellow school bus appliqué on her sweater was in fact moving along in jerky spasms. The motion and flashing light intensified my already present headache.

The dichotomy of the Montgomery manor home with warmly lit and comfortably upholstered areas for students on the main level contrasted greatly with the almost brutalist dungeon-like classrooms and the actual dungeon that was the lower level.

"Lunch." I held up the stacked containers with my hands. "As promised."

"Goodness, I can't believe it's almost one o'clock already. The day's just flying by." She hung her lanyard, heavy and jangling with keys, around her neck, and veered toward the couches in the waiting area just in front of her desk.

I handed her a fork and a box. We wasted no time digging into the food. Although it was lukewarm, neither of us minded.

"Lenny said people have been talking about me leaving with Chance," I grumbled, unable to keep it from her and desperate to know what she had heard herself. Jolene was *the* eyes and ears of Montgomery.

She shrugged. "I mean, everyone seemed a little surprised when he returned so quickly..."

I gave an exasperated sigh. "I'd like to keep my job. I'm not a rule-breaker or a risk-taker. That means nothing will happen. Ever."

"Everyone knows the headmaster doesn't enforce that rule, or he'd have to resign himself." She quietly snorted. "You could date him if you wanted to."

"I don't want to do anything with Chance Harper," I hissed. "In fact, I think I might despise him."

"What he'd do? Try to kiss you?" Jolene laughed through a bite of her food.

When I went rigid next to her, feeling the telltale burn of a blush staining my cheeks, she went silent. Again the kiss flashed through my mind. I shook my head. "It's not like that. It *can't* be like that," I replied adamantly.

"Okay, okay." She held up her hands in defeat. "He's cute though," she hedged. "I wouldn't blame you if you changed your mind."

I huffed indignantly, shoving my half-eaten lunch aside, having already lost my appetite at the thought of everyone talking about me. I worked so hard to not be a topic of conversation, and yet there I was, in the spotlight once again.

"I don't want people talking about me. Don't they have anything better to do than gossip?" I asked more rhetorically than anything.

"All *we* do is gossip." Jolene giggled, taking a sip from her water bottle. Just like her car, there were funny cat stickers covering almost all of the hot pink aluminum.

Hang in there, baby, indeed, I thought, as I read the block lettering below a cat clinging desperately to a tree branch.

"Did I miss anything after I left?" I asked, trying to change the subject.

"Well, I saw Serena leave with Doctor Bryant, but you didn't hear it from me." She gave me a conspiratorial nudge. "The headmaster seemed pleased; I think he set it up."

My stomach soured at the thought of him pimping out the staff to eager donors. "Gross," I muttered.

A knowing smile crept across Jolene's lips. "Don't worry about Serena. She knows how to take care of herself and wouldn't agree to anything she didn't want to do."

"And has the headmaster managed to keep Daniel's disappearance secret from the donors?" I threw at her out of left field.

Jolene choked on her food a little, disarmed by my sudden inquiry. "Violet," she hissed. "He's in his office." She nodded toward the hallway, where I could see light from his open office door spilling into the more dimly lit hallway.

"Sorry." I shrugged.

"Actually, one of the donors caught wind of it at the mixer and made a big fuss, which took him a while to diffuse. The headmaster told me to give everyone on staff strict instructions not to mention it. Not to the students. Not to the parents. Not to the donors. Not to anyone." She glared at me. "He wouldn't even let me send out an email or print a memo. 'In-person only.'" She used air quotes around the last part to denote what he'd said to her.

"What is he trying to hide?" I scowled.

Jolene waved me off. "Let the police handle it. If they say he ran away, that's probably what happened. You won't hook up with Chance Harper to avoid breaking an antiquated rule that nobody follows, but when the headmaster himself orders everyone to keep quiet about a runaway, you're ready to throw caution to the wind?" she correctly pointed out my contradictory actions.

"You don't find it suspicious at all?"

"I don't want you to get in trouble," Jolene argued.

We both looked up upon hearing a door open down the hallway. The disembodied voices of a student arguing with one of the guidance counselors drifted closer.

"All it will take is one call from my father to get you fired," a young woman's voice snarled.

"That's fine, Miss DeLongpre." The counselor sighed, no doubt having been threatened by plenty of students.

"I won't let this go." Claire DeLongpre emerged from the hall-way, pointing a perfectly manicured finger at the counselor.

"Have a nice day, Miss DeLongpre."

Claire turned on her heel to glare at Jolene and me, before snapping, "What are you staring at?" and then promptly stormed up the stairs, not bothering to wait for a response.

"What was that about?" I wondered aloud.

"She's always down here making the staff miserable." Jolene rolled her eyes.

10

A Most Unfortunate Discovery

"Who can tell me which Greek city-states fought in the Peloponnesian War?" I asked my class, leaning against the front of my desk to alleviate my aching feet after a full day of classes.

Nobody answered.

Predictable.

Three students were asleep, five were messing with their phones, a couple were lazily flipping through their textbooks, attempting to look like they were searching for the answer, and in the very back, Queen Bee Claire DeLongpre was touching up the top coat of her manicured nails.

The bell sounded over the ancient PA system. Everyone stood in unison, packing their things to take a quick exit.

"Athens and Sparta," I yelled the answer over the cacophony. "Turn in your essays on the way out, please," I requested beseechingly.

A good third of the class probably wouldn't even bother. I knew better than to put up a fight. I merely deducted points for days late, eliminating any awkward conversations or made-up excuses. If they couldn't write a five-paragraph essay on any topic of their choosing, they deserved to fail.

"Claire," I called out as the girl passed me, surrounded by her usual gaggle of friends.

"What?" she replied sharply.

"No more nails in class—someone will pass out from the fumes, and the windows are painted shut," I explained.

"Fine." She rolled her eyes, flipping her long hair over her shoulder as she marched out the door.

I had noticed I wasn't getting quite as much resistance from the students as the year before. Montgomery was small, with only around one hundred students per grade level. "Keeps things competitive," Headmaster Winston had noted of the small student body when I'd once asked him.

With eight periods in the day, I taught two classes per grade each day and was able to cycle through the entire student body between the fall and spring semesters. I was fortunate for the smaller class sizes. I'd heard so many horror stories from other teachers while earning my teaching certification of how public schools were bursting at the seams and funding went down every year.

But as with any job, Montgomery had its own set of challenges, despite the benefits. Fearing any interaction with a privileged student could lead to professional disgrace was definitely high amongst them.

Six weeks.

We'd already been in session for a month and a half.

And those first six weeks at Montgomery had thankfully passed almost uneventfully. The autumnal foliage in the surrounding woods had started to turn early. The colors deepened as the temperatures dropped with each passing day.

I watched leaves fluttering to the ground as I made my way across the back lawn to the storage shed where Lenny had kindly left a few parcels of chopped wood for me to take up to my room and the lounge, as the weather had also begun to turn with the leaves.

There was some sort of primitive central air system in the carriage house, but I had never figured out how to work it and my maintenance requests the previous school year had gone unanswered. So instead, I took to using the wood-burning fireplaces to keep warm, which suited me just fine. I found the smell and sound of a crackling fire quite soothing.

Chance had finally taken the hint and had thankfully been keeping his distance from me. Although occasionally I'd catch glimpses of him around campus snapping photos on the antique camera he had mentioned to me on the drive home the first night we met.

I often wished I could see the photos he took. If things had turned out differently between us, maybe I would have become his muse, as he had joked. I found my anger toward him waning slightly, but it didn't change the fact that we were from different worlds, or that he had lied to me.

As fall sunk in, he began to wear sweaters over his button-up shirts, which made him look positively swoon-worthy. And swooning I still was, much to my dismay.

"He probably smells good too," I grumbled to myself as I hauled one of the heavy parcels across the back lawn to the carriage house.

The thought occurred to me as I lugged the wood up the three flights of stairs, thumping on each step as I went, that it sounded like I was dragging a body, so I wasn't surprised when Chance poked his head out of the door to his apartment, just as I made it to the fourth-floor landing.

"What are you doing?" His eyes darted from me to the parcel.

"Nothing," I grunted, trying not to think about how my fingers were burning from the exertion and that I definitely felt at least two blisters forming.

"Sure you don't want help?" He quirked a brow, his head swiveling as he followed my progress down the hall to my own door.

"No—go away," I retorted petulantly as I passed him.

"Violet..." He trailed off, as if it pained him not to be able to assist me.

"It's still Miss Price," I scolded him, more to stop myself from giving him a chance to speak to me like the civilized human being I should have been, or worse, admitting to myself that I not only wanted his help, but was pleased that he had even offered.

I was extraordinarily good at holding grudges. But it was a talent I didn't wish to harbor.

I didn't want to snap at Chance at every opportunity.

I wanted to be friends with him.

Hell, I wanted to be much more than friends.

That was the problem.

And *that* was why it was easier to be cold and distant with him.

It was the only thing I could do to keep from acknowledging how my heart still fluttered around him, and that I thought of the kiss we'd shared so much more than I ever reminisced over any other kiss I'd ever received.

I sighed in relief when I heard the click of his door latching.

Per my usual routine, I threw some pasta on the stove to cook while I unpacked my bag. Pasta and PB&J sandwiches had been a dietary staple for my entire life. While it would have been nice not to live like a broke college student, I was, unfortunately, a broke adult. So when I didn't want to eat what they were serving in the dining hall (which was eggplant parmesan that night, yuck!), or didn't want to make the trek back over to the main building, I resorted to old habits.

While I changed out of my work clothes into the only pair of pajama pants I owned and a hoodie from my collegiate alma mater, idly I wondered if my small stature had been a product of potential malnourishment when I was very young. My mother had done her best, but ends hadn't always met.

Slipping on a pair of fuzzy slippers that had been a Christmas present from my mom a few years prior, my heart tugged a little thinking of her, as it always did, and I made a mental note to give her a call over the upcoming weekend. The slippers were almost worn through, but I didn't have the heart or the budget to get new ones.

Next I gathered the stack of essays from my bag, along with a green felt-tipped pen, my grading weapon of choice, and set them on the small table between the kitchenette and bathroom door.

I made two trips up to the lounge: the first with half the wood, and the second with the papers and my simple dinner.

I had found my lounge quite by accident during my first winter break at Montgomery. I didn't normally take it upon myself to go exploring where trapdoors in bathroom ceilings led to, but I'd had nothing better to do in the few weeks I had been practically stranded on campus by myself.

I had initially hoped it wouldn't be filled with bugs or animals, then absently thought it might be nice to have even a little bit of room to store some extra wood, so it wouldn't be strewn about my apartment. But what I discovered was so much better than I could have ever hoped for.

It seemed to have just been used for storage, based on what I'd found up there. Although I still wasn't exactly sure how they'd managed to get the large furniture up to the fourth floor. However, I only had access to the half of the room above my room and Chance's.

The opposite side was inaccessible, from what I could determine, completely separated by an entire wall lined with bookshelves. I thought perhaps there was a stairway, long forgotten, like everything else up there, that led to the other half of the floor, and that the partition had been erected after everything had been brought up. But that was all just a guess.

Either way, the attic at one point had been completely refinished: hardwood floors, fireplaces on either end of the room that aligned with where the fireplaces were located in my room and likely in Chance's.

I found pool, Ping-Pong, and air hockey tables amongst a few other similar indoor activities. All were brand new, half assembled, and wrapped in moving blankets that kept them in pristine condition. Accessories like pool cues and table tennis paddles were neatly stacked in factory packaging nearby.

I had spent the whole break cleaning, arranging furniture (which was not easy to do solo), and alphabetizing textbooks. The latter had taken me the longest. The entire length of the interior wall was floor-to-ceiling shelves, full of well outdated materials, but what a phenomenal time capsule they were.

On the side of the room directly above my apartment, I situated a sofa and armchairs in front of the fireplace, with a study table and chairs just behind it.

The table was excellent for spreading my work out, and was much more preferable to the floor of my apartment.

In the middle of the room, I spaced out the game tables, and at the far end, above Chance's apartment, was a terribly out of tune baby grand piano. Luckily I hadn't had to move that anywhere; I just removed the blankets covering it.

But my absolute favorite find in the room was a neat little console table that I situated between the fireplace and window seat on my side of the room. Atop the table sat a very old phonograph, with a big trumpet-like speaker. And on the shelves below was a fantastic old record collection, full of jazz, classical, and big band instrumental records, as well as some music artists from the forties and fifties. My favorite was a Motown album that I often played while I read on the couch.

Judging from the labels on the recreation tables and the most recent books, I figured nobody had been up there in a good thirty years, which would have aligned with the last renovation of the carriage house in the early nineties, when it had been turned into the faculty apartments.

How someone had forgotten the treasures in my lounge was beyond me, but I was glad for it. Having my own space, and a secret space at that, made a piece of Montgomery feel like mine. The lounge was the one place on campus where I felt like I belonged.

It was as if the room existed solely for me. Like it had been waiting its whole existence just to bring me joy.

I selected a jazz album that evening and took to lighting my first fire of the season in the large hearth. The sound of crackling wood and the flickering firelight put me at complete ease. I exhaled in contentment, settling at the study table to eat first, then started to work.

It began to rain halfway through grading my essays. The gentle pitter-patter on the paned windows made me drowsy...the soft jazz didn't help either. My eyelids drooped, heavy with exhaustion. I gave in, closing them for just a moment, only to be startled out of a dead sleep moments, or maybe hours, later when something came crashing through the window at the far end of the lounge.

On instinct, I released a bloodcurdling scream.

"Violet?" a familiar male voice called out from the dark.

A shadowy figure moved toward me, and once he reached the study table, I finally recognized his blue-grey eyes.

"What the fuck, Chance!?" I shouted, scrambling off my chair and promptly tripping over the leg, falling to the floor in a heap.

"Sorry." He grimaced, reaching a hand out to help me up.

I swatted it away and righted myself without his help, taking a few steps back to increase the distance between us once again.

"What is this place?" he breathed in awe, craning his head to look up and down the long room.

"My lounge..." I frowned, willing my heart to stop racing.

Chance paced toward me, but his attention was on the seating area situated in front of the still crackling fire, just behind me.

"This is your secret cozy space." An impressed grin spread along his face, but quickly faded when he took me in. "I didn't mean to frighten you."

I folded my arms over my chest defensively. I wanted him to leave...immediately. Nobody else had been up in the lounge. Jolene and Lenny were the only two people on campus who even knew it existed, or at least they *had been* the only ones who had known I knew it existed.

"How'd you find me?" I pouted.

"I've heard you puttering around up here for weeks. I thought it was an animal." He paused abruptly to chuckle at himself. "Or maybe a ghost. But rodents and ghosts don't usually start fires and play jazz, as far as I'm aware."

Chance looked around, searching for the source of the music. "Where's it coming from?"

I pointed to the console. "It's a phonograph."

"Actually, it's a gramophone." He grinned, walking over to look at it up close. "And a beautiful one at that." He traced the edge of the horn with the tip of his index finger. "Well, technically, a gramophone is a type of phonograph, but they play cylinders, while gramophones play records like this."

Ignoring his unsolicited correction to my terminology, I asked, "How'd you get up here?" I squinted, trying to see how he might have entered from the end of the room, but failing.

"The fire escape." He beamed, proud of his ingenuity. "The window was unlocked."

I fought back a grimace, remembering the last time the weather had been pleasant and I'd opened up all of the windows, knowing it would be one of the last opportunities for a while. It hadn't occurred to me that I needed to be concerned about intruders on the fourth floor that nobody was supposed to know existed.

I studied him as he continued to gawk at everything. His hair was wet with rain, rivulets of water running down his face and neck, disappearing beneath the casual grey zip-up hoodie he was wearing. Like me, he had swapped his slacks for pajama pants, but had put on a well-worn pair of sneakers to scale the fire escape. Small puddles formed in his wake as he traipsed across the floor in earnest exploration.

Without thinking, I reached over the couch to grab a blanket. "Here," I called out, just before throwing it to him.

He looked down at the blanket and then back up at me, a curious expression etched upon his face. He took a beat before using it to dry off, wrapping it around his broad shoulders afterward.

"How'd *you* get up here?" He raised an eyebrow in interest.

"There's a trapdoor in my bathroom ceiling," I admitted.

"Huh." He nodded his head, seemingly amused at the thought.

"Please don't tell anyone," I blurted out.

Chance gave me a predatory grin as he contemplated my request.

I tried desperately to ignore the flutter in my stomach at having his eyes on me so intensely.

Taking his time to respond, he strolled past me, elegantly seating himself in the armchair closest to the fire.

"I might have a few conditions." He turned his gaze on me, crossing his ankle over his knee, then leaning back into the chair.

Chance was already acting like he owned the place. But he wasn't the one who had painstakingly arranged everything. I had. This was my lounge. MINE!

I said nothing, letting the anger stew just below the surface as I waited for him to continue.

He watched me closely as he spoke. "If I wanted to join you up here occasionally, do you think you could tolerate being in the same room as me?"

No.

"Fine."

"I'd also like for you to allow me to call you Violet," he challenged.

No.

"Fine."

Chance slowly rose from the chair to approach me. "And I'd like to put the past behind us, so we can call a detente and be done with all this contention."

My jaw clenched involuntarily. I knew he wasn't asking for much. I knew I should just agree and be done with it all. But I found myself speechless.

"Perhaps you're just determined not to like me." He took a step closer, tilting his head down to meet my fiery gaze.

He wasn't wrong.

I couldn't help but let out a soft gasp when his warm fingers connected with the sensitive skin at my wrist. "Or maybe you like me too much—is that it?" he whispered softly.

That hit too close to home.

"I have to go," I choked out, abruptly severing the connection and rushing to gather my papers strewn across the study table.

"Violet, you can't run away from me forever," Chance simpered, but made no move to stop me.

"Doesn't mean I won't try," I replied flippantly, kneeling down between the pool and Ping-Pong tables to open the trapdoor and extend the ladder into my bathroom.

"I'm glad we can discuss and solve our problems like adults," Chance called out sarcastically.

I slammed the trapdoor closed in response.

Chance Harper was mistaken if he thought all it would take was one conversation and a handshake for me to move on—to forget that he'd lied to me. Fool me once and all of that. But I'd been made a fool of too many times before, and I was dead set on holding my ground.

Maybe I *was* determined not to like him, but I knew if I gave in, it would only lead to ruin.

11

DANGEROUS LIAISONS

Every time I spoke to Chance, he threw me off-kilter.

I'd spend hours analyzing what he'd said and how he'd said it, or if it meant something deeper than the surface layer words. And don't get me started on the time I'd spent replaying our physical interactions. Just the tips of his fingers grazing against me had set me on fire.

Curse him for having such power over my body, with only the slightest touch. Despite everything, I still found myself drawn to him. I couldn't get him out of my mind.

Was it possible I was being too harsh and only seeing things through the jaded lens of my own circumstances?

I understood that I was being quite indignant over the whole situation, but the feelings he stirred inside made me uncomfortable in my own skin. When he was near me, I wanted to go against every instinct I had to stay away and protect myself from not just potential heartache, but more importantly, from losing my job.

Perhaps it was immature of me not to find a way to get over myself and simply maintain a polite but distant acquaintance with Chance, but I knew he felt it too. The chemistry that undulated, just below the surface, when we got too close, felt like a constant threat to my sanity. So instead, I chose to keep my distance.

And all the mental hemming and hawing was a simple way to protect myself, clinging to any desperate attempts to ignore the fact that Chance Harper appeared to be a decent guy. I supposed I didn't know him well enough to be sure, but I sensed it. I think in my own twisted logic, if I was an asshole to him, he'd get the hint and stay scarce.

But in fact, it seemed as though my strategy was having the opposite effect, drawing him to me like a moth to a flame. Or maybe I was the moth...surely I was the one bound to end up burned to a crisp in the ashes of whatever combustion that was likely to spark between us, should I decide to give in to my desires.

I tortured myself, running through all the awful things Harry Ainsworth (yes, of *those* Ainsworths), my most recent ex, had put me through. Namely love bombing me for the better part of a year, then suddenly pulling the rug out from under me and accusing me of being a gold digger and opportunist.

I had taken all the grand gestures and offers to help with my finances as generosity born of love, but it had merely been a way for him to extort control over me and feel superior to me.

Without a formal education (and why would he need one, when his family paid for everything?), I realized later, piecing together many of the common jabs he'd make at me, especially toward the end, that he was just an insecure, privileged man-child.

I still wasn't sure if he had turned so spiteful and mean to push me away, validating his self-fulfilling prophecy of me having used him for his means and money, or if he truly couldn't get out of his own head and his own way to see that I cared little for any material objects. He'd set me up to fall into his trap. I was barely scraping by when I'd met him. I'd never asked for anything from him, but I had accepted it when offered, because I'd thought it was a sign of his affection, not because it had been my goal from the start.

I had seen a future with him. I had planned for that future. And I was still grieving the loss of merely the illusion of having a secure, kind, and loving partner to share my life with.

The last words he'd ever spoken to me as I stormed out of his high-rise penthouse in the city perpetually bounced around my head. They were louder on days when I struggled with my near-constant feeling of inferiority.

"You're just desperate to be loved. Even your own mother didn't want you," Harry had snarled, watching me pack up what little I owned into a single suitcase.

He was definitely right about the first part, though it pained me deeply to admit it. I didn't think I'd ever known what love felt like, because everyone I thought I had come to love had found a way to betray me, my own mother being one of those people.

But he wasn't exactly correct about her not wanting me. She had wanted me, but I had left her alone, and in her loneliness, she had betrayed me as well, although I felt that I was the one to blame for it.

I had let my guard down with Harry because of an initial physical spark, and there I was, wanting to do the same thing with Chance. I should have never let him give me a ride home, or asked him to walk me up, or kissed him. I'd created this mess. I would have to wallow in it.

The fact was, I knew better. So how could I give Chance the opportunity to break me? And he *would* break me. I was already so broken, there would be no putting me back together if my heart was shattered again.

After Harry, I vowed I would never again be made to feel so foolish. And unfortunately, that meant closing my heart to anyone who showed they couldn't be trusted.

But I did have to find a way to co-exist with Chance. He wasn't going anywhere, and the one refuge I had from him had been infiltrated. There truly was no escape.

It had been weeks since Chance had discovered the lounge. My heart ached for my cozy space, but I knew the moment I set foot up there, he'd join me. So I stayed away.

Occasionally I'd hear the floorboards creaking overhead, as if he was pacing by the fireplace. Some nights I thought maybe I should just go up there and get it over with, but I was nothing if not stubborn.

I knew eventually I'd have to see Chance again, but I wasn't ready.

Undeterred, Chance was the one who wound up finding me.

With Halloween quickly approaching and midterms well underway, tensions were running high throughout Montgomery with both students and faculty. I was on the way to my classroom earlier than normal, needing to write instructions for my midterm on the whiteboard, when I heard Chance's hushed whispers just beyond the threshold.

I paused in the hallway to listen.

"I'm not joking around—you can't tell anyone," he pleaded with someone.

"I won't say anything," a young female voice replied, but her tone was uncertain.

"Because things aren't like they used to be at Montgomery. If the wrong person finds out, we'll both be in danger," Chance warned her.

What did he mean about how things "used to be at Montgomery"? What kind of danger would they be in?

I had asked Jolene to check the school records after the mixer because Chance seemed so familiar with the headmaster, but she confirmed that nobody named Chance Harper or similar-sounding names had attended Montgomery Prep in the years that would have aligned with his age.

"You want to pursue this, don't you?" he tried to confirm her intentions.

"Yes," she said more vehemently. "You know I do."

I could feel my heart racing as I pressed my back against the hallway. Alarm bells were blaring in my mind, but I tried to quiet them to continue listening. Because at best, he was conspiring with a student over something that was likely unauthorized, but at worst...I shook my head. Their tone wasn't romantic. I didn't want to consider the potential of a relationship.

I had just spent weeks feeling guilty over giving him the cold shoulder, thinking he was a good guy—that it was me who was fucked up—and here he was, sneaking around, having hushed conversations with a young girl.

"Good." Chance sighed in relief. "Meet me after dinner, okay?" he asked kindly.

"Okay," the girl agreed.

I only had a moment to gather myself. I stared in shock as none other than Claire DeLongpre strolled out of my class, appearing completely unbothered.

"Hey, Miss Price." She gave me a tight smile as she passed me, but oddly didn't seem to be concerned about having been overheard. What on earth was going on between them?

I took a moment to gather my thoughts and rein in the confusion that was likely showing on my face.

Apprehensively, I walked into my classroom.

Chance was also oblivious to the fact that I had overheard his rendezvous with a student.

"Good morning, Violet," he simpered, leaning against my desk, almost provocatively, with his eyebrow raised in anticipation of my terse response. That day, he wore a vest over his button-up shirt, which only accentuated his criminally lean and tapered waist.

"What do you want?" I grumbled.

"It wasn't my intention to chase you out of that room, you know." He pushed himself off the desk and followed me as I placed the midterm packets on each of the student desks.

"Why does it matter to you if I like you or not?" I was quickly becoming aggravated with him, despite how good he looked in that damn vest.

"You know why." He attempted to block my way, but I side-stepped him. "I don't know what I've done to incite such contempt."

It further angered me that he was always so elegant with his words. But he had all but confirmed my suspicions that there was something more sinister to Chance Harper. And I had a feeling that whatever he was up to with Claire was far from the only secret he was keeping.

"I don't have time for this." I again pushed past him to make my way to the dry-erase board to begin writing the test instructions.

"They all think very highly of you." Chance suddenly switched tactics.

I spun around, eyes narrowed. "What are you talking about?" I hissed.

There was no humor in Chance's stance. "You're so concerned with what everyone thinks of you. You've convinced yourself they hate you—that they'd get rid of you in a heartbeat if you so much as looked at a student the wrong way."

"This is not the time—"

"Violet, nobody is out to get you—least of all me."

Chance paced toward me, trapping me against the whiteboard.

"They might be a little put off by you, but they think you're a good person and a great teacher." He raised his hand slowly, delicately combing his fingers through the ends of my hair. "You isolate yourself, but if you give them a chance..."

Again I found myself furious with my heart, for pounding so fast, and with my body, for angling toward his touch.

He could be a predator...

I shook my head, trying to regain my wits. "Why are you telling me this?" I said through my teeth, though I wasn't mentally strong enough to push him away from me.

"Because I don't want you to hate me," he whispered, leaning in.

The sound of feet shuffling and male laughter in the hallway pulled us both from our daze. Chance stepped back from me, just in time.

A few boys sauntered in, joking with each other.

"Hey, Mr. H," Jonathan Walters, a sweet, but rather dim student said, looking around the classroom, completely unaware of the sparring match he and his friends had interrupted. "Is this the right classroom?"

I glared at Chance, wordlessly commanding him to leave.

He stood his ground as the boys settled in their usual seats at the back of the room, having come to the conclusion that they were in the correct place.

I didn't know what he wanted from me, so I spoke the truth at that moment, hoping it would be enough to end the conversation. "I can't hate you, Chance. I don't *know* you."

He gave an exasperated sigh at the sentiment, and I thought he might leave, but he just had to get the last word in. "Whoever made you feel like you need to be so guarded at all times, I'm not him. And I'm not giving up."

"Get the fuck out of my classroom," I growled under my breath.

12

A VEXING EXCHANGE

"**E**arth to Violet." Jolene waved her fingers in front of my face, pulling me from my thoughts.

"Huh?"

"You don't usually let me prattle on about sewing and knitting techniques for this long." She chuckled, amused by my vacant state.

I'd been replaying both my interaction with Chance and the conversation I had overheard between him and Claire all day. I was missing something, and I couldn't put my finger on it. Whatever it was, it was burrowing deeper under my skin, determined to gnaw at me until I figured it out.

"Sorry." I stared at the midterm papers in front of me. I'd resolved to keep Jolene company while she worked late to finalize the quarter-end finances, which needed to be mailed out before the last mail pickup. I hadn't wanted to go back to the carriage house, afraid I might run into Chance and blurt out that I'd heard him talking with Claire, giving up the only leverage I had.

What do you need leverage for?

"Are you going to tell me what's up, or do I have to coax it out of you?" Jolene smiled at me over her desk, the orange sequins from the giant pumpkin on her sweater flashing upon the movement.

I did trust Jolene, but I was torn about sharing all the details of what I'd witnessed. Something weird was definitely going on, but the only thing I'd really been able to discern from the bit I'd overheard was that Chance and Claire seemed to know each other and were working together on something, which they were trying to keep under wraps...something dangerous, Chance had pointed out.

I needed to tread incredibly carefully with what I said and who I said it to. If I said the wrong thing to the wrong person, I might get someone hurt, or find myself without a job.

"What do you know about Claire DeLongpre?" I asked Jolene.

Her eyes narrowed on me. "Enough to know you don't want to mess with her," she warned.

Anxiously, I chewed on the corner of my mouth. "Has she ever gotten in trouble at Montgomery—like *real* trouble?"

Jolene considered me for a moment. "Not that I know of, but her parents are donors, so anything could have easily been swept under the rug." Her brow furrowed. "Are you going to tell me what this is about?"

I didn't know why exactly I was protecting Chance, but something about the way they spoke to each other indicated there was fear underlying whatever they were working on.

"Violet," Jolene scolded me for stalling.

"I overheard her having a weird conversation with someone. I don't know what they were talking about exactly, but it sounded...I don't know, it sounded like they were up to something." I sighed, not knowing how exactly to explain without divulging everything.

"Who was she talking to?"

"I—I don't know," I stuttered.

Jolene seemed to see through me, but rather than call me on it, she leaned back in her chair, appraisingly. "You should report it to the deputy headmistress," she finally suggested. "She'll take you seriously."

"But I wouldn't even know what to report." I raked my hands down my face, trying to figure out the best course of action. Maybe I could try to talk to Claire and just make sure she was okay?

What I really needed was more information.

I tried to hide the light bulb going off over my head when I realized the answer was right in front of my face.

"What are you going to do then?"

Spy on their dinner meetup.

"Maybe if I sleep on it, I'll figure it out," I lied.

Jolene's eyes narrowed on me, suspecting I was up to something.

"Can I grab you dinner before I head to my room?" I offered, in a poor attempt to distract her.

Her lips pursed, seemingly well aware of what I was trying to accomplish. "Okay."

Luck seemed to be on my side that night.

I scanned the dining hall from behind the kitchen service window and spotted Chance first, just before he casually strolled out of one of the dining room doors. A moment later, Claire got up from her table, leaving her tray for the kitchen staff to clean up, rather than returning it to the racks near the exit, and she slowly followed the same path Chance had taken.

"Don't move these," I instructed a bewildered kitchen assistant as I abandoned the to-go containers I was filling for myself and Jolene and dashed back through the kitchen. Lenny raised an eyebrow in my wake, following my gaze out of the service window to Claire's retreating form, but didn't say anything.

They'd left through the front entrance of the dining hall, and in theory could have gone in multiple directions. Finding the entrance hall empty, I knew they hadn't gone downstairs into the administrative offices, where they would have found a harried Jolene stapling and collating finance paperwork.

That left either going outside, which would have led to a whole slew of possible paths, or ducking into the hallway that led to the classrooms. I chose the latter, thinking that with the chilly fall weather and bright lampposts illuminating the front lawn, the dark and likely empty hallways of the school were a much better bet.

Stepping lightly and keeping to the shadows, I hadn't made it far before I heard hushed whispers.

"Where are the photos you mentioned?" Chance asked.

"On my phone," Claire replied.

"Send them to my personal email address, and don't show anyone," Chance commanded the girl. "If we don't do this the right way, we could be implicated."

My brow furrowed. I was even more convinced this wasn't some kind of affair. If there were photos of them together, why would he want copies? He'd want her to destroy them. No, this had to be something else.

"Nobody knows, I promise." Claire's tone turned flirtatious.

"Keep it that way." His voice was stern. "Don't follow me right away."

I tucked myself into an alcove, holding my breath as Chance strode past, oblivious to my presence, and holding a laptop he hadn't been in possession of when he'd left the dining hall only a minute earlier.

Claire followed his instructions and waited a while before making her way down the hall and back toward the front entrance.

If Jolene suspected I had been up to something when I'd taken a half hour to grab her dinner, she didn't mention it when I returned with her lukewarm food.

"Hey, I meant to ask you," I began, "did you say you checked into Chance Harper being an alumni?"

Jolene's gaze turned devilish. "I knew you liked him."

"I don't."

She clicked her tongue.

"Like who?" Milton, the IT guy, sauntered out of the shadows in the hallway. I wondered how long he had been eavesdropping on our conversation. He had a habit of working late some evenings, but coincidentally, it was always when Jolene was working after hours and I was keeping her company.

"Nobody," I said quickly.

His eyes scanned me from head to toe, lingering too long for my comfort. I turned back to Jolene, not wanting to make eye contact. But her eyes were decidedly fixed on Milton. I might have even seen hearts in them.

Yuck.

"Want anything from the faculty lounge?" he offered, eyes squarely on me.

"Rain check?" Jolene piped up sweetly.

His gaze slid to hers. "Okay." He gave her a half smile and continued through the front office up the main stairs.

I waited until he should have been out of earshot before I continued. "You're sure about Chance? I just keep getting the sense that he's familiar with Montgomery, but if you say you looked him up..."

With a few clicks and keystrokes, she pointed to the screen. "No records for a Chance Harper. In fact, the only person with the last name Harper was a girl who attended in the eighties." She turned the monitor so I could look at the screen. "See."

Sure enough, there was only one record showing on the screen for a "Cindy Harper," graduated class of 1987.

"And even if he was a transfer student, he'd show up in the records?"

"Definitely," Jolene confirmed. She let out a small gasp as her sweater snagged on a splinter from the wood desk, causing a small waterfall of sequins to scatter across the floor before she was able to stop the thread from hemorrhaging more.

I took a beat while she was distracted, trying to find the emergency sewing kit stashed in her desk.

The faculty that had attended Montgomery were quite vocal about the fact, finding it a point of pride. And Montgomery was very prestigious, which made having attended a badge of honor in certain circles. So if Chance had attended Montgomery, as I suspected, why would he hide it? What could he gain from keeping it a secret?

"Does it matter if he went here?" Jolene's attention was solely focused on mending her sweater.

"I guess it doesn't. It's just been bothering me. I think he's lying."

"Sounds like you're grasping at straws to justify disliking him, and if you can prove he lied about something, it will give you a valid reason."

I hated that she hit a little too close to home on her assumption. But it was worse than that. I think in some weird way, I needed to find something wrong with him. Because if I didn't, it would only be a matter of time before I wouldn't be able to fight my attraction to him.

This little research project might have been a last-ditch effort to prove once and for all that Chance wasn't who he appeared to be.

And if he really was, then I'd surely give in. Maybe giving in to Chance wouldn't be so bad, as long as I knew for sure he was being honest with me...about everything.

Because the last time I'd let myself fall for someone, I hadn't done anything to protect myself, and it had almost ruined me. I wouldn't let that happen again. I had to know what I was getting myself into. I needed to learn from my past mistakes.

"I have to get these in the mail." Having fixed her sweater, Jolene stood, collecting the organized and sealed mailers from her desk.

"I'll walk you to your car."

13

OLIVE BRANCH

I still had half my midterms to grade when the weekend came around. Having unintentionally woken up early on Saturday morning, I decided it would be more productive to actually get something done, as opposed to lying in bed and thinking about Chance.

I was no closer to figuring out what he was up to, but I was at least sure that a romantic entanglement was quite unlikely, though I still worried about what danger both of them thought they might be in. It felt as though the answer was on the tip of my tongue, but no matter how hard I tried, I couldn't figure out how to arrange the pieces to make them fit together to form a bigger picture.

Rolling out of bed, I refused to change out of my pajamas, wanting to be as comfortable as possible.

I glanced up at the string dangling from the trapdoor to the lounge while I brushed my teeth in the bathroom.

I missed my lounge. I was going stir-crazy having only my apartment to occupy.

"Screw Chance Harper," I declared after spitting out my toothpaste into the sink. "It's my lounge. Not his."

I scurried about my room, making a cup of coffee, gathering my papers, and tidying as I went.

It was chilly when I at last made it upstairs, and the grey light streaming through the windows from a gloomy autumn sky made it feel that much colder. I regretted not bringing my sweatshirt up with me, but I had blankets on the sofa, and the room would warm up considerably once I got a fire going.

The lounge didn't look any different since I had last been up there, but the energy had shifted, and I could almost smell the spice of Chance's cologne in the air, confirming that he'd been there. It rankled me that he knew my secret. It felt as though his knowledge of the space had somehow tainted it.

I was surprised, but pleased, to find that Chance had more than replenished the woodpile next to the fire. I scowled as I felt my heart flutter at the thought of Chance doing so to make things easier for me.

Once the fire was blazing, I found a suitable record to play on the *gramophone*, I remembered, as I had been so eloquently schooled on the difference between the various models by Chance.

I was able to work in peace for a few hours before I was startled by a tap on the far window.

I groaned when a second tap sounded, and got up to traipse across the lounge, finding Chance struggling to juggle two steaming mugs with one hand as he used the other to attempted to lift the window on his own.

"Hey." He beamed the moment I opened the window. He handed me both mugs so he could climb through without falling on his stupid, pretty face.

Chance was also dressed casually in a long-sleeve Henley that accentuated every single sinew of his muscular torso, arms, and shoulders. But that day he had opted for a pair of dark wash jeans instead of the pajama pants he had been sporting the first time he had invaded my space.

"What's this?" I motioned to the mugs as I stepped back to allow him space to enter the room.

"A peace offering." He chuckled sheepishly as he closed the window behind him, shutting out the cold air from outside.

I followed him as he started toward the far end of the room, but stopped abruptly alongside Chance as he wistfully gazed at the piano. "When do you think was the last time somebody played her?"

Her?

"Thirty or forty years."

My eyes widened as he took a seat on the bench, dust puffing up from the velvet upholstery. Lifting the cover from the keys, he got out a few bars of "The Entertainer" but pulled his fingers back as the notes soured, wincing at the sound. "Hasn't been tuned in longer than that."

I said nothing. I hoped he couldn't hear my heart thundering in my chest. An image of me sitting next to him on the bench, my head on his shoulder as he played a soft tune, flitted into my mind, but I quickly shoved it from my thoughts.

Chance stood from the bench and wandered toward the wall of books on the interior of the room. "Were the books already organized when you discovered them?" he asked vacantly, crouching down to read some of the titles on the bottom shelf.

"No," I said quietly, fondly remembering the hours I had spent categorizing by genre, then alphabetizing, then organizing them neatly shelf by shelf.

"Really?" He looked at me over his shoulder. "I bet it took you forever."

I nodded. I didn't think he was making fun of me.

He smiled, seemingly impressed, but quickly turned back to the shelves. "Cool! Old yearbooks!" he exclaimed, grabbing a stack from one of the shelves.

I must have audibly gasped because he quickly replied, "Don't worry, I'll put them back where I found them." He carried the books over to the study table on the opposite side of the room. "Come here."

Without permission, my legs carried me to Chance. He held up his hand and gently took one of the still-steaming mugs from my hand.

"It's hot chocolate," he noted before taking a sip.

When I said nothing and made no attempt to move, he looked up at me, eyebrow raised in jest, and said, "It's not poisoned."

I looked down at the cup, wondering what it would mean if I took a drink.

"You're not lactose intolerant or allergic to chocolate, are you?" He laughed.

"No," I replied quietly. Feeling his eyes on me, I took a sip to appease him. A soft moan escaped as the liquid hit my tongue. It was perfect. Of course. Cooled to just the right temperature, and creamy because he'd used milk instead of water. I couldn't help but go back for another taste.

Daring to glance up at Chance, he displayed only the hint of a satisfied smirk.

"Truce?"

I frowned. "Don't press your luck."

His smirk broadened in amusement as I couldn't help but take another drink.

"What does it matter if we're on good terms or not?" I leaned my weight against the heavy wood study table.

"Why do you insist on pushing everyone away?" he countered.

I scoffed.

"I like you, Violet." His gaze turned hungry. "I know you like me too. I think you hate that you do." Chance chuckled darkly.

Was I so easy to read?

I could only glare in response. My stomach flipped at his admission.

He leaned forward, slightly invading my space, his voice was low when he said, "From what I can tell, the school doesn't enforce this non-fraternization policy you keep using as justification for keeping me at arm's length. So unless you tell me to stop, I think I'll keep pushing."

"Maybe you should stop," I whispered half-heartedly, internally cursing the tremor in my voice.

"You sure about that?" Chance cocked his head.

I clenched my jaw. I didn't mean it. I knew that. He knew that.

"What are you working on?" Chance changed the subject suddenly, his fingers sliding over the stack of papers behind me on the table.

"Grading midterms." I swallowed; he was still achingly close.

"Is it okay if I stay up here for a while?" He took a step back from me, picking up the stack of yearbooks.

"Sure, whatever." I waved a hand flippantly.

He flashed me a grin, then strode past me to settle on the couch. Chance was surprisingly respectful while I worked. Save for the sound of him flipping through yearbooks and the tension still lingering in the air, I barely noticed he was there.

I had expected to feel more put out with him in the room, but I continued to feel drawn to him in a way that made me question everything. I regretted not allowing myself to enjoy the lounge for the past few weeks. Maybe things wouldn't be so bad with him around after all.

Make no mistake, I was still going to figure him out, but I didn't have to force myself to be miserable in the process.

After a couple hours, satisfied with the progress I'd made on my stack of exams, I began to pack my things. My stomach grumbled on cue, suddenly realizing it was past lunch.

"Heading out?"

"For a while," I replied. "I want to grab something to eat from the dining hall."

"Can I come?" he asked eagerly, already striding over to the bookshelf to replace the yearbooks in their proper spots, as promised.

"I need to change first." I sighed, knowing it would be awkward if I refused.

"Just knock on my door when you're ready." He gathered the empty mugs and made his way over to the far window to descend the fire escape back into his apartment.

I took a moment to gather myself as I swapped the loungewear for slacks and a polo, not wanting any students to see me looking less than professional.

I rolled my eyes as I found myself primping in the mirror. I wondered if part of the frustration I felt regarding Chance was that my mind was at war with itself when I was close to him. It was exhausting to ping pong between thoughts of desire and physiological reactions when I was near him, to having to remind myself that he had already proven himself untrustworthy between the stunt he had pulled the first night we had met and whatever he was doing with Claire DeLongpre.

But I was finding it impossible to stop the butterflies in my stomach every time he smiled at me, or spoke in that soft and low voice, trying to entice me to him. It was much easier to avoid him entirely, but he had seemingly decided to thwart that tactic.

Walking in charged silence to the dining hall, there were a million things I wanted to ask Chance; most of them were completely irrational, inappropriate, or were about what the hell he was doing with Claire. I decided keeping my mouth shut was a better approach.

"I didn't realize how late it was." Chance was disappointed when we found the dining hall had stopped serving lunch for the day. Only a few students lingered in the dining hall, either studying for classes, or eating food they'd brought themselves.

"Give me a sec."

Chance looked puzzled, but took a seat at an empty table near the entrance to the kitchen.

"Chef Lenny." I saluted upon entering.

"Lunch is over, Violet." Lenny scowled. But it was an affectionate one.

"There aren't any leftovers?" I asked sweetly.

He rolled his eyes, but tipped his head toward the service area.

I was easily able to fill two plates and quickly returned to Chance in the dining room, only after offering Lenny a "thank you" on my way out.

"Oh thank god." Chance sighed in relief. "I'm starving and the only food I have in my room other than the hot chocolate is a box of crackers."

I couldn't help but give a genuine laugh at the thought of him angrily munching away at crackers alone in his apartment.

"You have a car, you could have driven to get food in town," I suggested as I took a seat next to him on the long bench, intentionally angling my body toward him, so I could keep an eye on him.

"Been too busy," he sighed. "I didn't know you had a connection in the kitchen."

There was a glint in his eyes that made me nervous. "Yeah, well, I don't often abuse it, so don't get any ideas."

He snorted a laugh.

But then a light bulb went on over my head, and I realized he had just provided me with the perfect opportunity to ask him about his potential history at Montgomery.

"Was Chef Lenny working here when you attended?"

He froze.

GOTCHA!

"I never went here." He recovered quickly, but the damage had been done.

"You sure about that?" I glared at him, mimicking his words from earlier that morning.

"I think I'd know where I went to high school." He chuckled, but I could sense his nerves along the edge of his tone.

He was only digging his own grave.

"Who told you I was a student here?" he asked cautiously, focusing his attention on the food in front of him to keep from looking me in the eyes.

"I don't remember," I lied. "One of the faculty, I think."

Chance's eyes narrowed. It was more obvious than ever that he had gone to Montgomery at some point and that he was trying desperately to keep it under wraps.

"So when are we going to talk about the elephant in the room?" he inquired nonchalantly.

"What!?" I choked. Did he know I had seen him and Claire?

Chance laughed. "What is it going to take for you to forgive me for not telling you I was teaching here the night we met?"

"Oh." I breathed a sigh of relief.

My reaction seemed to puzzle Chance.

He glanced around the dining hall. The couple of students that had been around when we'd first arrived had since left. We were alone. He leaned in so close that his lips almost brushed against the shell of my ear. "I thought we had a lovely evening, and I was looking forward to spending more time with you."

"Then maybe you should have taken me up on my offer that night because you're definitely not getting another invitation." I found I was starting to quite enjoy antagonizing him.

"Tell me how to make this right?" His fingers grazed the outside of my thigh, under the table, sending sparks of electricity up my spine.

"I don't owe you anything." It was taking everything in me not to lean into his touch.

"Do you want me to beg? I will." He smiled against my ear.

I pulled away from him, not trusting myself in such close proximity. "We're in public." I swallowed.

"You haven't answered my question," he pleaded.

"Honestly?" My tone came out short. I was frustrated and confused, and it was all his fault. I was tired of being polite. "There is something off about you—something that doesn't add up."

The corner of Chance's mouth turned up in an intrigued smirk.

"I can't put my finger on it, but I'm going to find out what you're hiding," I threatened.

Chance leaned forward one last time, his face so close that if I moved at all I could have closed the gap to kiss him. "I bet you will."

14

TRIPPED UP

"Has anything come from that conversation you overheard?" Jolene hedged. As we were close to Halloween, she was donning a bright orange sweater featuring white ghost appliques with beady little eyes (literally) sewn to both the front and back.

"No." I shook my head.

"And you're certain you don't know who Claire was speaking with?" She eyed me, definitely suspecting I knew more than I was letting on. "Because if you do, you should report them."

"I can't do anything...yet," I told her. "I can't go around leveling accusations without more information or any evidence to back up my claim. I still don't know what they were even talking about."

"I'm not sure if you need evidence. Let the headmistress dig into it," she disagreed with my assessment.

But she hadn't been there. She hadn't heard what I had. I was still certain it wasn't any kind of romantic relationship—I would have reported Chance if I suspected it was. That was crossing a line no teacher should ever come close to. Still I worried about the "danger" Chance referenced. I thought maybe if I could get closer to him, maybe I could convince him to tell me, or I'd have more information to figure things out for myself.

Things had been decidedly more cordial between us since he'd extended an olive branch over the weekend, but I was more suspicious of him than ever. I just didn't know what or why he was hiding things. Basically, I had nothing.

"What happens if you never find any evidence?" she posed. "You're just going to let her get away with doing whatever shady stuff she's up to?"

I huffed. "You know it's not that easy. The wrong kind of accusation could ruin her future."

She let my words sink in before responding, "Who cares? They're all rich. They'll just throw money at it to make it go away." I couldn't miss the simmering fury behind her words. She'd worked at Montgomery for just over twenty years and hadn't come from money either. We had bonded over similar backgrounds and being jaded by the wealth that was flaunted around us.

"Jolene, it's about integrity." I shook my head.

I wished I hadn't told her.

She clicked her tongue in disagreement.

"If I find anything, I *will* turn her in. I'll do the right thing."

"Turn who in, Miss Price?" Headmaster Winston had materialized in the hallway behind Jolene's desk.

I paled, mentally scrambling for a decent lie. "A student turned in an essay that seemed familiar."

"Oh?" He raised a bushy eyebrow and pursed his lips simultaneously.

"I don't believe the student would cheat, and I have to go through my records from last year." The lies continued to unravel before me.

"See that you do; we don't tolerate cheating of any kind at Montgomery Prep," he confirmed.

His gaze was wary and I thought he still suspected he was missing the truth of our conversation.

"Yes, Headmaster." I nodded. "I don't want to jeopardize the student's academic future if the similarities are merely coincidental." I eyed Jolene as I spoke.

A scowl formed on her face.

"Good." The headmaster seemed to be appeased. "I appreciate your thoroughness and caution with such a delicate matter."

I blinked and he was already down the hall, closing his office door.

I pointed my finger at Jolene. "Not a word of this to anyone. Not even your cats."

She sighed in defeat.

I was up in the lounge, just after dinner, finishing grading the last of the midterm tests later that evening, when I heard the sirens off in the distance. I knew immediately they could only be for someone at Montgomery because the campus was so far removed from the closest town and residential homes that I would have never heard them otherwise.

Scrambling down the trapdoor ladder, I threw on a coat and shoes and raced out into the hall. Chance almost ran right into me, exiting his apartment the same moment I passed his door.

"What's going on?" he asked in a rush, hurriedly following me down the stairs.

"I don't know, but it can't be good."

A crowd had gathered in front of the main building, consisting of both students and staff. The headmaster was instructing the dorm monitors to escort the students back to their building in one breath and telling the staff to go back to their rooms with the next.

I spotted Jolene, her bright orange sweater making her stand out in the crowd. Her arms were gathered tightly around her waist, as if she was self-soothing.

"Jolene?" I called out to her when I was closer.

She turned, her face red and blotchy from crying. Smears of red blood marred the previously white ghosts on the front side of her sweater.

"What happened!?" I wanted to hug her, but was wary of the blood, so instead I put a reassuring arm around her shoulders.

She glanced up at Chance, who had followed me. Her gaze narrowed before she turned her attention back to me. "A student fell down the stairs to the admin offices. It was horrible, there was blood everywhere."

"You saw it happen?" I began gently combing my fingers through her hair, trying to comfort her.

She nodded, sniffling.

"Who was it?" Chance asked softly.

Jolene looked at Chance, studying him for a brief moment, then back to me when she replied, "Claire DeLongpre."

My jaw went slack at the revelation.

"You're sure?" I breathed.

"Yeah I'm sure!" Jolene shouted, then fell into another fit of sobs, perhaps disturbed by her own outburst.

"It's going to be okay." I rubbed circles on her back as she cried.

I looked up at Chance, who had gone deathly still and pale.

His shocked blue-grey eyes met mine. He looked devastated.

Claire had her whole life ahead of her. Could it really have been so cruelly snuffed out before she'd had the chance to reach any kind of potential?

As I soothed Jolene, I watched my hand move of its own volition to reach for Chance, lacing my fingers through his, trying to offer him some sort of comfort.

We stood there for a while and watched as the paramedics entered the building with an empty gurney and returned a while later with a closed body bag supported on the frame. I stayed with Jolene until the police found her and asked to speak with her to get her account.

Security cameras were sparse at Montgomery, only present in common areas, so I wasn't sure what help they could be in seeing what had happened.

Slowly most of the staff drifted away, leaving only Chance and me standing on the lawn. I'd reluctantly released his hand at some point, not wanting anyone to see it. A police officer came by and politely asked us to leave after a while, and when I tried to say I was waiting for Jolene, he let me know she would be escorted home when they were finished talking to her.

"She'll be okay," Chance told me as we walked back to the carriage house.

But he didn't know. He didn't know Jolene. She could be so sensitive. I knew she was hurting.

He was quiet otherwise, still quite shaken. I wanted to tell him I knew he had a connection to Claire, but I couldn't find the courage in that moment. It seemed so callous.

He paused in front of his door, and I can't say what compelled me to do so, but I embraced him. He sunk into my hold, pulling me close, needing the comfort. I could have sworn I heard him say, "It's my fault," but his voice was muffled by my hair.

I pulled back from him, wiping an errant tear that had fallen down his cheek. "You're going to be okay," I told him.

He swallowed, then opened his mouth to speak, but he shook his head, closing it only a second later, as if he'd thought better of saying whatever he had been going to.

"I'm here, if you want to talk," I offered, sensing that he was on the verge of revealing something.

He nodded.

I moved to step away, and was surprised when he stood in the doorway watching me as I made my way to my own room. I remembered what he had said to me the first night we'd met as he departed. "I want to make sure you're safe inside your room." He had watched me the same way then.

And sure enough, when I closed my door, I heard his click shut a moment later.

Exhausted, I stripped out of my clothes and collapsed into bed. As I fell into a fitful sleep, I kept replaying his whispered confession in my mind.

"It's my fault."

And I realized with a creeping dread that Chance didn't think Claire's death had been an accident.

15

PROM QUEEN

The atmosphere at the school was somber.

Both Jolene and Chance were quiet and pensive, leaving me feeling anxious and out of sorts.

Chance seemed to have been in his room when Claire had fallen, so I was almost certain he hadn't physically caused her death, but he clearly knew so much more than he was saying, and based on how withdrawn he had become in the few days since she'd passed, I felt that he was blaming himself for her fate.

I had a sinking feeling that Jolene suspected I was keeping something from her; maybe she'd seen me comforting Chance and her feelings were hurt that I hadn't discussed it with her. As a result, I sensed her pulling away from me.

She wasn't quite as cheery as her usual self, didn't share gossip as readily, and her smile didn't feel as bright as it used to. I hated to think I had a part in dimming her light.

In an effort to redirect Jolene's discontentment and distract her from what she had witnessed, I pulled her in to help me figure out what Chance Harper was hiding and just prayed it wasn't something completely nefarious.

Watching Chance pore over the yearbooks in the lounge had given me the idea to go through the more recent years, which were, unfortunately for me, located in the creepiest room in the basement: the records room.

Nestled behind Jolene's desk, the door locked from the outside, and I had on more than one occasion rescued her from the door having closed on her, trapping her inside. And once inside, the buzzing from the overhead lighting was even more intense in such a small space. Sounds echoed off the stone walls, making it constantly feel like someone was right behind you. And then there was the smell...

Normally I loved the smell of books, the older the better, but the books and papers in the records room smelled as though they were rotting from within, despite there being no evidence of mold or anything else that was causing the odor.

The one benefit of working in the records room was that it offered a hidden space where I could work without the headmaster or any of the other nosy admin staff bothering me or giving Jolene snotty glares because she had allowed me into an area typically reserved for staff of their level only. God help me if they knew she had shared with me the secret location of her master key set.

Nestled away in the records room, after classes had been dismissed for the day, I was thankful Jolene had propped the door open with a stone block that had long ago detached from part of the main building and been relocated to the basement offices for such an appointment.

On the first day, I studied the six years Chance could have attended Montgomery, given his age. The second day, after taking another look at the student records on Jolene's computer and having no luck finding a student with a name even close to his, I broadened my search, thinking perhaps he was lying about his age, but I soon gave up on that theory as well.

"Can rich people pay to have their name changed without having to make a public announcement?" I asked Jolene on the third day of *Project Expose Chance Harper*.

She'd grown increasingly annoyed with me as the days passed, worried someone on staff would see me rifling around the records room and report her to the headmaster. She had decided that Chance hadn't gone to Montgomery, and while she had initially teased me about him at the beginning of the school year, it seemed the idea of something going on between us wasn't sitting well with her. She had soured on him, and I wasn't sure why.

"Is that still a thing? Having to put that in the paper or something?" She munched on a snack at her desk, the black and silver metallic pom-poms on her sweater, forming a colony of bats of all different shapes and sizes, glittering as she moved.

"In Maine it is," I confirmed. "I already tried looking at the public records and couldn't find anything. And the only thing I can find about him on Google is about his college degree being from Oxford, but the page with the information is the Montgomery faculty page."

"What about his family?" Jolene suggested.

"Yeah, I could stand to turn over a few stones there," I grumbled. The work was tedious, but I really felt like I was so close to breaking the whole thing wide open.

Another quick round on Google didn't turn up anything about Chance or his family that I could find. Maybe he had paid a service to scrub search engines of his information?

Then I had a thought. I recalled a lecture I'd given recently in class about how the Greek family unit worked, and it got me thinking about how everything is passed down and how the Greeks, just like so many families today, expected their children to follow in their footsteps.

I was willing to bet anyone that Chance Harper was a legacy at Montgomery—the vast majority of students admitted had family members who attended before them, and being a legacy gave applicants a leg up in admissions. So did cash, consequently.

I jumped up, tearing into the records room, digging through the stacks of old yearbooks to find the one from 1987.

"What's going on?" She poked her head through the door, watching me with curiosity.

"I can't find 1987," I huffed, eyes scanning the pile again. They were in numerical order, but occasionally there would be duplicates of some years, while others would be missing entirely.

"I'm not sure. Sometimes the headmaster sends yearbooks to alumni if they call to request them." She worried her lip. "Why?"

"Remember there was one other Harper? I thought maybe they'd be related." I slumped against the wall, having reached yet another dead end.

"I've heard there's more yearbooks in storage on campus somewhere. I can ask the headmaster," Jolene offered.

"I'm such an idiot!" I laughed.

It was how I'd gotten the idea to look at the yearbooks in the first place. I could only hope there were yearbooks up in the lounge that were as recent as 1987. I couldn't remember the last year, but I knew that within the range, no years were missing.

"I gotta go." I scrambled to grab my bag and coat. "I'll see you tomorrow; thanks, Jolene!" I shouted, already halfway up the stairs.

I booked it across the courtyard to the carriage house, thundering up the three flights of stairs and dumping my things on the floor, just inside the door, in a heap before launching myself up the trap door to the lounge.

The most recent yearbook in the lounge was 1988, and sitting neatly on the shelf right before it was the one from 1987.

Plucking it from the bookcase, I immediately settled at the study table and flipped to the graduate mugshots. And there I found her: Cindy Harper.

Cindy was beautiful, despite the big eighties hair and bright blue eyeshadow. The makeup perfectly emphasized her striking eyes—the same blue-grey eyes that belonged to my nemesis, Chance Harper.

I flipped to the index to see where else she appeared in the book, only to find out that she had been voted Prom Queen that year, with her high school beau, Thomas Roberts, voted as Prom King. The two had also been voted "Best Couple" in the superlatives.

Thomas also looked vaguely familiar, which might have been because Chance clearly shared some of his features as well. But after staring at their posed prom picture for longer than I cared to admit, it hit me.

Chance's father was *the* Thomas Roberts, multi-gajillionaire business mogul, and in recent years, a congressman. He'd gained his fame in the late nineties, being one of the few who had seen the dot-com bubble burst coming and making sure he'd profit off the crash. And then he had repeated the same foresight and success just before the 2008 housing crash and subsequent recession.

"Unbelievable..." I muttered to myself.

"What is?" Chance asked from behind me.

I slammed the book closed and covered it with a research paper I'd left on the table over the weekend.

"Nothing," I squeaked.

Chance's eyebrows raised, immediately recognizing I was up to something.

As usual, he was looking rather dashing in a navy blue sweater and grey slacks, along with a pair of shiny black wingtips. Taking the brief moment to assess him caused a flash of desire to mingle with the fear of being discovered, while I worked to expose him and his true identity.

The anger and resentment that no matter what he did, no matter how mad he made me, no matter what secrets he was keeping from me, I still wanted him, continued to bubble beneath the surface, threatening to explode at any moment.

And who knew how that explosion would manifest? I was just as likely to shove him out the window as I was to climb on top of him.

"I brought you dinner." He produced two takeout containers from the dining hall and set them on the table.

Chef Lenny and I were going to have a talk about consorting with the enemy. And also, why the hell had he gone and done something so thoughtful? He made me feel like a monster...a lonely, desperate monster.

"You didn't have to do that." I tried not to smell the food, but my stomach betrayed me, grumbling in protest. I might have forgotten to eat lunch while going down Google rabbit holes trying to find references to Chance's family.

"I saw you run outside like a bat out of hell when classes finished, so I figured you hadn't eaten." He pulled out the chair next to me.

Jolene's bat sweater flashed in my mind, and a giggle erupted from my lips.

Chance cocked his head, amused by my demeanor. "What has gotten into you?"

I slowly slid the books farther away from him, trying to be discreet, but failing miserably as his gaze tracked the movement for a beat before landing back on me.

"You must be on to some big breakthrough," he said while taking the lid off his food.

"What?" I quacked.

Chance's brow furrowed. "You're writing a research paper to publish, aren't you?" He nodded toward the large report covering the yearbook.

"Something like that," I laughed, sounding a little too relieved at the suggestion.

"You don't have to keep it a secret. I won't tell anyone," he said between bites of his food.

My heart began to race. I needed to get away from him. If he saw the yearbook, I knew he'd put two and two together. If he felt threatened, what would he be capable of? I was 99% sure he hadn't hurt Claire, but there was still that 1%. We were alone in the lounge. Nobody was around to help me if he did something.

Chance surprised me when he started packing up his half-eaten food. It seemed he had realized my prickly behavior meant I wasn't in the mood for company. I flinched when he got up from his seat, and I could have sworn I heard him sigh in disappointment.

"I didn't mean to disrupt your work." He picked up the container, pausing for a moment to add, "Let me know if you want another set of eyes when you start editing." He smiled sadly.

"Thank you for dinner," I replied softly.

He looked me up and down, studying me for a moment, perhaps considering asking me why I was suddenly so jumpy, but thankfully he eventually decided against it and padded to the far end of the lounge, taking his leave.

I'd never been more relieved when I heard the window snick as it closed.

My heart told me Chance was innocent, but my head couldn't just ignore all the facts against him. At the very least, he was a Roberts, and he was lying about it.

What it meant...I didn't know. But I was determined to find out.

16

ALEXANDER ROBERTS

The next morning, I was up early, a feat in itself, with the intention to sneak into the records room before class to look at the more recent yearbooks since I had a new name to search for.

"Violet!" Jolene exclaimed with her usual exuberance. Only I hadn't expected her to be working so early, so her excitement startled me. The cartoonish, green-skinned witch on her sweater, on the other hand, may have frightened me just a bit more.

"Jolene," I stuttered, hands clasped over my chest. "Hi."

"I don't think I've ever seen you up so early." She giggled.

"Ha, ha," I replied sardonically. It was only seven in the morning.

"Did you need help with something?"

"Actually, yes." I couldn't help but grin conspiratorially. "I got a new lead last night. Can you pull up all the students with the last name Roberts who attended the school between 2000 and 2015?" I decided to be overly generous with the time frame, just in case Chance had also lied about his age.

Jolene's eyes widened at the request. "I have so many questions, I don't know what to ask first." She paused to take a deep breath.

"Do you mean Roberts as in relatives of Montgomery's most prolific alumni, Thomas Roberts?"

"Yeah, those Roberts," I confirmed. "I'll explain more later." I grabbed the keys from Jolene's desk to open up the records room, holding my breath as the odiferous miasma emanating from the room enveloped me.

I plucked six yearbooks from the shelf: the four that would have ranged from his freshman through senior year, if he was indeed thirty-one, and two more to add a year on either end, in case he'd been enrolled at an earlier or later age, and began combing through the student portraits each year.

There were plenty of Roberts, that was for sure, but none of them looked anything like Chance—or his parents, for that matter. I recalled reading that Thomas Roberts came from a large family when I had tried to do more online research the night before.

Checking through the class photos was taking longer than I planned, so I had to abandon the task to make it upstairs for my first period—Greek Mythology—my most popular class, with a promise to Jolene that I would return later to pick up where we had left off.

My abrupt arrival and disheveled appearance amused my students, but I was able to easily pick up the lecture I'd started the day before on the many lovers of Zeus and his penchant for turning into animals to seduce women who were not his wife. It was a rather salacious topic, in my opinion, but it kept a room of hormonal teenagers interested, so it was worth it.

The morning dragged, but eventually the lunch bell sounded, and I rushed out the door, down to the kitchen to grab food for myself and Jolene. I nearly avoided literally running into Chance, but he caught me around my waist just before I could face-plant into the food containers.

"Geez, Violet," he chuckled, "where are you off to in such a hurry?"

"I—ugh…" I stammered, trying to think of an explanation, but failed. "I gotta go." I ducked past him and scampered down the side hallway that spilled out into the front entrance and the stairway down to the basement offices.

"Nice seeing you!" Chance called out after me.

"Whoa—whoa—slow down." Jolene grabbed my arm after I threw the boxes at her. "I have your list." She held up a piece of yellow lined steno paper, filled with her eighth-grade bubble script, complete with little bubbles over the letters "I" and "J."

"This is great!" I exclaimed, snatching the list from her and scanning it. She had written out names, years of attendance, and birthdays. "I'm going to cross-reference these." I grinned.

"Helping Jolene with her work?" The headmaster appeared behind me, startling both Jolene and me.

My lips parted, at a loss for an adequate answer.

"Actually, Violet is still trying to figure out who wrote the research paper that might have been plagiarized." Jolene stepped in. "Since she brings me food from the kitchen *every* day so I can work through lunch, I didn't think you'd mind if I gave her a roster of her students from last year."

Bravo, Jolene!

"Carry on," he replied, with no hint of remorse, making his way up the main stairs, likely heading for the faculty lounge to eat lunch with the rest of the teachers.

A loud, relieved exhale escaped me, when he was out of sight.

"Nice cover, Jolene." I gave her a high five.

She blushed at the appreciative gesture. "He wouldn't get any-thing done if I wasn't here." She smirked, folding her arms over her chest. The action made the orange sequin eyes of the witch appear as though she was winking.

Of the twenty or so names that Jolene recorded, only four didn't have mug shots, and two of those were girls. As such, I focused on finding any evidence of the two male Roberts that were left, Alexander and Edward.

I quickly ruled out Edward when I saw photos of him with the basketball team; he was tall and gangly, with large ears and spiky hair. There was nothing about him that looked remotely like Chance.

Alexander was considerably harder to locate. He only attended Montgomery Prep for part of 2010, his Junior year, before trans-ferring. Coincidentally, his arrival lined up with the completion of the swimming pavilion Thomas Roberts had donated. I recalled thinking that Chance's upper body reminded me of a swimmer's physique. And the time frame put the elusive Alexander Roberts perfectly within the range that would match up with Chance's age.

There wasn't anything listed in the index for him, and nothing in the athletics section, other than photos of the grand opening of the swimming pavilion. But my persistence paid off.

Buried in a collage, I found a photo of a cute, but scrawny boy with braces, sitting in the library, and the caption beneath listed the boy as one Alexander Roberts. It was lucky that the photo was printed in color; otherwise, I might not have recognized those angsty blue-grey eyes.

Alexander Roberts was Chance Harper.

"I found him!" I cried, scrambling to my feet and bounding out of the records room to show Jolene.

"You did!?" She clapped excitedly from her desk.

I spotted the time on a cat-shaped clock resting next to her computer. It was quarter to one. "I have to go! I'll be late for class!"

"Wait, who is he?" Jolene asked.

"Alexander Roberts." I grinned. "Can I take this with me?" I lifted the 2010 yearbook in front of me.

"As long as you bring it back."

I nodded, tucking the book under my arm. "I don't suppose you'd do me a favor and see if you can find anything about him online?" I pleaded.

"Sure," she agreed in earnest.

"And don't let anyone know what you're up to, in case they're in on it," I warned her under my breath.

"Our secret." She beamed, happy to be included.

"I've got some tutoring after school. Will you still be here around dinner?" I asked, walking backward toward the stairs.

"Yes, the headmaster has me transcribing old board meetings, which is taking forever."

"I'll bring you food from the kitchen, and thank you!" I gave Jolene a small wave before ascending the stairs, feeling a sense of euphoria in my vindication.

Over dinner I'd brought down from the dining hall, Jolene recited every piece of information she could find on the ghost that was Alexander Roberts. Except he wasn't a ghost, he was an exceedingly handsome pain in my ass.

He was Thomas and Cindy's oldest child and only son. He had one younger sister, Amanda, who was my age. His father seemed to revel in the spotlight, but his mother and sister were phantoms similar to him, although I was able to locate a few images of his parents together at charity functions.

There was so much information on Thomas Roberts that it was next to impossible to find anything on Chance, or Alexander...whoever he was.

"The Roberts moved to London for two years around 2010 after Thomas opened up a new UK branch of his business," Jolene said after slurping her soup. "That must have been why he transferred."

"Makes sense then, how he ended up going to college at Oxford, and why we can't find much information on him stateside." I sighed. We didn't know much more than we had at lunch.

I needed more.

I fully realized my vendetta had gotten out of hand, but I think I had convinced myself that if I discovered his secret and confronted him, he'd finally be honest with me about everything. And if nothing else, at least I would have the satisfaction of knowing that I hadn't let another person pull the wool over my eyes and make a fool of me.

"Come upstairs with me." I tugged Jolene up by the wooly sleeve of her witch sweater.

"What? Why?" she whined, but followed me anyway.

I led us up the side hallway to the back door of the dining hall and opened it a crack. I'd noticed before that Chance liked to eat his dinner with a few of the other faculty members who preferred the noisy dining hall to the confines of the stuffy faculty lounge, where the more elitist of the teachers sequestered themselves during meals.

I spotted Chance in the far corner, intently listening to a story that Dr. Stephen Albert, one of the math teachers, was regaling him with.

"I need twenty minutes," I told Jolene. "Keep an eye on Chance and keep him occupied if he tries to leave before then. Text me if you lose him."

"What are you going to do!?" she asked in a hushed whisper, eyes wide with concern.

"I'm going to break into his room," I told her matter-of-factly.

Jolene's mouth gaped. "Violet..." she practically gasped.

"Twenty minutes!" I called out to her, already jogging down the hall to the front entrance.

Once back at the faculty dorms, I pulled down the ladder in my bathroom and rushed through the trapdoor to the lounge. I fumbled around in the dark to get to the far window and thanked the universe I was wearing slacks and flats that day, while I crawled down the precarious fire escape.

The metal rattled and creaked with even the slightest movement, and I couldn't believe Chance was comfortable using such a dangerous method of entry without batting an eye. As I'd hoped, Chance had left his window unlocked.

I didn't know exactly what I was looking for, only that I'd know it when I saw it. I needed to find something—anything, that would give me more information about who he actually was, and maybe point me in a direction to help me discover why he was hiding his identity. I'd exhausted all other avenues at that point.

His room was just as dark as the lounge, save for a dim red light emanating from behind the closed bathroom door.

Like a moth to a flame, I was drawn to the door.

Thankfully Chance kept his room tidy, and it seemed to be a mirror to my own, so I had no trouble making my way toward the bathroom, even in the dark. Turning the knob slowly, perhaps already sensing something sinister lay behind the closed door, I was not disappointed.

I stifled a gasp as the door swung open.

He had converted his bathroom into a darkroom to develop the photos he took on his old camera.

There were photos strung up everywhere...and all of them were of me.

17

THE DARK ROOM

My heart was pounding so loudly that I could only hear the sound of blood rushing in my ears. It was most likely the reason why I didn't hear anyone at the door or feel my cell phone vibrating in my pocket.

I was temporarily blinded when Chance's bedroom light switched on, but there was no mistaking Chance's voice when he angrily called out, "Who's in here!?"

I froze.

Chance rounded the corner of the kitchenette and flipped on the bathroom light, finally able to see that I was the intruder.

A knowing and defeated look crossed his face, and he put his hands up defensively when he said, "Violet, I swear, this is *not* what it looks like."

I said nothing, still too shocked to speak.

Of all the things I had considered finding in Chance's apartment, dozens, if not hundreds, of images of my own face staring back at me was not one of them.

"Let me explain..." he said softly, but he made the mistake of taking a step toward me.

Without warning, adrenaline surged through me, sparking my fight-or-flight instinct. I backed up until I hit the edge of the bathtub, almost missing the wall as I reached for something to help stabilize my body before I could tilt backward.

"What could you possibly say to explain these!?" I hissed in a shrill voice that sounded unrecognizable to my own ears. "How can you explain what happened to Claire, Chance?" I panted. "Or should I call you Alexander Roberts!?" I challenged.

All the color instantly drained from Chance's face upon hearing his given name from my lips. If he hadn't been wearing a green sweater, I would have thought my vision had gone greyscale.

"Jolene knows I'm here, so if something happens to me, like it did with Claire, you won't get away with it."

Chance's jaw set in defiance. "Whatever you think you know, you don't—this has all been one big misunderstanding."

"Misunderstanding!?" I waved my hands around at the photos surrounding me. "You've been stalking me! You have me cornered in your bathroom!"

He slowly backed out of the doorway into the larger room, allowing me space to exit, but I didn't trust him enough to think it wasn't some sort of ploy.

"Violet, please—you can come out."

"No!" I shouted stubbornly.

"Just come out here and sit down so I can explain everything." He glared at me, continuing to slowly back away from the door, farther into his room, until he made it to the foot of his bed, where he gently sat down at the edge, leaving me a path to his front door, if I could make it there faster than him. "Please."

I swallowed, my gaze bouncing between Chance and the door.

Taking slow steps, I approached the threshold of the bathroom, eyeing him warily. "You're a murderer *and* a stalker," I accused him, still formulating my exit strategy.

"I most certainly am *not* a murderer," he replied adamantly, folding his arms over his chest, blue-grey eyes blazing.

"What happened to Claire then? You said it was your fault," I spit. "And I see you're not denying the stalking."

Chance huffed in frustration. "How did you even know I knew her?"

"*Knew* her!?" I pursed my lips, glancing again at the door. "I heard you in my classroom! I've been wondering for weeks what you were up to with her—worried you might even be having an affair with her."

"WHAT!?" he half-yelled, half-laughed.

I was thoroughly confused by his response, but continued to slowly inch my way through the kitchen.

"If you'll just sit down." He pointed to the small bistro table and chairs next to me, just outside the bathroom door, exactly the same as the set in my room. "I'll answer all your questions."

"I'm fine right here," I replied, almost to the front door. "I'd be better still if I was away from you entirely, *stalker*."

"Fine, have it your way." He uncrossed his arms and leaned back on his hands. "And yes, you figured out my legal name. Are you happy?" He seemed particularly put out by that revelation.

"Why did you lie?" I asked.

"Because I didn't want anyone to know I was a Roberts. And I've never gone by Alexander. Chance is my middle name—it's what everyone has always called me." He crossed his legs at his ankles. His posture was so casual, it almost made me want to laugh.

"And what about Claire?"

"I'd never even look at a student like that, let alone touch one." He grimaced at the thought, and his sentiment felt genuine. "She was dating my cousin—Daniel Graham."

On cue, so many pieces fell into place. And while I didn't have every single detail figured out, things slowly began to come into focus.

"You came here to try and figure out what happened to him?" I guessed.

"Took quite a bit of money to bribe Jennings to retire early and recommend me for the position," Chance admitted.

My lips parted in shock.

"But if he's your cousin, why was he on a scholarship?"

"It's complicated. My family didn't know about him for a long time, and because they didn't like his mother, he doesn't—didn't have access to the same things I did." Chance winced as he corrected his tense. "I only got to know Daniel a couple years ago, but we got close really quickly. And then suddenly he just disappeared off the face of the earth and wouldn't respond to any type of contact. It wasn't like him. I don't care what the police think. I knew something was very wrong." He leaned forward, running his hands over his face.

"Claire was helping me...then whoever got to Daniel found out and took care of her too."

I blinked. The photos, the laptop, it all made perfect sense then. "Was he working on an article that got him into trouble?"

Chance nodded. "I think so."

"You're not a very good detective," I said indignantly. "I knew from the get-go there was something off with you."

Chance gave a humorless laugh. "That's fair—you're much more perceptive than I ever gave you credit for. I won't make the same mistake again. Here I thought the only reason you disliked me was because I couldn't manage to tell you the truth about working here the first night we met."

"There are a lot of reasons." I glared at him.

Chance laughed again, this time with a bit more mirth. "I look forward to hearing each and every grievance you have with me."

I huffed.

"You make it so easy to push your buttons, and you're adorable while doing so—I can't help myself."

"You're a jerk."

"Just a shitty detective, like you said. Now will you sit down so I can get you up to speed?"

"You want to work together?" I asked incredulously.

"Yeah." He shrugged, his brow furrowed as a result of my reaction.

"But I still don't trust you. And none of what you've said explains the stalking." I hazarded a glance back at the bathroom. I wasn't nearly satisfied. "What kind of a creep takes pictures like that, Chance?" I demanded.

"Well, before we met, I suspected you might be involved," he admitted begrudgingly.

"You've got to be kidding me!" I shouted. "I was trying to help! Was the whole thing in the bar a setup!?"

"No, no!" He waved his hands at me. "That was a coincidence. I swear!"

"But you already knew who I was when we met."

"I knew your name before coming into town, but I didn't know it was you when I saw that asshole slip something in your drink." He shook his head. "And then when you told me your name and I realized who you were, I—I was intrigued. I saw it as an opportunity to talk to you without you being suspicious."

"You let me kiss you," I growled. "You took advantage of me being drunk."

His jaw ticked at the accusation. At least he had the decency not to outright deny it.

"Do you really think I'm capable of hurting anyone?" I was disgusted at the thought. I'd sacrificed so much to keep the people I cared about happy, and he had no idea. He didn't know a single thing about me.

"Of course not. It's just that you were the only new teacher last year. I was looking for variables. And on paper—listen, it was stupid and I realized right away that it couldn't have been you. You're right, you wouldn't harm a student. Besides, you're tiny—even if you wanted to, there isn't much you could do."

I audibly growled at the insult. He wasn't wrong, but I still *hated* when people assumed my size meant I was weaker or less than.

"Violet—"

"The photos in the bathroom are recent." I spoke aloud as the gears in my brain were working simultaneously. "If you stopped suspecting me right away, why did you keep taking pictures of me?"

Chance's face blushed crimson in embarrassment.

"Why are there recent pictures of me, Chance?" I ground out, refusing to let it go.

"You wouldn't give me the time of day; I needed to firmly rule you out as a suspect," he offered, but there was still something behind his words.

There was more, I was sure of it.

"Chance," I snarled.

"I told you it would happen that first night." He drew in a deep breath, preparing himself for the truth that remained. "You kind of became my muse."

I scoffed at the thought.

"I didn't mean to be creepy. I never followed you. But if you were around, and I had the opportunity to take some shots—"

"That doesn't make it better." I shook my head. I didn't know how to take his admission. Because I knew I should be absolutely repulsed, but there was a part of me that was flattered.

What the fuck is wrong with me?

"It's the best work I've ever done," he confessed quietly, more to himself than to me.

"No more pictures," I told him firmly.

"Okay…" He frowned.

"And I want you to let me leave."

Chance sighed, but motioned to the door. "I won't stop you."

Without hesitation, I flung open the door, not bothering to close it behind me, and sprinted down the hall to my room, struggling only for a moment with the keys before I was able to lock everything behind me.

I pulled my phone out of my pocket. I had a dozen missed calls from Jolene.

"He snuck out! I'm sorry!" she wailed upon picking up the phone.

"I'm okay," I told her, my voice sounding far calmer than my mind.

"Did he find you? What happened?" She sounded distraught.

"We worked it out," I half-lied. "Everything is fine."

"You left your bag by my desk." She sniffled.

"If you don't mind tucking it under, I'll come by tomorrow and grab it," I told her. She didn't work over the weekend, but the faculty had access to the main part of the admin offices during off-hours.

"You're sure you're okay?"

"Yeah, I'll see you on Monday," I told her before hanging up.

My heart was still racing, but the adrenaline was starting to wane.

I wasn't sure how to deal with the situation. But as I slowly began to calm down from the rush of everything, I tried to parse through my thoughts.

I believed Chance's story about Daniel and Claire, although I certainly wanted to ask him a few follow-up questions about being related to Daniel and having only found out about him recently.

I had occasionally seen a fashion column, written by Claire, in the student paper, but it hadn't occurred to me to ask her about Daniel. I had thought about trying to talk to some of his known friends, but as a teacher, it felt like I would be overstepping. And I didn't want to stir up feelings, as they were likely traumatized by losing a friend at such a young age.

The thought occurred to me then that if Daniel and Chance were as close as he said, he was likely deeply affected by the loss as well. I felt a brief pang of guilt at the idea of him having to process that grief alone.

But then I reminded myself that he had been taking unsolicited photos of me while I was unaware, for the last two months. Though the photos I remembered seeing in the bathroom were exactly as he had described, just candid shots, usually from a distance, of me in common areas, like the entrance hall, front courtyard, and rose garden.

Could I really trust that he hadn't meant any harm? The same confused feeling washed over me as I was both discomforted and pleased at the thought of him being drawn to me to the extent that he felt compelled to photograph me.

Lucky for me, because it was a Friday, I had the weekend to cool down and figure things out before I'd be forced to deal with Chance in person.

Unfortunately, Chance had other ideas.

18

KNIVES & PASTRIES

At eight in the morning, on a Saturday, I was abruptly woken up by a sharp knock at my door.

Too tired to think straight after a fitful night of sleep, I tumbled out of bed, stomping to the door to answer it in nothing but a tank top, sans bra, and my pajama pants, one leg still stuck around my knee from all the tossing and turning the previous night.

I looked like a complete mess.

"Hi," Chance greeted me with a cheerful smile. A cup of coffee in one hand and a bag of what I presumed was some sort of breakfast food in the other. He shoved the items into my hold and waltzed right past me into my room.

"I have..."—I looked around, panicked— "...knives in here," I sputtered.

"Really?" He chuckled, looking inexplicably dapper in his regular uniform of slacks, a sweater, shiny wingtips, and his wool coat, having likely come directly from outside. I wasn't sure where he had procured the food, as it definitely wasn't from the dining hall. "That's what you're going to go with? Knives?"

"Shut up, Chance," I barked. "You can't just barge into people's rooms without asking." I set the coffee and bag of what I could see were actually pastries on the kitchen counter, trying to ignore the lovely smell that wafted from both items, setting my senses alight.

"I knocked." He shrugged, taking a seat at the small table next to my kitchen.

"What do you want?" My fingers twitched with the impulse to straighten my hair, or at least wipe the sleep from my eyes, but instead I folded them over my chest in a poor attempt to hide his view of my nipples through the thin material of my tank top.

"I want to finish our conversation from last night, and I want an answer from you." He folded an ankle over the opposite knee. He had no right to look so casual and yet so goddamned attractive at my kitchen table, uninvited.

"What answer?"

"If you'll help me find out what happened to Daniel," he said. "You cared about him. I can tell. So help me."

His tone was so sincere...his argument so simple, it caught me off guard. I slumped against the counter, giving in and grabbing the cup of coffee, relaxing slightly as the sweet liquid warmed my throat.

Would it really hurt to hear him out?

I glared at him in realization. "How do you know how I take my coffee?"

He rolled his eyes. "It's hard to miss you spending an hour pouring so much sugar into it that there's none left for anyone else."

I scoffed.

But he wasn't wrong.

"What did he mean to you?" he asked cautiously.

"I didn't know him that well, but all the students take a class with me each year." I took another sip.

He waited, knowing there was more.

"He reminded me of myself, I suppose—he was determined and scrappy, and never let his circumstances get him down." I frowned, worried I'd given too much away about my own insecurities.

So much wasted potential. Both he and Claire were gone, their lives snuffed out too soon. And for what?

"He mentioned you once." Chance's eyes were trained on the ground.

"He did?"

"He liked your Greek mythology class."

I blushed, tickled by the idea that anything I taught mattered to my students. So many of them seem disaffected, but it was all worth it, if it mattered to even a single one.

"What do you know about the article he was writing?" I turned to pull two plates from the kitchen cabinet.

"Only that it was something big. He wouldn't even tell Claire about it because he was worried she'd get caught up in it."

"I overheard you talking to her in my classroom that morning, then I saw Claire give you the laptop." I plucked a pain au chocolat from the bag and placed the bag with the remaining pastries and the second plate in front of Chance on the small table.

"You devious little thing." He flashed me an impressed smile.

"You weren't very discreet." I shrugged, licking some errant chocolate off my fingertip, trying to ignore the triggering adjective he had again used to describe me.

Chance's gaze turned hungry as he watched my tongue dart over my lip to catch the last of the chocolate. The desire in his expression sent shivers down my spine.

He swallowed, his throat bobbing in response, and averted his gaze, seemingly aware that I had caught him not just staring, but coveting.

"As previously admitted, I have grossly underestimated you. I promise I won't make the same mistake again."

"What was on the laptop?"

"I don't know. Claire was supposed to help me figure out the password, but she..." He trailed off. "We never got the chance." He cleared his throat, visibly affected by the thought of her demise.

My heart ached for him. He really did blame himself.

"I know this sounds callous." I took a step toward him. "But something came out of what happened to her. Now you know that whoever hurt Daniel is still here. Even more, you were on the right track, and they felt threatened."

He gazed up at me, his blue-grey eyes a stormy sea of emotion.

"It's not your fault. If she really was killed..."—I paused; I didn't want him to think I didn't believe him, but the idea still felt so awful—"whoever hurt her is to blame."

"There was something I didn't get a chance to mention to you last night before you left." He took a beat, perhaps debating if he could trust me with the information.

I crossed my arms over my chest, waiting patiently for him to continue.

"Daniel isn't the first student to go missing from Montgomery."

"What!?" My eyes went wide. But then it sparked a memory about something I had overheard the police talking about when I'd gone to the station in town trying to file an official missing person's report, which they had refused.

I couldn't remember exactly what they'd said, but it had been something about how it was lucky they couldn't afford to go to Montgomery so they wouldn't disappear too. I thought it had been odd at the time, but it hadn't made sense, so I'd assumed I'd misheard them and had quickly forgotten about it entirely.

"Over twenty years ago, two students—sisters, went missing. The school almost got shut down. I'm surprised Winston managed to keep his post. This time around, I think he instructed the staff to withhold information from the police and to keep the whole thing under wraps so they wouldn't lose funding, or worse."

"And the police have told you the same thing they've said to everyone else, that he ran away?" I asked.

Chance nodded. "I can't even get my hands on the police report for either of the cases because they're both still technically open. And I certainly don't have access to Montgomery's records."

I took a deep breath, carefully considering what I was about to offer; however, I truly felt that Chance was being honest with me and that there was nothing left to discover.

He seemed physically relieved now that the burden of his secret was shared by at least one other person he could talk to. I also felt like

I owed something to Daniel and Claire. They didn't deserve what had happened to them, and if I could do something to help resolve this injustice, I felt a sense of duty to do so.

"I do," I replied meekly.

"You do what?" Chance was confused.

"I have access."

"You really think it's wise to bring Jolene into all of this?"

"We don't have to."

His eyes flashed.

"I know where she keeps the keys to all the administrative offices, including the records room." I pursed my lips in thought. "But we might consider asking her if she knows anything about the girls who disappeared. I don't think she was working here that far back, but maybe she saw or heard—" I stopped.

Chance had the biggest shit-eating grin on his face.

"What?" I snapped, placing my hands on my hips.

"You said 'we.'" His grin grew impossibly larger. "Does that mean you're in?"

I huffed in annoyance. He was so aggravating. "Yes," I sniped.

"I'll pretend you put up more of a fight if it'll make you feel better," he mocked.

"I have a few conditions." I tried to mimic his tone from when he'd used the same words against me the night he had discovered my lounge.

"I'd be disappointed if you didn't."

"No funny business." I managed to say it with a straight face.

"Don't worry, you're not funny, so no funny business will be had," Chance quipped.

"I mean it." I glared at him.

It was bad enough I was still attracted to him despite everything, which should have had me running for the hills. I needed to be careful and keep protecting myself if we were going to work together, so I wasn't at risk of losing my job for violating the faculty code of conduct—whether or not it was frequently enforced remained irrelevant.

"Define 'funny business' then," he challenged, folding his arms over his chest.

"You cut out all the flirting. I won't lose my job because of you."

"I had no idea my fondness for you was such a temptation."

He was incorrigible.

"And what if the policy didn't exist?" He leaned forward in his chair. "What then, Violet, darling?"

I clenched my teeth, refusing to answer, because I couldn't say out loud what he seemed to already know, that I was still very much interested in him, or at least my body was.

An awkward silence ensued. Our physical chemistry palpably filled the room.

"Can we at least be friends?" Chance finally broke the tension.

"Maybe—I haven't decided yet," I stuttered.

His lips curled into what had become his trademark smirk. I hated how entirely pleased he was with himself, knowing he had won me over, much to my chagrin.

"I would also like it on the record that you're practically unbearable, and that you're lucky I'm agreeing to this." I pointed my index finger at his face.

Chance captured my finger, forcing me to lower it, and twined his fingers through mine, causing heat to travel from his touch to other areas I wasn't exactly proud of. "It's been noted."

I pulled my hand from his grasp and took a step back.

"Get changed and come upstairs. I need to get you up to speed on my notes."

"How about you go upstairs and I'll go back to bed." I crossed the room, flopping onto the mattress.

He barked a laugh at my dramatics. "I'll see you up there." And then the asshole had the audacity to fucking wink at me before making a casual exit from my room, bag of pastries in hand.

19

OUTSIDERS

"Do you know what's on the other side of the wall?" Chance asked when he heard me ascending the trapdoor stairs twenty minutes after he'd taken his leave.

"No." I was still grumpy from a restless sleep and early morning wake-up call.

The clack of pool balls echoed through the long room. Chance rounded the table to line up his next shot. "I figure there's another room over there. Probably the stairs too—there's no way they got all of this bulky furniture, let alone the baby grand, through your trapdoor, or even a window."

"I've looked for stairs, but I've never found anything." I set a cup of black coffee on the pool table next to him, hating that I'd noticed how he'd taken his preferred morning beverage, just as he had mine. I'd made myself another cup after finishing the first one he'd brought me, and as if on autopilot, brewed enough for more than myself.

"My charms must be working—you're already warming up to me." He grinned, setting the pool cue against the table before grabbing the steaming cup of coffee.

I had been too tired to really take him in earlier, but the cut of his slacks perfectly emphasized his lean legs, and his black V-neck sweater, without a button-up beneath that day, exposed just a hint of his clavicle. And he was scruffy.

It was as if the universe had carved him from my dreams and dropped him right in front of me. Why did everything have to be so complicated?

My cheeks heated when his brow arched. He'd caught me staring.

"Shut up," I snapped.

"I didn't say a word." Chance chuckled.

Deciding it was too cold, I gathered what I needed to start a fire.

"Can I watch you?" Chance had abandoned his game of pool to sip his coffee next to me. "I don't know how to do it." He took a seat on the edge of the big leather sofa that faced the hearth.

Of course, he wouldn't know. He'd have servants for that.

"How have you been staying warm in your room then?"

"Flannel pajamas and three blankets." He laughed.

"Fine, come here." I beckoned him over.

He watched with rapt attention as I explained and demonstrated the process, noting things I had learned along the way, like having to make sure the flue was open while in use, but to make sure it was closed when there wasn't a fire, especially if he wanted to avoid bats in the summer.

"Sounds like you know that from personal experience." He smiled over his cup of coffee.

"That's a story for a different day." I shook my head, recalling how freaked out I had been when I found one flying around only a few weeks into summer break. Thankfully a quick web search revealed that opening the windows so they could sense the fresh air would help, and it hadn't taken long for the bat to exit the lounge of its own accord.

I showed him how to best position the wood and kindling to catch and burn longer, as well as what the tools beside the fireplace were used for.

"I'm surprised you made it the entire time without making fun of me for not knowing how to do any of this." He waved his hand at the now roaring fire.

"I did, I just didn't say any of it out loud." I stuck my tongue out at him in jest.

We both settled on either end of the couch. I curled my legs under me, and Chance rested his on the coffee table, stretching his arms over his head as he yawned.

"I'm sorry about what happened to Daniel," I said softly.

"Me too." His tone was somber.

"You said you were close, but only recently?" I hoped I didn't come across as being nosy, although, let's be honest, I was. But I thought if I understood Daniel the way Chance appeared to, maybe it would help us figure out what had happened...and maybe it would make it easier to trust Chance.

"Daniel is—was..." Chance paused. "Was one of the few people in my family I'm on good terms with. His mom, my aunt, was the black sheep of the family. She married young, and my grandfather didn't approve, so he completely cut her off, and the rest of his family did too, to stay in his good graces. I didn't even know I had an aunt while

I was growing up. But a few years ago, she died in a car accident, and I guess Daniel's dad didn't stick around very long after he was born.

"He had to be placed in the foster system for a while, as It took the better part of a year for the state to actually get ahold of my dad, who had been named his legal guardian, without his knowledge. At first I thought it was a mistake, given how many layers of people stood between him and the public, but now I'm sure he knew earlier and thought it might go away."

"Wow."

"Yeah." Chance snorted.

"How did you find out about Daniel?"

"I overheard my dad arguing with one of his advisors on the phone and got the gist of the situation. I confronted him, and he pretended not to know what I was talking about. But then I took the matter to my mother, who I knew wouldn't let it stand. She runs and donates to a million different charities, and all of them are for children. She's always had a soft spot for kids, and wouldn't let Daniel's circumstances, which were completely out of his control, be the reason he suffered.

"A few days later, she came to me and told me it had been taken care of and that they had found a boarding school for him and would cover his tuition. But I didn't think it was fair that this kid, who had lost everything, would just be shipped off to figure shit out on his own. So I started reaching out to him, and we just clicked. I'd always wanted a brother. And he was so lost in his grief...I suppose I was a little lost, myself. So we just kind of were there for each other. I needed him to know he wasn't alone."

Chance stopped to chew his lip, silently contemplating as he gazed into the fire.

"*I* didn't want to feel alone."

"Why did you feel alone?" I asked softly.

Chance glanced at me over his shoulder, then looked back into the flickering flames. "I've never quite fit in with my family. My father tried to raise me to be this perfectly crafted, younger version of himself, but I rebelled. Sure, I have a business degree, but every spare moment, every elective was in something creative. I've always been interested in writing and photography and art, but that wasn't what he wanted a son for. Being a Roberts, I was under so much pressure to follow in his footsteps. It was too much."

He took a deep breath, letting the sound of the crackling fire take up all the space for a while before speaking again.

"I was never enough for him. I will never be enough. So I left."

"You left?"

Chance gave a mirthless laugh. "I haven't talked to him in two years, and I've been going by Chance Harper since college, because I didn't want the family name hanging over me while I was trying to figure out my own path. I don't think he ever forgave me for that, so when I took Daniel's side and called him out on being a piece of shit, well, I don't think he's missed me much either."

"But you're still on good terms with your mom and sister?"

"Yes, thankfully. They were the reason I was able to get enough cash so quickly to pay off Jennings into retirement."

I hummed in response, more pieces falling into place, and the puzzle that was Chance Harper becoming that much more clear.

"What? No jokes about me being a poor little rich boy?" He grinned at me, but there was no joy in his eyes.

"No," I said firmly. "Your dad sounds like an asshole. I'm sorry you fell out with him over you trying to befriend a kid who lost everything he'd ever known in the blink of an eye."

Chance relaxed into the couch. "I'm sorry I lied to you, Violet." Chance's expression was sincere. "I had my reasons, but I never meant to hurt you."

I was regretting telling him nothing could happen between us, despite the stupid school rule, because the more I learned about Chance, the more he opened up to me, the worse my stupid crush deepened.

I swallowed hard.

Was I about to forgive Chance for everything?

No.

Because, I realized, I already had.

"I'll admit it would be so much easier to stay mad at you, but given the situation, it feels inappropriate." I tried to joke to avoid admitting more than I was ready to.

"When has appropriateness ever stopped you when it comes to me? Miss 'I have knives in here.'"

"That was completely justified!" I threw my hands up. "You all but admitted to stalking me! You still could be a serial killer, for all I know."

Chance laughed as he rose from the couch. "About that..."

I craned my neck around to watch him walk to the study table, where there was a stack of papers and the laptop I'd seen Claire give him. "I'm not a serial killer. Scout's honor." He held up two fingers, smiling at me before pulling a thick manila envelope from the top of the pile and making his way back to me. He extended his arm, handing it to me.

"But you were right—I was being a creep."

He scratched at the stubble on his chin, nervously watching me as I opened the envelope and found all the photos from the darkroom.

"Prints and negatives," he told me, coming back around to reclaim his spot on the couch. "I didn't want you to think I would just turn around and make more."

"I—" I didn't know what to say. I closed the envelope. "Thank you." I clutched it to my chest, feeling the warmth of the gesture from the top of my head to the tips of my toes.

"So, we're okay?"

I looked down at the envelope again and back up to meet Chance's stormy gaze. "Yeah, we're okay," I confirmed.

"Friends?" He raised a brow, the corner of his lip curving ever so slightly.

"Don't push your luck," I scoffed, but there was no venom behind the sentiment.

Seeing how Chance valued integrity and was so loyal to Daniel, I thought I wouldn't mind considering him a friend.

20
SECRET PARTNERSHIP

e spent most of the weekend comparing notes.

Chance had a lot of questions about the weeks preceding Daniel's disappearance. I had replayed them over and over in my mind so many times, trying to remember if anyone had been acting strange or if I'd noticed anything out of the ordinary, but I simply hadn't. I hadn't been looking for anything at the time, and I was more caught up in finals and graduation.

"What were you saying yesterday about the laptop Claire gave you?" I asked late Sunday afternoon.

"I can't get in."

"Why not?" I raised a brow.

"It's issued by the school. Claire thought she had his password saved somewhere, but she was gone before we had the chance to connect again."

"I have an idea, but you're not going to like it." I tapped my finger on my chin.

Chance cocked his head, intrigued.

"Milton Cox has access to all the passwords," I stated.

"So?"

"Milton Cox also has a habit of leaving his computer open when he leaves to grab lunch, or when he's distracted."

Chance narrowed his eyes at me. "Distracted?"

"I've noticed he's easily distracted around me."

Chance sported a lopsided grin. "That makes two of us, then."

I rolled my eyes.

"What about the photos you mentioned to Claire the night she gave you the laptop?" I tried to bring the conversation back to the task at hand and pretend that Chance's flirtation wasn't affecting me, despite the fact that it very much was.

"Ended up being nothing." He shook his head. "They were from his article last year about the drugs. But he wrote three other articles in addition to that one. Do you know who he pissed off when each one came out? I know he wasn't exactly without enemies. I just never thought any of the articles were serious enough to make someone want to hurt him." Chance's shoulders slumped.

"What could you have done?" Against my will, I watched as my hand reached out to take his, in comfort.

He nodded, squeezing my hand in return, and then refusing to let it go when I gently tried to pull away.

I sighed, but decided not to fight him on it. I *definitely* wasn't actually enjoying the feeling of my hand in his. And it *most certainly* wasn't giving me butterflies...

"A dorm monitor was fired over the drug article, but the last I heard, she moved back home to the West Coast. I asked Kenneth if he'd gotten any flak for the article during the faculty mixer. He said a little, but he didn't seem to mind, and if he did, he's the newspaper advisor and has final say, so he could have just refused to publish the article."

"I agree. And the other articles?"

"He wrote one about bribery and another on favoritism between certain students and faculty his sophomore year, but that was before I got here. I don't think he named any names, and I didn't hear about anyone being angry with him. If anything, it gave him a somewhat elevated status amongst the students, who seemed to be largely on his side."

"What if the students he was referencing were worried he would speak out and cause problems with college applications? Sometimes arguments can escalate quickly," Chance surmised.

"It's possible, but they seemed largely anecdotal without any hard evidence, which is why Daniel didn't print any names. It was more of an editorial with fact-based arguments, versus the other investigative pieces he did that were more hard journalism."

"And the last one?"

"The one about the scholarship students not receiving the same opportunities as the others?"

"Yeah."

"I mean, the administration and donors were definitely unhappy, but I got the sense they were more annoyed than anything. I remember overhearing the faculty talking about not biting the hand that feeds you." That was the last day I had tried to hang out in the faculty lounge and was only a few weeks after I'd started at Montgomery. They saw people like me and Daniel as nothing but dogs at their feet. It was disgusting.

"Who said that?" Chance's eyes flashed in anger.

"The headmaster."

"He's a piece of shit."

"Well, if he really cared, he could have easily found a way to kick Daniel out."

"I'm not so sure," Chance argued. "He was one of very few people that knew who was paying Daniel's tuition. There was no way he would do anything to piss off my dad. Half the school's funding comes from him."

"Geez." Even thinking about that kind of money being just something Thomas Roberts could throw around without blinking an eye was too much for me to stomach. "Did, umm, Daniel ever talk to you about what he was working on next?" I tried to stop thinking about how I'd be set for years with that kind of cash.

"Nothing specific, only that he was working on something big, but he liked to keep his work close to his chest. I just told him to be careful and to do his due diligence. Once I can get on his computer, I know we can find more."

Chance began tracing shapes with his fingertip in the palm of my hand, which was entirely too distracting.

"I don't even know who our potential suspects are." I swallowed. "They would have needed motive, means, and opportunity. I don't even know where to start."

"Winston has always been the highest on my list," Chance offered.

"After me," I deadpanned.

A grin broke out on his face. "Yeah, after you." He threaded his fingers through mine, sliding his thumb back and forth across my skin.

Finally having had enough, and sick of being turned on by such a shameless flirt, I pulled my hand back into my lap, away from his reach.

Chance shook his head, holding back a chuckle. I hated that he knew exactly what he was doing to me. I think he also knew that even if I pulled away, I didn't want him to stop.

"Just think about it." Chance leaned back in his seat. "He was here when the first girls went missing, which is already suspect, but he had a lot to gain by getting someone like Daniel out of the way. He was making him look bad and exposing the underbelly of the school and all the corrupt people greasing the wheels."

"Just because he was here when those other girls went missing doesn't mean he had anything to do with it," I countered, feeling a little ill standing up for someone like Winston.

"No, but he has a reputation for being a creep around women. You even said it yourself that he's made sexist comments to you before."

"Being a misogynistic asshole doesn't make you a killer." I felt like he was taking it a step too far on pure conjecture, with no real evidence. "Don't make me defend him, but we need solid proof, not just our opinions."

"I know." Chance sighed, pushing his chair back from the table before standing. "Let's go grab some lunch from the dining hall. I need a break."

I'd been meaning to bring something up to him sooner, but I was worried I'd shatter the tenuous alliance we were slowly building, so I'd been gathering the courage to say something.

"Wait," I called out to him. He was already heading for his fire escape.

Chance turned around.

"I've been thinking—"

"Uh oh," he joked.

"Shut up." I couldn't help but laugh at the jab.

"Go on," he encouraged me to continue.

"We both agree that whoever is doing this is at Montgomery?" I asked.

He nodded.

"We also agree that they're aware of what we're doing, enough to know that Claire was helping you. Which means they likely know why you're really here—"

"Violet, my lovely muse, where are you going with this?"

I narrowed my eyes at the new nickname. "I don't think we should let anyone know we're working together."

He cocked his head, not understanding.

"We need to keep up appearances at school, where I've been very vocal about my dislike for you." I eyed him nervously, unsure of how he would take my suggestion.

"You're right."

I straightened. "I am?"

Chance crossed his arms over his broad chest. "Yeah. The faculty definitely knows, and I'm sure some students are aware—plus, you rarely eat at the dining hall. We should go about our business as usual and keep our investigation between us…"

He paused.

"That means you can't talk to Lenny or Jolene about anything," Chance finished hesitantly.

"I wouldn't involve Lenny, but I don't think I can lie to Jolene—she'll know something is up. Plus, she helped me figure out who you are—or were. She's going to ask me what happened on Monday. What am I supposed to say?" I didn't disagree with him, but I felt guilty not including her in some capacity.

"You don't have to lie to her, but maybe just don't tell her the whole truth," he suggested.

"So I shouldn't tell her you've been stalking me and taking creepy pictures?" I held up the folder he'd given me.

He shook his head, amused. "Never going to live that one down, am I?"

"Not ever."

"I know she's your friend, but we need to be careful. We can't trust anyone. She's too close to the headmaster."

"She wouldn't tell him anything," I argued.

"Not intentionally, but her desk is right by his office. And other than you, he's the only person who knows I'm a Roberts. I'm sure he's wondered what my motives were for applying to teach here." Chance wasn't going to budge.

"I'm not good at lying." I slumped against the table.

Chance paced back to me, leaning against the table. "Don't look at it as lying. You're only keeping information from her to protect her, and to protect us. She would understand." He placed his hand on my shoulder. "We can't risk her knowing anything, especially if it means she could become the next target."

I let myself look up into his darkened eyes. He was trying to protect all of us.

"Okay…"

"When can we get into the records room to check on those missing girls without worrying about running into Jolene or any of the other admin staff?"

"We'll have to wait until tomorrow night—the staff is usually all gone by nine."

"Not tonight?" Chance asked anxiously.

"Too many students around. Remember they have evening study sessions on Sunday nights in the dining hall."

"Shit, I forgot. Okay, Monday night it is." He took a beat. "I'll go grab us food."

"I have some tests I need to grade." It wasn't that I didn't want to work on the case anymore, but it felt like we were at a bit of a standstill.

"You don't mind if I'm up here, do you?" he asked sincerely, giving me an out if I wanted to be alone in the lounge.

"No, I don't mind."

Somehow, Chance Harper was weaseling his way even further into my heart.

21

A CASUAL HEIST

All day Monday I was on edge, knowing what I planned to do with Chance that night.

"What's up with you?" Jolene threw a crouton at me while we ate lunch at her desk.

Having passed Halloween over the weekend, she was transitioning into more Thanksgiving-inspired sweaters. That day she wore one in a deep russet, with brightly colored leaves in different mediums and textures adorning the front.

"Nothing..." I replied absently.

"I'm still waiting to hear the full story about what happened on Friday night. Is that it? Are you still mad at me?" Jolene pouted.

"I'm not mad at you." I looked up, making sure she felt the truth in my words.

"Then what is going on? What happened after you broke in?"

"I didn't find anything before he stormed in." I recalled the feeling of dread when I had seen dozens of eyes, all my own, staring back at me, through the photographs he'd taken, in his makeshift darkroom.

I was glad he'd given me the photos, and while I initially would have been upset if he hadn't, after more carefully inspecting them in the privacy of my apartment, I started to feel guilty about having the negatives as well.

While I was the primary subject matter, the photos were his art. He was clearly a skilled photographer, even if he considered himself a novice. The way he framed the shots, the angles, and the diffusion of light...they were beautiful. I hadn't seen other photos he'd shot, but I believed him when he admitted that he was proud of them.

If I hadn't been the subject, or they hadn't been taken without my permission, and I had stumbled upon them at a gallery, I would have thought them something special. I was considering returning the negatives to Chance, under the agreement that he not shoot any more photos of me without my permission.

"Did you ask about his name?" Jolene extracted me from my reverie.

"He said he didn't want special treatment." Just like Chance had coached me, it wasn't the whole truth, but it wasn't an outright lie.

"Oh." She set her fork down, disappointed in such a banal reason. "Then what?"

"Then I apologized for breaking into his room like a crazy person and asked him not to report me." That was a little bit of an exaggeration.

"And he let it go? Just like that?"

Jolene wasn't convinced.

"I'm not sure." I sighed. "He'll probably hold it over my head until he wants something."

Why was it getting easier to stretch the truth?

"What a jerk," she sneered.

I nodded, picking at my salad mindlessly. All I could think about was how awful it would be if Jolene got hurt because I couldn't let Daniel's disappearance go, and put her in the crosshairs. I wouldn't be able to live with myself.

"You're sure you're okay?"

"Just stressed over fitting everything in for class before Thanksgiving break," I replied honestly. But then the thought occurred to me that I could use the opportunity to spend more time with Chance—for the investigation—*obviously*. And in the process, slightly distance myself from Jolene, so if someone was observing us, they would be less likely to target her to get to me.

"Actually," I began, "I don't know if I'll have time to do dinner for a while, just lunch."

"No worries." Jolene smiled sweetly, making me feel awful for lying and using her understanding nature to my advantage.

"I'm sorry."

"Violet, you're just doing your job." She laughed. "Speaking of your job, you better get up to your class—the next period starts in five minutes."

"Shit."

Whereas the morning crawled by at an excruciatingly slow pace, the afternoon passed in a blur.

All too soon, I found myself knocking on Chance's door, dressed in all black. Black sweater. Black yoga pants. And, thankfully, my only pair of sneakers were also black.

"Your ass looks great in those pants," was the first thing Chance said when he got a good look at me. He snapped his mouth closed—dare I say, mortified—as if he hadn't intended to voice his thoughts aloud.

As for me, my body was suddenly on fire, blushing from head to toe.

Not knowing how to respond to his comment without embarrassing myself, I turned on my heel and walked toward the stairwell. A moment later, Chance's footsteps were close behind.

As we had hoped, at ten o'clock at night, the school was deserted, so we were able to make it down to the administrative offices undetected.

I'd instructed Chance to bring flashlights, as I didn't want to worry about getting caught, knowing that without some form of light, the basement would be pitch-black and impenetrable. The lights he had procured were barely adequate, but we'd make do.

"I hate it down here. It's definitely haunted, right?" he joked, keeping close enough that I could feel his body heat through the thin leggings.

"I'll protect you," I replied sarcastically.

"Oh yeah?" he challenged. "Who's going to protect you?"

"Shut up, Chance," I hissed. "I said no talking other than what's necessary when we walked through this harebrained plan last night."

"I didn't think you were being serious. I thought you loved the sound of my voice."

I scoffed, feeling around under Jolene's desk for the hook hidden in the back corner, where she stashed the master key set she got tired of taking home every evening. "Gotcha!" I whispered victoriously.

Chance moved the beam of his flashlight to the lock on the records room door to help me see what I was doing. I sighed in relief when the door clicked open at the behest of the key. Careful not to allow us to be locked in, I instructed Chance to move the stone block against the door to hold it open.

"What is that smell?" Chance half-gagged when he entered the room.

"You'll get used to it."

"God, I hope not." He placed a gentle hand at the small of my back. "What exactly should we be looking for, do you think?"

"I don't know? A big red folder that says 'Montgomery Prep Secrets'?" We hadn't really thought much further than the idea that there had to be some record on campus about the missing girls.

"Hey look! Old trophies." Chance grabbed one, but the gold-coated star must not have been securely fastened to the rest of it because the base landed on the stone floor with a loud *crack*.

"Chance!" I barked. "Stop messing around! We have to make this quick so no one walks in on us breaking and entering."

Snatching the top of the trophy from him and placing it on the ground, I gave him a gentle punch on the arm.

"Such a violent little muse." He chuckled, rubbing his bicep, as if I could have actually hurt him.

"Stop calling me that."

Chance hooked his arm around my waist from behind, pulling my back flush against his front.

"What? Little or muse?" he whispered, his lips right next to my ear.

"Both." I shoved him away. "Do you want my help or not? I can't think when you're so close to me."

A smile curved along Chance's face, pleased at my admission.

"The school should keep incident logs—try to find those." I ignored his continued advances and moved to the opposite side of the room, away from him and his infuriating magnetism.

"What are you going to do?"

"See if I can find any thicker-than-normal student files from the year the girls went missing." I paused, having a sudden thought. "We should grab the 1992 yearbook too. That was the year you said you thought they went missing, and the yearbooks in the lounge stop at 1988."

He gave me a thumbs-up in agreement, and we got to work.

For the next hour, we searched through the records room with absolutely no luck, except for the yearbook.

"Chance—there's nothing here." I set my flashlight down, completely exhausted, my eyes bleary from squinting in the dark at the tiny typewritten font.

"There has to be a record somewhere." He leaned against the wall, just as tired as I was. "Two girls went missing—it was a big fucking deal."

"Well if there's information about what happened, it's not here."

Chance snapped his fingers. "Violet, you're a genius."

"What?"

"Those keys open any door on campus?" He looked through the door to Jolene's desk, where I had left the ring of keys.

"Yeah..."

Chance raced through the door, grabbing my hand as he went.

"Wait—the yearbook!" I stopped him to go back and get it, closing the records door behind me. "Where are we going?"

"Headmaster Winston's office." Chance grinned, keys in hand.

"Chance..." I pulled on his hand, hesitant to go with him. If he got fired, he still had money and a family he could go back to, in theory. But I didn't, not really.

"I won't let anything happen to you." He seemed to sense the reason for my concern. "I promise."

"If we get caught, I'll tell them you drugged me or something." I tried to make light of the heavy situation.

"Stockholm syndrome would be more believable. What with all the shameless flirting."

I couldn't help but roll my eyes.

"We should have worn gloves." I wrung my hands nervously as he used Jolene's keys to open up the headmaster's office.

We'd only just entered the room when we heard someone coming down the stairs. Our panicked, wide eyes met in the near dark.

Chance silently closed the door, flipping the lock back into place, then grabbed my arm and hauled me into the large wardrobe situated behind the door. We clicked off our flashlights in tandem, waiting to be discovered.

Chance's warm body was pressed flush against mine, as well as something long and hard, which was digging into my thigh.

"Please tell me that's the yearbook," I whispered pitifully.

Chance shifted his arm and lifted the book, which at some point had ended up in his custody, shoving it against my chest and relieving the spot on my leg.

"Is that gorgeous mind always in the gutter?" he snickered.

I was happy to be in the dark then, as my full-body blush returned. "Do you ever turn off?"

"You make it extremely difficult when everything you do turns me on," he whispered. I could feel his lips at the crook of my neck, and I thought for certain he might try to kiss me.

The door handle clicked open, and we both stilled, holding our breaths as the light switched on.

"I told you Janice—I left it in my office—I'm sorry." The headmaster was speaking to his wife over the phone.

We listened with literal bated breath as he rummaged around his desk for what was probably only a minute, but felt like it stretched on for hours, as Chance and I waited to see if we'd be discovered.

"Found it," he proclaimed suddenly. While a very thin stream of light came through the door of the wardrobe, we couldn't see what he was doing or what he had come back to retrieve. "I'll be home in half an hour." He hung up the phone, switched off the light, and locked the door. His footsteps slowly faded down the hall.

We waited another couple of minutes to be sure he was actually gone before tumbling out of the wardrobe with no grace whatsoever. I tried to forget about having almost kissed Chance.

"Too bad we didn't find Narnia," Chance quipped.

"I can't do this," I said, my voice shaky. "That was too close of a call. It's bad enough we're putting our lives in danger, but I can't lose this job."

"Hey." Chance rounded on me, placing his hands on my shoulders. "It's going to be okay. Just give me five minutes, Violet."

I started shaking my head.

"Five minutes and we'll leave, with or without the records."

"Five minutes?"

"Five minutes." He nodded.

"Okay."

But he didn't need that long.

In the top drawer of the headmaster's ancient filing cabinet, which mercifully sported a broken lock, Chance found a dark brown accordion file with everything we'd been looking for: the student records, school records, newspaper clippings, faculty and student accounts of the incident, and even a copy of the police report.

I wasn't sure how the headmaster had managed to get his hands on the report, but I was beginning to think he was capable of much more than I had initially thought possible. And maybe Chance was right that he could be behind everything.

Initially Chance wanted to just grab the folder and leave, but I was concerned the headmaster might notice its absence, so we used our phones to go through document by document and take photos that we could review without as much worry over being caught.

While we both wanted to start going through everything right away, it had taken a while to document everything, so we agreed to retire for the night. Chance left me only after ensuring I was safely tucked away in my room.

Finding it impossible to sleep as my thoughts ping-ponged between the mystery we were unraveling and trying to forget the way Chance's body had felt against mine, I gave in, letting my hand snake down my stomach and under the hem of my underwear. Only after I was sated did I finally fall into a restless slumber.

22

ADOLESCENT SECRETS

It seemed to take ages for Chance and me to slowly make our way through the information we had ~~stolen~~ liberated from the headmaster's office, because with the end of the term fast approaching, it only left us with maybe a couple hours on weeknights and half of the weekend, if we were lucky. Still, we persevered, poring over everything together in the lounge.

Most of what Winston had amassed were things we already knew or could be easily found online. Twin sisters Faith and Hope Marshall, aged 17, juniors, disappeared in the spring of 1992. They supposedly left Montgomery Prep for spring break, but never arrived home. The problem was that there were no witnesses who saw them depart, which was why Montgomery had been the focus of the investigation.

The authorities and locals combed the woods for weeks after their disappearance, with no luck. There were newspaper clippings from all across the country, showing that the case had made national headlines, but as it was just before the 24-hour news cycle shifted into high gear, the fanfare died down rather quickly after they had failed to be found.

Although, the fact that Winston had kept so many articles showed that he was tracking the case. But his tracking news about students that had gone missing from the school he ran didn't say much about whether or not he'd had anything to do with their disappearance.

The school records for the two girls were also fairly standard. They'd had average grades, no incident reports, and they'd both seemed to be on track to apply for college by the end of their tenure at the school, even though, sadly, they would never make it there.

The police report, on the other hand, was much more valuable.

Wayne Davies, the head detective on the case, was very thorough in both his investigation as well as his documentation. There was a fair amount that was redacted, but nothing that Chance and I were overly interested in, as it was mostly student names because they were minors at the time.

Winston, it seemed, was quickly ruled out as a viable suspect because he had a rock-solid alibi during the time that the girls went missing, seeing as he was on a flight to the Maldives to start his spring break early.

In my opinion, and certainly Chance's, who was still very much convinced he was guilty of something, his alibi didn't exonerate him entirely. If he'd had a reason to want to get rid of the girls, he was wealthy enough and had possessed plenty of connections to find a way to make it happen.

The police's main theory was a botched kidnapping, seeing as the Marshalls were exceedingly wealthy and the twins' father was a politician. However, no ransom demands were ever made. No evidence was ever found in the woods during the searches, or anywhere else on campus.

DNA testing had still been an emerging field at the time, from what I could tell, but I wasn't sure what the police would have been able to test with such a lack of physical evidence, other than the girls' belongings, which had been untouched in their room. Their purses had gone missing with them, however, which had led Davies to surmise that they had been on their way home, but it was unclear where along the way they had gone missing, as their driver had never connected with them.

Reviewing the multitude of interviews with the girls' parents, friends, family, as well as faculty and staff from the school, was exhausting and turned up nothing. The girls seemed to have been well liked, they'd had no boyfriends, and had made no enemies or rivals that anyone could think of.

"I don't think there's anything here." Chance sighed, closing his laptop after we finished the last of the interviews. "They're a dead end."

"For now." I leaned back against the chair at the study table. Chance followed the movement of my arms as I stretched them over my head.

"It was always going to be a long shot that two girls, twenty years ago, had anything to do with Daniel." Chance sighed.

"Do you really think there wasn't a single person that had an issue with them? In all the interviews, it seemed like everyone loved them, but they were teenage girls. There had to have been at least one or two petty arguments that could have escalated."

Chance's brow furrowed, considering my assessment.

"Reading through the interviews, it felt like everyone was protecting the girls, but what if, in their desire to show them in the best light, they left out something that would have mattered?" he added.

"Would Daniel have hidden anything from you? I mean, I know he was trying to work on the article by himself, but something else...something that was going on in his life."

Chance's shoulders slumped. "I'm sure he could have. We were fast friends, but considering how my father treated him, he would have been within his rights to keep anything from me. Don't all teenagers have secrets?"

He was so nonchalant with the last bit that it made me curious. I leaned toward him, resting my elbows on the table. "What was your teenage secret?"

Chance gave a soft laugh. "Probably not what you'd expect."

I raised a brow, encouraging him to continue.

"I questioned my sexuality a lot when I was younger."

I reeled back, definitely not expecting that answer.

"Because I was into art and more creative endeavors, I used to get teased a lot about it; even my dad would call me gay sometimes, like it would have been the worst thing in the world if I was attracted to men. And after a while, I wondered if they were seeing something I wasn't. But the more I learned—when I actually met people who were queer—I knew for sure I was not. I was just subjected to a lot of bullying, but nothing compared to what actual queer people go through."

Chance sighed. "It was around that time I started to realize that the pressure my dad put on me, the pressure of my family name, that it wasn't normal. It was probably around the same time that I started trying to figure out an exit strategy."

"I'm sorry you went through that. It must have been very confusing and difficult." I had the urge to reach out to him, but held back. The deeper things got with Chance and me, the harder they would be to manage, and they were already so complicated.

Considering why Chance had come to Montgomery, I didn't think he planned on staying, once he discovered the truth about Daniel's disappearance. Combined with my concern over violating the faculty rules of conduct, I felt even more strongly that I needed to keep my walls up and maintain distance from him. But he made it next to impossible, when he was so very open and raw with his words, as if nobody had ever stopped to listen to him...to comfort him.

"What was your secret?" he threw the question back at me softly.

I chewed my lip nervously, debating how much I wanted to share. But Chance had been so vulnerable, it only felt fair to let him have a peek behind the wall that I kept built so high around my heart. Maybe a small part of me wanted to test him too. Would he judge me, like others before him?

"Growing up, I was responsible for a lot more than most kids my age were. My mom has always dealt with depression, and some years were better than others. But nobody knew how bad things were, because I was terrified that if they did, I'd be taken away from her, and I didn't know what she'd do without me." I folded over the table, resting my chin on the tops of my hands, but keeping my eye contact with Chance.

It was as if talking about my complicated relationship with my mother and everything I had gone through in my youth continued to physically exhaust me, even though it had been years since I'd been subjected to the worst of it.

Chance reached out, when I couldn't with him, and rested his hand on my arm to comfort and encourage me.

"I had to get a job at fourteen, the second I was eligible for a work permit. I worked every hour I could get, bagging groceries for minimum wage, which was pennies back then, just to try to keep the electricity on. We got checks from the government, but they rarely stretched far enough to cover everything without my mom being able to hold down a job."

Chance's lips parted, as if he wanted to apologize, but he closed them and said nothing, letting us sit in a comfortable silence for a while.

"I almost didn't go to college. I was worried she'd hurt herself. But she encouraged me to go. Despite it all, she was always supportive of everything I did; she did the best she could." I bit my cheek, hating that I was always protecting her, even now. "When I left, I couldn't afford to support her as much because I had to cover my own bills, so she got a reverse mortgage on the house. Those assholes are so predatory," I spit.

Chance nodded in agreement.

"Every cent I get paid here that doesn't go to pay off my mountainous student loans gets sent to the bank to pay them back for taking advantage of her at her weakest moment." I closed my eyes. "The house is too big, and she really should sell it, but it's all that's left of my dad. I can't take that away from her. She wouldn't recover."

Again the stillness surrounded us.

I opened my eyes to find Chance watching me, a melancholic expression upon his face. I wondered what he was thinking, so I asked him.

"What am I thinking?" he repeated. "That it's a lot for someone so young to take on. That it must have been painful to try to work through the contradiction of loving your mother so deeply but feeling resentment for not getting to be a child and not having been taken care of the way a child ought to be."

I let out a quiet sob. I had never had someone put it so eloquently before.

Chance leaned forward, his fingertip gently wiping away the tear that was trailing down my cheek. "You're not alone, Violet."

23

RECONNAISSANCE

Whatever was going on between Chance and me was evolving into something else entirely. There were some moments where it felt natural and I was eager to explore the way he constantly sent my heart soaring. But other times, it gave me so much anxiety, fearing opening up to someone after having been betrayed and rejected over and over again by those that I trusted.

If he broke the trust we had built—if he broke my heart...I would not recover.

Thankfully, after the heavy discussion of the crosses we had born as teenagers, splitting both of us right open for the other to examine and dissect, we turned our attention to our next mission: obtaining Daniel's laptop password.

On the Thursday before Thanksgiving break, the perfect opportunity presented itself.

Jolene had left school early for the day, for a dentist appointment. It was imperative that she wasn't in the office, as she would easily spot Chance, and it could not only expose our tenuous alliance, but then we'd have to reveal everything to her, which could put her at great risk.

In the days preceding our second heist, Chance and I strategized on how best to distract Milton to give Chance enough time to poke around on his computer to find the student laptop passwords.

"Can you wear the leggings you wore when we broke into the headmaster's office?" Chance asked seriously. "Those will easily distract him—they did a number on me."

"Be serious." I shoved him playfully.

"I am!" He threw his hands up, feigning innocence.

"They're not work appropriate," I argued. "There's a no leggings rule in the Montgomery dress code."

"There are a lot of ridiculous rules in the dress code. Interestingly, most of them apply only to women," Chance observed.

I snorted a laugh. "I wouldn't expect any less from Montgomery Prep."

"What about a low-cut shirt?"

I rolled my eyes.

"Can you unbutton like one or two more buttons than usual?"

"Why don't I just show up in nothing but a bra?" I suggested sarcastically.

"That would definitely work." Chance grinned.

I huffed, hating that we had to resort to overt sexuality to get what we needed...but we really did need that password. "Fine."

Chance's eyebrows raised in shock. "Just a bra then?"

"No! The button thing," I snarled.

He nodded his head in understanding. "You know you'll have to bend over so he can see down your shirt, right?"

The thought made me queasy. "I'll do what I need to do to give you as much time as possible."

"I'm only sorry I'll be missing your acting debut."

I pursed my lips into a flat line, unamused by his flirting that evening.

Taking a deep breath, I set my laptop on Jolene's empty desk, unfastened two buttons—Chance insisted it had to be two—and set off down the hall to enact the plan that he and I had devised.

"Milton?" I asked sweetly, leaning against the doorframe.

Milton started at my appearance, closing a window on his computer before I could take a step in to see what he had been looking at.

"Uhh—hi, Violet." He straightened his mustard-colored shirt, then righted his thin-framed glasses on his nose. "Did you need help with something?"

"Urgently." I sounded breathless; the effect was unintentional, but worked like a charm.

Milton scrambled out of his chair, not bothering to lock his computer, just as we had hoped, and strode toward me. "Tell me what happened."

"I just finished writing my final exam—it took me weeks—and my computer got unplugged and shut down before I could save. When I started it back up, the file disappeared, and I can't find it anywhere,"

I lamented, leading him down the hall toward the front office and my waiting computer. "Can you help me?" I pleaded.

I positioned myself and the computer at just the right angle so Milton's back was to the hallway to his office. Chance slunk out of the shadows, flashing me a devious grin as he silently padded through the room.

Catching my line of sight, Milton almost turned to see what I was looking at, but I bent over, giving him a great view of my cleavage, pulling his attention right where I wanted him. "I had it saved in this folder." I pointed to the screen.

Chance was gone the next time I glanced up. The clock was ticking.

"But you had it partially saved when your computer shut down?" Milton asked, clicking away on the keyboard and searching through folders.

"I don't know. Doesn't it autosave?" I asked coquettishly, knowing damn well I wasn't that technologically illiterate.

"Do you have the autosave feature turned on?" He glanced up at me.

"I don't know." I shook my head.

He grimaced, but kept clicking. "Do you remember the file name?"

"ClassicsFinal-rev4," I told him.

"So you did have it saved?"

"That's what I wrote at the top of the document. Usually it saves the document as the first thing I write." I should have felt ashamed at how easy it was to sound like an idiot. Maybe I just had too much experience with all the neo-Luddites at the school who still wrote their papers by hand and had Jolene type them up.

To be fair, most of the teachers just reused the same tests for decades at a time, so Jolene didn't have to help them too frequently. More often they just took advantage of her to print and collate their massive stacks of paper tests, a task which she seemed to enjoy, but one that would have been hell on earth for me.

"But the paper comes out all warm, and it smells good," she had gushed to me one day when I had eyed her strangely as she had smiled brightly while sorting the stacks into an assembly line, grabbing one paper from each pile and then stapling each packet together, completing the process by creating a new stack of its own.

"I think I need to start it in safe mode to try to recover an older version." Milton stood back from the laptop. "I wrote down the instructions in a notebook because I kept forgetting. I'll just go grab it."

"Wait." I instinctively reached out, placing my hand on his arm.

He stood frozen, bewitched by my touch. "Can you tell me how you were looking through the files?"

He stared at me blankly for a moment, his mouth open like a dead fish. "Sure." He grinned suddenly, returning to the computer.

I had to stifle a giggle when I remembered the mission title Chance had settled on—without my agreement, I might add—which was "Project Seduce Milton." And if he could see me in action, he would have been pleased...and probably a little turned on.

Despite my hesitation, his tricks were working. I *hated* that he had been right about Milton's baser instincts.

"I'm looking at the root file directory here." Milton pointed to the screen. I tuned him out as he rambled and clicked through the windows. It was obvious he was working to throw in as many tech terms as he could muster, many of which I was pretty sure he was using incorrectly.

But after another minute or so of his explanation, I saw Chance hold up a piece of paper, a giant victorious grin plastered across his face as he snuck back up the stairs, with Milton none the wiser.

"Oh my gosh!" I exclaimed. "There's the file!" I pointed at the screen, at nothing in particular.

"What?" Milton blinked.

"You did it! Thank you!" I closed the laptop and pulled it to my chest, covering the spot where the buttons weren't fastened. "I owe you one, Milton." And with our mission complete, I turned on my heel and scampered up the stairs, leaving a bewildered Milton in my wake.

24

VIOLET, THE MALADAPTED GHOST

I bolted through the carriage house to make it back to the lounge where Chance and I had agreed to meet. If my legs were long enough to have taken the stairs two steps at a time, I would have. I dumped my laptop on my bed and rushed up the trapdoor stairs.

"You brilliant, beautiful woman!" Chance pulled me into his arms the second I made it into the lounge, swinging me around so forcefully, my feet left the ground for a moment before meeting the floor once more.

"You got in?" I tilted my face up to look at his expression, still in his embrace.

"Because of you and your connections and your clever mind and your perfect scheme," he panted, a bit breathless in his excitement.

And that was when I realized how close we were. My body was flush against his, his lips a mere breath away from my own. His blue-grey eyes searched mine, and I knew what permission he was seeking. His lips parted, but I couldn't do it. I pulled back before he could make the move. I didn't want him to feel rejected.

Throbbing guilt weighed heavy in my chest, and my throat felt tight.

I wanted him to kiss me.

I wanted to kiss him.

But I was still too scared.

"Have you found your smoking gun yet?" I asked cheerfully, knowing I was doing a shit job of playing off just how charged the air remained between us.

"Not yet." Chance shook his head, a small smile playing on his lips, but it was a sad smile, not the one filled with glee that he had sported only moments ago.

I had done that to him.

I had stolen his joy.

And I hated myself for it.

"How can I help?" I tried to dispel the awkwardness permeating the lounge.

"I'll load some of his files on a flash drive, and you can look on your computer."

"I might forget to save them," I joked, jabbing him playfully in the ribs.

"I could hear everything—you were a force to be reckoned with. You had him wrapped around your finger in two seconds flat." Chance lightened up a little, plugging the flash drive into Daniel's laptop.

I quickly snatched my laptop from my room and hurried back up the stairs. "What are you going to be doing while I dig through his files?"

"Sorting through his emails."

"Can't they see that someone is digging around in there?" I asked, taking a seat next to him on the couch, rather than my usual spot at the study table.

He cocked his head, watching me, as if he was considering asking me why I had chosen that particular spot. And if he had, I definitely wouldn't have told him the truth, that even though I was sure I would be the worst thing that could happen to him (maybe I already was), I liked being close to him.

"I'm using a VPN while logging in, which I think will offer enough encryption to look like it's just a random person, if they notice, rather than a targeted effort. It's not foolproof, but I doubt any of the local guys would be able to decrypt it easily," Chance offered.

He laughed when he saw how wide my eyes were at his complicated explanation.

"I've been doing my own research, and I want to keep us protected. Just because we think we're doing the right thing doesn't mean the authorities will see it that way."

"Better safe than sorry, I suppose." I took the flash drive from him and plugged it into my laptop. "Does the school know this laptop still exists?"

Chance shook his head. "The police assumed he had it on him when he went missing."

"Are they going to know you have it turned on?"

"They shouldn't be able to; once I'm logged in, I'll work offline."

I nodded, crossing my fingers that all of his preventative measures would be enough to keep us from being caught. I hadn't really paused to consider the consequences if the cops found out we had Daniel's laptop and were looking through something that was evidence. Jail time would be worse than losing my job for openly dating Chance.

I tried to remind myself that they had made their incompetence quite clear by how little they had investigated and how quickly they had declared Daniel just another runaway without doing their duty.

A couple hours later, I had only found school assignments, but I was going through each folder and each document one by one, so there was no telling if or when something of interest would turn up. Chance was focused on going through, email by email, to see what sort of trail he could find that might lead us to a break in the case.

Needing to stretch my legs, I offered to go grab us food from the dining hall.

"Huh?" Chance's gaze was firmly on the screen.

"I'll be right back." I gave his shoulder a reaffirming squeeze. The familiar sparks from the warmth of his body zinged through me like usual.

Walking through the chilly courtyard back to the main building, I found myself lost in thought over the battle waging inside me over what the fuck I was going to do about Chance.

I was still desperately attracted to him; the throbbing between my legs at merely being in close proximity with him was clear evidence of that fact. And worse, Chance continued to make it clear that he was still very much interested in me, beyond our cordial alliance.

Oh, who was I kidding? I could deny it all I wanted, but we'd become more than just cordial—one might even call us friends.

Ugh. I have no willpower.

However, between the looming threat of the school policy, as well as the fear and baggage I was harboring from past relationships, I was a ball of anxiety any time I wasn't near him. Maybe that was a sign in itself—how he was starting to calm me. Unless he touched me; then it was a whole other ball game.

Thinking through my reactions and ruminating on my fears, I wondered if part of the reason I was pushing him away and refusing to allow myself to give in, or not even letting him pursue me, was because I felt unworthy. And not just unworthy of Chance, but there was a part of me, buried deep, that didn't think I was worthy of anyone.

I had nothing.

I *was* nothing.

Why would anyone want me?

I hated the small, awful voice that echoed Harry's words in my head, over and over again. "You're just desperate to be loved. Even your own mother didn't want you."

I knew it wasn't completely true. But I also knew it wasn't completely false. That was the problem.

And what did Chance truly know about me? If he knew the full extent of how damaged I was inside, he'd see that I brought nothing to the table. I had come around on him, and I thought he deserved someone better...someone who could give him more than I could.

I had spent my entire life carefully constructing walls around my heart to protect myself, and after what I had experienced, I didn't know how to take them down anymore. I was too scared to let anyone in. So I remained safe in my castle, but alone, and lonely.

Even Jolene and Lenny didn't really know the depth of my struggles, because I liked being able to talk to them and share things with them, without those pitying glances I'd get at home, whispering about my misfortune the second I turned my back.

Because it wasn't just my mom that I had left behind. No, there were others that had let me down. I could no longer face them. I wasn't strong enough.

"I've lost count of how many times you've come in here and left with two plates, and I know that Jolene isn't who's getting the second," Lenny chided as I assembled the dinner boxes for Chance and myself.

"Maybe nosy chefs should mind their own business." I smiled up at him, teeth bared.

Lenny merely chuckled, shaking his head in amusement.

"How long are you going to let that boy chase after you?"

"I'm certain I don't know what you're talking about." I feigned innocence, sealing up the containers and knowing damn well, of course, Lenny understood exactly what was going on.

That was why Lenny and I had become such fast friends; he saw through people, and he saw things people tried to keep hidden. Never one to hold back his opinion, at a place like Montgomery, where most people were fake, having someone that would tell you like it was, was priceless.

"You should consider putting him out of his misery," Lenny advised as he cleaned up from dinner service.

I shot him a look.

"Well, then put yourself out of your misery and just give him a chance." He laughed. "Chance." He'd unintentionally made a joke.

I rolled my eyes. And then I wondered how many similar jokes Chance had previously had to deal with over the course of his life. I'd have to ask him.

"Sooner or later, you'll have to make a decision, or you'll both get hurt."

"I think we'll both get hurt regardless of what I decide," I said soberly, pausing next to Lenny.

He looked at me with his soft eyes, having transitioned into grandfather mode. "Give him a shot. He's smitten with you. What's the worst that could happen?"

"I could be fired, have my heart broken, break his heart, ruin both our lives—"

"Violet," he stopped me.

I glared at him, but there was no real malice behind the gesture, only indignance.

"You float around this place like just another ghost haunting the grounds. You're so young, you have your whole life ahead of you. Live it. Or you'll regret it."

"Yes, chef," I said softly, giving Lenny my customary salute. "Thank you, chef."

"Goodnight, Violet."

25

THE SOURCE

Over the next few days, I learned a lot of things about Daniel Graham.

Some good.

Some bad.

And some awkward.

I knew what books he read, who his favorite artists were, and what sites he frequented. Thankfully he kept most of his porn watching in a private browser (I assumed), as I only spotted two accidental slips in his internet history, and that was two too many.

Daniel and Claire had been dating for most of the last school year. Their instant messaging back and forth was cute, but very much between teenagers. It felt inappropriate to laugh at their banter, but I couldn't help myself from cringing occasionally. Often I found myself wanting to share something with Chance, but refrained.

Daniel had already been prepping his college applications for quite a few prestigious schools, wanting to pursue a career in investigative journalism.

"Columbia was his top choice," Chance shared with me. "Dad wasn't happy, but Mom told me she'd make sure wherever he wanted to go, his tuition would be taken care of."

There were certain sections of his computer files that were very organized, like his class work, but other folders, like his personal documents, and most of his journalistic research, that was a jumble of discombobulated fragments all jammed into a single folder with no naming conventions. I didn't know how he could keep any of it straight, and I had a hard time categorizing things in my mind as I went.

It would have been too much to ask for him to have kept a digital journal, but his email did have a calendar feature that had some appointments listed, unfortunately none of interest, unless he was using an incredibly advanced coding system to make it look like a dentist appointment was something else, despite Chance's parents having received the bill for the cleaning.

"We're going to be at this for days." Chance groaned, stretching his thick arms over his head, then settling them across the back of the couch.

We had the week of Thanksgiving break to really dig into everything before we'd be inundated with end-of-semester teacherly duties that would surely sabotage our fieldwork.

"Have you found anything of note?"

"I'm not sure that Ken can be one hundred percent ruled out," Chance offered, regarding his counterpart in the English department.

"Oh?"

"They argued back and forth about all of the articles. The last one about the drugs—Daniel threatened to go to the ACLU to help him argue for his First Amendment right of free speech if he wouldn't publish it," Chance revealed.

"I didn't know that." I turned to him. "Banks did a good job of positioning himself as a champion of free speech when he allowed the article to be published, knowing that however upset the board and donors would be, they would have a hard time working around the optics to punish him or Daniel."

Kenneth Banks had sometimes struck me as an opportunist; he'd sway wherever the wind was blowing. "Were their exchanges enough to escalate to something in person?" I asked.

Chance scratched the back of his neck, "I don't know Ken well enough. I don't think he'd have the guts to hurt someone, but I still can't help but wonder if whatever happened to Daniel was maybe an accident—something that got pushed too far."

"Maybe," I offered. "Everyone at Montgomery is so worried about their reputation inside and outside of these walls, that could be a reasonable motive for hurting someone, but it also could be motive to let things go, so they wouldn't make themselves or their families look bad."

"Exactly. Right back at square one." He sighed. "There were a few emails from some of his classmates after the last article was published. They weren't happy with him and didn't hold back, but it all felt very juvenile, internet troll kind of junk, not real threats."

"What about Winston?"

"Nothing yet. You?"

"There were a few stories he was working on, but the folders aren't as full as the others. I don't know if they were newer, although the documents in them aren't. Or maybe his research isn't on here." I frowned.

"It's possible he has another computer."

"Maybe on the cloud somewhere or an external drive?" I guessed.

Chance shrugged. We were grasping at straws.

"I think I'm going to call it a night. I'm going cross-eyed." I felt guilty leaving, but was surprised when Chance agreed with me.

"We'll have fresh eyes in the morning." He closed the laptop. "Remind me again what we're supposed to do for food while the school is closed down for break?"

"We're on our own." I laughed, surprised that it had taken all weekend for Chance to ask about it.

"Ramen noodles all week it is." He gave a sour laugh.

"I have food from the kitchen," I admitted. "I'll keep us fed." Lenny had made sure I was stocked for the week before he had left on Friday.

"Thank you, Violet." He ruffled my hair lightly, letting his hand linger on my head a moment too long, but I didn't think I minded as much anymore. I was becoming more comfortable with him by the day.

"He has a source!" I accidentally shouted in earnest the next day. While going through the remainder of Daniel's chat logs with his other friends, he had mentioned to Bryce Osbourne, the student editor of the paper, that he had found someone who was willing to talk to him, off the record. Daniel had told Bryce he was following a scandal so big it was going to give him "the pick of Ivy League schools without having to rely on family favors to get in."

I scrambled to show Chance everything and explain while he read.

The problem was that Daniel hadn't given any more details than that.

But then Chance found the reason why.

"He's got a drive—you were right." Chance pointed to a line I had missed in the chat thread.

Bryce was concerned about Daniel's safety, if this story was as big as he was making it out to be, and Daniel assured him that he was doing everything by the book and had everything backed up where nobody would find it.

"So how are we supposed to find it?" I slumped next to Chance.

"We'll think of something, but the point is, it's out there." I could sense a renewed energy in Chance that cold and rainy Monday. It didn't matter that, as it stood, we didn't have much, just the hope that there was something else out there for us to find, something that could give us a decent lead on what had happened to Daniel. That was all Chance needed—some luck and a little bit of hope.

As I stole glances of Chance while he continued to work through Daniel's emails, I let my mind wander, wondering what it would be like to be with him.

What would it be like to let Chance in and see me for who I was and what I had really been through? What would he think of all the remaining secrets I kept locked inside so closely guarded that I hadn't spoken of them after Harry had thrown them in my face to make himself feel better about dumping me?

Would I be capable of breaking down those walls, even for just a moment? Could I have enough courage to try?

I still wasn't sure, but the more I was around Chance, the harder it was to keep him at arm's length, and the more impossible it became to pretend that I didn't want to chip away at every last defense to see what it would be like to be loved by someone who cared as fiercely as he did.

26

A CHANGE OF PERSPECTIVE

"What are you doing up so early?" Chance's voice startled me from across the lounge.

"Yeah, you caught me." I snorted a laugh, building the wood structure in the fireplace to warm up the space for us while we worked.

"What are those?" Chance pointed to the large cardboard boxes I had moved out from under the pool table, where they normally hid.

"Decorations."

"For Christmas?" Chance's voice was much closer then.

I turned around to look up at him, only a few paces away from me, and nodded, before swiftly returning my attention to building the fire.

"With that black cat attitude, you don't strike me as the type to enjoy decorating for holidays." He took a sip of coffee from a mug he'd brought up to the lounge with him from his apartment.

"Well, I do," I replied curtly.

Sensing he'd inadvertently hit a sore spot, he crouched down next to me, placing a warm hand on my arm. "I can help."

I swallowed. Why did he have to smell so good? He was fresh out of the shower, his hair still damp, and he smelled clean, like soap.

We worked quietly in tandem to get the fire going, settling on the couch when we were pleased with the outcome. Chance sat down next to me, his thigh touching mine, sending warmth flooding through me. He leaned back into the cushions, closing his eyes and taking a deep breath, completely unaware of the effect he had on me.

"So Christmas decorations...on Thanksgiving?"

"Don't tell me you're one of those people who thinks you have to wait until December to put anything up? What a waste to lose out on a couple extra weeks of all the holiday cheer." I poked his arm in jest.

Chance laughed. "You can put them up whenever you want."

I felt his fingers brush against mine where our bodies met on the couch, and a moment later, he slipped his fingers through mine, his gaze still fixed on the fire.

I didn't pull away.

I couldn't.

"What were your holidays like growing up?" I asked.

"The only word that comes to mind is perfunctory."

"You're such an English teacher." I snorted a laugh.

"Jealous of my vocabulary?" he teased, gently squeezing my hand.

"Maybe," I admitted.

"My parents would throw big charity parties at our house over the holidays, and they would trot me and Amanda out like props. I can't remember a holiday season where I didn't feel lonely."

I sat with his words for a moment before responding. "Not even Christmas morning?"

"It was fine, but it was mechanical. Me and my sister would give my parents a list, and they would sit and watch us open the exact things we'd asked for, but there was no excitement or joy in any of it. I suppose my mom seemed happy, but it never felt like what you see in the movies, that sense of wonder and being surrounded by familial love. It was them checking off a box of what was expected of them," he finished, punctuating the thought by taking another drink of his coffee. "What about you? What were holidays like with your mom?"

"It was my favorite time of year because it felt like the only time that Mom wasn't completely down. I mean, the depression never went away, and looking back, I think it was really that she made more of an effort during the holidays, which made them feel more special. All of my favorite memories of growing up were during the holidays.

"She had a friend with a farm that would let her cut down a tree for us, and we'd string up a popcorn garland. We couldn't afford lights, but that was enough. She didn't have money to spend on gifts, but she'd make crafts with me and always create such unique things, so I always had at least one or two items to open on Christmas. She could make a lot from nothing."

I laughed, having an errant thought. "I wonder if that's part of the reason I liked Jolene right away. My mom would *love* her sweaters. Did you know she makes them all herself?"

"I didn't, but I might have assumed. They look handmade, and I don't know what store you could find something quite like them."

Chance smiled. "But they suit her, I'll admit. Nobody could pull them off quite like Jolene."

He took a beat, then asked softly, "You don't have to answer, but why was your mom always so sad?"

"Because of my dad."

Chance squeezed my hand again. I don't even think he was aware of it; it had somehow become second nature for him to try to comfort me, even though I had continually pushed him away.

"My mom was pregnant with me when he died while deployed overseas. He never got to meet me, but he named me. He found out I was a girl right before he left and begged my mom to name me Violet after his grandmother. She loved the name, so she agreed. So even though I didn't know him, I've always felt like he was a part of me."

"I'm sorry."

I cocked my head. "It's not your fault." I didn't understand why he was apologizing.

"I've been complaining so much about my dad, but at least I had one."

I couldn't help but laugh. Chance glanced over to me, unsure of my amusement. "Don't be sorry. Your dad sounds awful. I don't think I would have survived a parent like your father. I have enough insecurities as it is—I don't need someone I am hardwired to love and want to make proud constantly pointing them out to me."

"What could you possibly be insecure about?" Chance's tone was so genuine, I had to do a double take to make sure that his facial expression was just as sincere, and it was.

"Are you kidding me?" I snorted a laugh. "First off, I'm a woman, so there are a million things, thanks to society: my looks, my clothes, my height. Then there's the reality of having grown up in poverty, which makes me feel inferior to every single person at Montgomery, every second of every day. I worry about my teaching, about my student debt, about my education, my emotional unavailability, would you like me to keep going?"

Chance's lips were parted in shock. "How can you say all of that?"

I mirrored his confusion.

"I wish you could see yourself from my point of view. I think it would completely change your perspective. Because I don't see any of those things when I look at you. I see a strong, stunning, incredibly intelligent, kind"—he paused—"very sexy, and accomplished woman." He chuckled, likely due to the shade of red my face was turning upon hearing his complimentary words.

"In fact, the only thing I would change about you is that I wish you would be able to acknowledge all the wonderful things about yourself, like how deeply you care for those you let in, how you've dropped everything to help me chase some kind of vigilante justice for Daniel, whom you barely knew, but simply identified with, or how dedicated you are to making a difference for students who rarely give you the time of day, because all it takes is for a single one of them to need you, for all of it to be worth it.

"I wasn't lying when I told you that almost everyone I've talked to at Montgomery thinks very highly of you."

"Almost everyone? Was it Serena that was talking shit?" I couldn't help but interrupt, despite the tightness in my throat from his appraising words.

Chance gave a small laugh. "After myself, Lenny, and Jolene, she might be your next biggest fan."

My brow furrowed. "But she hates me." We couldn't be talking about the same Serena Lawrence.

"No, she doesn't." Chance gave a withering chuckle.

"You must have misunderstood her then," I replied firmly.

"*I* misunderstood?" His brows shot up. "I did not misunderstand her approaching me out of nowhere on my third day here, saying she had seen me making eyes at you and if I hurt you, she'd eviscerate me with her own bare hands."

I felt my jaw drop at his confession.

"She really said that?" I asked meekly, in disbelief.

"Yeah, and she wasn't the only one."

Again my throat constricted. I'd always felt like an outsider at Montgomery. How could he be talking about the same people that I'd felt so deeply shunned by? But like Chance suggested, it was all about perspective.

Maybe it wasn't that they had iced me out, but rather that I had positioned myself on the outside, assuming they wouldn't want to have anything to do with me. I couldn't remember having given them a chance, because I hadn't. I had just kept my guard up to protect myself from being hurt.

"You are wanted and needed at Montgomery, and you have more allies here than you realize, but you need to open your eyes to find them."

I nodded, still in a daze at this ridiculous revelation, but I couldn't help but ask, "But you did say 'almost'— who was the holdout?"

"Bernie." Chance shrugged.

"Bernie!?" The mild-mannered, sweet, bearded chemistry teacher whom everyone loved. "Not Bernie!? Why does Bernie hate me?"

"He doesn't hate you," Chance said through laughter. "He's just scared of you."

I scowled at the thought, already running through a few different ideas for how I could win him over. I didn't want Bernie to be scared of me. I wondered if he liked cookies…

"Does knowing that you aren't their enemy change things for you?" Chance asked.

I shrugged, playing it off, but obviously it made a difference. How could it not? "I mean, it's nice to know, I suppose."

"You suppose?" He laughed, clearly sensing that it meant a great deal to me that maybe I wasn't as ostracized as I had always felt.

I shrugged again, just to see his reaction. But I couldn't help the smile adorning my lips, so he merely shook his head, suppressing a grin.

"C'mon, these decorations aren't going to put themselves up." Chance looped his arm through my elbow and pulled me toward the boxes.

27

JAKE & JENNY

I'd never seen the lounge looking so festive before.

Putting everything up with Chance went so quickly, and his height certainly helped to expedite the process. It was nice to decorate with someone as well. The fact that that someone was Chance was a nice bonus. I had a lot of opportunities to admire his figure as he stretched in various ways to assist me.

"Did you bring these from home?" Chance asked as we worked together to fluff the faux tree. From a distance, after it was all done up, I swore you couldn't tell the difference.

"Actually, Lenny and Jolene got them for me last year." I smiled, thinking about how Lenny and Jolene had conspired together after they learned I would be alone at Montgomery over the entire break, pretty much on my own.

They still didn't know the extent of what the holidays meant to me, or how much their act had impacted my life. It almost made me tear up to think about the shock I'd felt as Jolene had shown me everything and told me that Lenny had picked up each item at her instruction.

There was a fake tree with all the trimmings, a giant pack of ornaments, and a star for the top. They'd gotten a dozen packs of Christmas lights to help cover the entirety of the lounge, although Chance and I hadn't gotten to those just yet, and even a single stocking for me to hang on the mantel.

"That was very nice of them," Chance commented.

It was a selfless and incredibly thoughtful gesture. I had never had anyone do anything so meaningful, just for me, with no motivations other than to make me happy.

"It was the nicest thing anyone has ever done for me." I smiled up at him, and he returned the expression.

It took us all morning to finish stringing the lights around the perimeter of the lounge. I'd had the foresight to leave up the nails I had used last year, as it had been an even more arduous task by myself, on a very tall, but rather unsteady ladder I had procured from the garden shed, at the reluctance of one of the groundskeepers. He had been very grateful when I returned it, seeing that both myself and the ladder were unscathed.

At some point, Chance had put on a record, and when the last string of lights was strung, he pulled me into him, swaying with me to the rhythm of the soft jazz coming out of the gramophone's horn-shaped speaker.

"I'm positive this is the best Thanksgiving I've ever had," Chance whispered, using his palm splayed on the small of my back to press me closer to him as we danced.

I looked up at him at the exact same moment he looked down at me. Maybe it was the music or the lights or my heart beating so fast

I thought I might be having a stroke, but I pushed up on my tiptoes, and he lowered his head to meet me in the middle.

My second kiss with Chance Harper didn't lack any of the heat from the first, but the heat burned low and slow, embers flickering so hot that if anything got near them, they would combust, needing no flame.

Chance kissed me sweetly, cupping my jaw with the hand that wasn't at the small of my back and letting me lead, as if he knew that if he pushed me too far, I'd pull back. My skittishness wasn't intentional but the fact that he sensed it and knew just how to counteract it made me even more drawn to him.

I opened my mouth, allowing him to deepen the kiss, and his tongue mimicked my movements, only going as far as I was willing to dare myself. Without the buzz of the liquor from our first kiss to taint the experience, I thought I knew what it would be like to kiss him again, but I didn't. I really didn't.

His clean smell was overwhelming in the best way possible. The warmth of his body seeped through every place where we touched, and I liked how he tasted of his morning coffee, strong, and slightly bitter, but in that moment, all mine.

Every fiber of my body was vibrating with every touch, every sensation, every new angle. Chance released a soft moan that had heat pooling low in my body, wanting more of him. I couldn't help myself from whimpering in response.

But then, oddly, Chance started to physically vibrate.

Hesitantly and breathless, I pulled back from the kiss.

Chance groaned in agitation, withdrawing his phone from his pocket. "I—" He looked down at the device. "I need to go downstairs." He pointed a finger at me. "Don't go anywhere. And we're not done with this."

I watched him hurriedly make his way to the fire escape, and pressed trembling fingers to my swollen lips.

Oh fuck. I just kissed Chance.

What on earth had come over me? And I'm pretty sure I had initiated.

I staggered to the couch, my knees weak, and was only able to manage leaning against the armrest, taking in deep and measured breaths as my mind continued to spin.

I shouldn't have done that. Because now how am I supposed to stop?

"Violet?" Chance called from outside the window.

I realized I had no idea how long he'd been gone while I had spiraled and tried to remember how to breathe.

"Can you help me?"

"Coming," I replied, my voice as unsteady as my legs.

When I made it to the window, I couldn't help but let my jaw drop. Chance had two giant bags of takeout food.

"What is all this?" I asked, grabbing the bags from him so he could make it through the window without falling.

"It's not Thanksgiving without good food." He grinned at me, taking both of the bags back the moment he was inside the lounge.

"What?" I squeaked, following him as he strode toward the study table.

"Lenny mentioned a place in town that puts together Thanksgiving meals for those who are less inclined to cook," he explained as he pulled out box after box of food from the bags. "Or for people like us who might be willing or able, but can't fit more than a drumstick in our ovens, let alone a whole turkey."

I watched in awe as he began to open the containers. He'd thought of everything; there was a perfectly cooked and sliced turkey breast, mashed potatoes and gravy, vegetables, rolls, and even an entire pumpkin pie.

"Why?" I hadn't realized I'd spoken the thought aloud until Chance paused to look at me.

He cocked his head, as if he didn't understand.

"I've been awful to you. Hot and cold, keeping you at a distance, threatening you with knives..." I half laughed.

Chance smiled, his eyes crinkling at the edges. "I like a challenge."

"I'm serious, Chance. Why?"

Chance took two steps toward me, closing the distance between us. He gently placed his palm flat on my stomach. "Because I think you feel it too."

"Feel what?" I asked, my voice shaky.

Chance smiled softly as he replied, "The butterflies."

The heat of a blush flooded my cheeks. Looking up at him through my lashes, I slowly nodded, breathing the confirmation he was waiting for, "Yes."

He tilted his head down, his nose skimming the column of my neck, eliciting a hitched breath from my lips.

"I can be very patient. I know you'll be worth the wait."

I swallowed hard, holding my breath as Chance placed a soft kiss just below my ear, before he withdrew.

"We should eat before it gets cold." He dug out plates and plastic utensils from the very bottom of the bag and handed them to me while he made work to open the bottle of wine that had been stashed with everything else. It was only a screw top, so it required no corkscrew.

I worried over how much he had spent on the food. I knew in my heart that he was doing it out of kindness, but I'd felt that before, with Harry, and been proven so wrong, so it was hard not to feel some weird sense of guilt knowing I couldn't pay him back with money. And I was desperate to know how and when he had arranged all of this with Lenny. But I pushed my questions aside and tried to just enjoy the moment, a feat I wasn't often capable of.

This moment, making idle chitchat with Chance over this unexpected but lovely shared meal, felt like one of those times you knew you were creating a memory you would look back upon fondly for years to come. It wasn't just that we had kissed.

God. I can't think about the kiss right now.

No, it was everything that had happened that day. And then it dawned on me that it was the first holiday I had spent with another person in years—nine years, to be exact.

I must have stopped eating or looked like I was on the verge of tears because Chance put down his fork and rubbed gentle circles across my back. He didn't ask me what was wrong. He just knew something was, and on instinct, he comforted me.

"I've been alone for every single holiday for almost a decade," I confessed.

"I'm sorry," he replied sweetly, continuing to rub my back.

After a beat he asked tentatively, "You don't want to go home?"

"I can't." I swallowed the lump in my throat, knowing what was coming next, and having already decided to tell him the only secret that was left to share. If he judged me or ever used this against me like Harry had, that would be it between us.

"Why not?"

"The last time I went home for Christmas was during my freshman year of college. I was terribly homesick. I was constantly worried about my mom, my relationship with my high school sweetheart, Jake, was crumbling, and my best friend—my only friend, Jenny, had been super distant, and I couldn't figure out why.

"Jake was over at my house on Christmas Eve, and while he was in the bathroom, he got a text on his phone from Jenny."

"Shit." Chance grimaced, already seeing where this story was going.

"Yeah, so I guess they hooked up toward the end of our senior year, and then it turned into this big thing, and neither of them knew how to tell me, because they knew I'd be devastated, but they also were fucking in love, so they didn't—couldn't end things." I sighed. "It seems naive now, but we'd been together for years. I thought I was going to marry him. And Jenny—god, I think the worst part was that when I confronted them, she seemed disappointed that I wasn't happy for them. But I was eighteen, still a child, and I'd had my heart broken by the two people whom I had centered my world around, outside of my mom."

"Anyone would have been destroyed if that had happened to them. It doesn't mean any less because it happened when you were young. Getting cheated on is incredibly painful to go through, not just because of the immediate damage, but because you end up blaming yourself. Or at least, I did," Chance offered.

I felt my shoulders soften. Somehow, knowing he had gone through something similar made me feel connected to him through that specific kind of heartbreak.

"Do they still live in town? I hope they wouldn't bother you." Chance was trying to piece together my exact reasoning for avoiding my hometown.

"Oh yeah, they still live there. They have a whole gaggle of kids—they're like this golden couple in town that everyone fawns over. Verona is small, only a couple thousand people. My high school was the same size as Montgomery. Everyone knows everyone, and everyone is in everyone's business. I think half the town knew they were fucking before I did. And years later, everyone's forgotten how their relationship started and how it completely changed my life, but I guess I don't really blame any of them. Who am I to stand in the way of true love?" I hadn't meant to sound quite so sarcastic, but it couldn't be helped.

"You're not meant for a place like that. You need to be somewhere where you can blend in, where you can decide when and where you want to be seen," Chance offered, understanding me on a level I wasn't sure anyone else had before him.

I found myself nodding in agreement. Wherever that place was, it sounded nice. I could blend in reasonably well at Montgomery, but as a teacher, I still felt like the spotlight was on me while I was giving lectures or at the front of the room, so I couldn't quite disappear like I wanted to some days.

The fact that Chance could sense that about me continued to chip away at my walls, which he was expertly dismantling brick by brick.

"Is it really so bad that you can't visit your mom though?"

"The problem is that my mom was just as close to Jake and Jenny as she was to me. They didn't know in school what was going on at home, but when I almost decided not to go to college, they practically staged an intervention, and I told them everything. They were both staying in town, so they offered to check in on her, and they became like family to her.

"I wish I could hate them for what they did to me, but the truth is that I don't know if my mom would have survived without them after I left. She was so happy when all of us were back home that single Christmas, and when I told her what happened, I think she already knew what was going on. She tried to argue that I'd find someone else and that I should forgive them.

"And I know she was just trying to keep the peace, but what I needed was for my mom to comfort me and tell me that everything was going to be okay and agree that Jake was an asshole and Jenny was a lying bitch. But she stood up for them and made me feel guilty for being upset. So now I can't go back. They've made her a part of their family. When I call her, she tells me about them. She's an extra grandparent to their children, she's happier than she ever was when I was with her. I can't take that from her. So I've just stayed away. It's easier that way. For everyone."

I took a long sip of my wine. It was cheap, which I was used to, but it still burned on the way down.

The soft jazz music felt stilted in the background as silence hung between Chance and me.

"I'm so sorry that happened to you, Violet. You didn't deserve that." He gave my hand a gentle squeeze, having moved it from my back while I was speaking.

"I just—" I paused, thinking through what I wanted to say. I looked up at Chance. "Please don't ever use that against me. I don't think I could bear it, not from you."

"I would never." He shook his head.

"I've only ever told one other person—but I shouldn't have, and I can't help how guarded I am, because the most important people in my life have let me down in such spectacular fashion that ten years later, I still haven't figured out how to get over it."

"Violet," Chance breathed, then a moment later, he had scooted forward in his chair and pulled me into a hug that was so tight it rivaled only the way my mother used to embrace me. "What happened was not your fault."

I let out a sob I hadn't realized was bubbling up inside of me, begging to be released. Chance held me there for a while, soothing me with his warmth and the simple comfort of his arms around me.

Eventually he released me, wiping an errant tear from my cheek and tucking my hair behind my ear. "We need to make sure this is a good holiday season for you then. We have a lot of bad memories to overwrite." He cut a piece of pie and slid the plate toward me, again sensing what I needed was a way to lighten the mood to pull me out of my dark memories.

"I've already got down the perfect Christmas Eve," I admitted. It was something nobody knew because I'd always been alone to celebrate the holiday.

"Oh yeah? I want to hear all the details." Chance grinned in between forkfuls of pie.

"Well, the perfect day always starts with sleeping in," I began.

Chance laughed. "Of course it does for you."

"You're just mad because you're a morning person not by choice," I argued, knowing he swam early most mornings. If he was running late, I could smell the chlorine on him if I passed him in the hallways at school.

Chance shrugged at the accusation.

"For breakfast, I get these frozen croissants from the market in town. I have to put them out the night before to proof, but they bake like a dream, perfectly flakey and crispy."

"We're definitely getting some of those." Chance nodded in agreement.

"I watch holiday movies all day on my laptop. Last year I watched them up in the lounge, with the fire going—it was perfect. And I only stop them to make mac and cheese from scratch for dinner."

Chance half choked on his bite of pie. "You can make it from scratch?"

I nodded, unable to hold back the smile on my face, so pleased that such a simple feat impressed him that much.

"I also have to get a bottle of sparkling cider. That was the one thing my mom would always splurge on for Christmas, so I have to have it."

Chance continued nodding.

"With the lounge at my disposal, I added one last part to the tradition. In the evening, when I was ready to wind down, I put on the Bing Crosby Christmas album, made myself a cup of hot chocolate—you can be in charge of that this year." Chance smiled, nodding emphatically. "And I watched the snow fall while sitting in the window seat." I motioned toward one of the window benches that was perfectly nestled in the bay windows along the wall opposite from the bookshelves.

"What happens if it doesn't snow?"

"That's the best part. As long as there's snow on the roof, it blows off the eaves and always looks like it's snowing from the window seats." I took in a deep breath, smiling as I remembered how cozy it had felt last year. I had been able to arrange everything in the lounge by then, but was just starting to alphabetize the books. But finding the lounge had been the best Christmas gift I'd ever gotten. I needed it. My soul had needed it. It still did.

"And you're really going to let me enjoy your traditions with you this year?" Chance asked hesitantly. "Last I checked, you weren't sold on even being friends."

I chuckled, shaking my head. "Yes, I suppose I would consider you a friend at this point."

"Maybe we can just be friends that make out occasionally?" Chance's trademark smirk turned devilish.

"Let me finish another glass of wine and you might get your wish." I grabbed the bottle.

Chance rolled his eyes. "That's not—" He stopped himself, turning serious all of the sudden. "I meant what I said earlier, about waiting."

I glanced up at him, setting the now empty wine bottle on the table between us. "I know," I said softly. "I don't think I'm ready yet..." I paused, averting my gaze while I gathered the courage to complete my thought. I looked back up at him, his eyes a storm of emotion. "But I want to be. I'm—I want to try."

Chance's throat bobbed as he swallowed, the impact of my admission hitting him with the full force with which I had intended it to. "You mean something to me, whether you want to or not, so I'll be here when you're ready."

I nodded. I knew I should have been more concerned about the school catching wind of everything, but maybe everyone who had been encouraging me was right, that the school didn't enforce their stupid rule. And as my trust in Chance bloomed, I really believed that he would do whatever he could to keep it a secret.

"Do you think we could maybe start your holiday tradition a little early?" he asked.

I cocked my head. "A month early?"

"It's Thanksgiving. I know the perfect movie." He smiled.

"Okay," I agreed.

After getting his laptop set up with the movie, Chance wrapped his arm around me, pulling me into his chest. He must have sensed me stiffen at the closeness, so he said, "Don't worry, I won't try anything. I promise."

I relaxed upon hearing his words, and felt myself drifting off not long after. As I was surrounded by the warmth of his body, I listened to the steady beating of his heart and realized I wanted it to belong to me. I needed to find a way to trust him with mine; that was the only way—a mutual exchange.

I had to get over the fact that uncertainty would always be a possibility, but it didn't mean I shouldn't try. There were no guarantees in life. There were no guarantees that love would last, but we were also not guaranteed there would be another tomorrow to try again.

As I ruminated over the possibilities, I felt Chance's warm breath against my skin just before he placed a soft kiss at my temple and whispered, "Goodnight, little muse."

28

THE RETIRED DETECTIVE

Startled out of my sleep by a loud pounding on my door, I scrambled out of bed, pulling on the closest thing I could find, the hideous, but thoughtful Christmas sweater Jolene had made for me as a gift before she left for break days earlier.

"I'm coming!" I shouted.

Chance got one look at my sweater and burst out laughing. I let him have his giggle fit while I stood in the doorway and waited with my hands poised on my hips.

"I'm sorry—I can't—" he stuttered through his laughter.

"Just get it all out now." I sighed, looking down at the monstrosity.

Last year, the sweater had been a festive Christmas tree with metallic pom pom ornaments and a star made of sequins, but this year she had outdone herself, with a giant reindeer face taking up the entire front of the sweater, complete with large red sequin nose, and she had attached brown felt horns that started at either side of my clavicle and ran over the shoulders. I had to admit, the literal beady eyes were a bit creepy.

"Done yet?" I drawled, rubbing the sleep out of my eyes.

"I think so." Chance attempted to compose himself. "Listen, I need you to get dressed and come with me."

"Chance. It's Christmas Eve. You've already ruined the most important tradition of sleeping in." I pouted.

"I know, but it's important." He took both my hands in his. "Please. I wouldn't ask if it wasn't. We'll be back in time to make mac and cheese, and we can watch the movies we don't fit in today, tomorrow."

I studied his handsome face, blue-grey eyes alight with excitement. "Fine. But you're letting me sleep in tomorrow then," I told him.

"Absolutely, and we'll cuddle on the couch as much as you want."

I narrowed my eyes at him. That was all we'd been doing since Thanksgiving, thanks to me putting the brakes on things, and because of the sheer amount of finals prep we'd had, which had completely derailed our investigation. "And what makes you think I want to cuddle with you?" I teased.

"Oh Violet, what a smart mouth you have." He leaned forward and swiftly pecked me on the lips. "We'll stop for coffee and a quick breakfast, my treat."

"It better be," I sulked.

"I'll be in the car. Meet me downstairs in ten." He turned to leave.

"Fifteen!" I argued.

Chance laughed, glancing over his shoulder at the sweater one last time. "You should keep that on."

I rolled my eyes and slammed the door. We were the only faculty that had stayed behind on campus, so there would be nobody around to complain about the noise.

Wanting to be comfortable and realizing Chance hadn't told me where we were going or what we'd be doing, I threw on my black leggings, the ones that Chance affectionately referred to as my "hot cat burglar pants."

I considered wearing Jolene's handcrafted sweater, but I wasn't sure I could handle the potential stares and attention it would garner if we were going somewhere more public. Instead I opted for my two sizes too large, but coziest hoodie from my college alma mater.

Grabbing my winter coat, a scarf, and mittens, as the temperatures had recently plummeted, I took a wistful glance around my room, my heart sinking as I spotted Chance's Christmas present sitting on the bistro table in the kitchen.

I'd made an online order for a monogrammed stocking that matched the one Lenny and Jolene had gotten me the year before. It wasn't much in itself, but inside were the negatives that Chance had surrendered to me.

The longer I kept them in my possession, the guiltier I felt. I didn't want to take his art from him permanently, so I planned on returning them and had a whole speech planned out. A speech I intended to give over breakfast on Christmas Eve. I hoped I'd still have the courage to tell him later.

The second I slid into the passenger seat of the warm car, Chance smirked and asked, "Did you wear those for me?" referring to the leggings.

"In your dreams."

"Yes, I do dream of them often." He chuckled, giving my knee a gentle squeeze before slowly pulling out of the Montgomery parking lot. It had snowed the first week in December, but not since; however, the cold temperatures had kept it from melting.

"Are you going to tell me what the hell we're doing at"—I glanced down at my phone—"seven thirty-two in the morning?" I groaned.

Why did it have to be on Christmas Eve?

"You remember the police report we snagged from Winston's office?"

I nodded.

"I've been hounding Wayne Davies for weeks, begging him to talk to me about the old case. And I woke up this morning to an email saying if we can make it down today, he'll give us twenty minutes." Chance beamed.

I wasn't sure what exactly I had expected all of this to be about, but that hadn't been it.

Chance mistook my silence for acceptance, rather than confusion. "He's a few hours away, so that's why we had to leave so early. Plus, I didn't want to risk him changing his mind. But I promise we'll be back in time to fit in your traditions." He glanced at me, suddenly unsure of my silence.

"But we're still stopping for coffee, right?" I leaned my head against the chilly windowpane, realizing the last time I'd been in

Chance's car had been the night he had driven me home from the bar...the first night we'd met.

"Yeah, I'll get you coffee." He reached out over the console and grabbed my hand, squeezing it lightly. "You can go back to sleep if you want."

I nodded, my eyes already drooping.

"Chance!" I squealed. "Can we get a puppy!?"

"Where would you keep it?" He laughed, shaking his head.

"In the lounge, obviously." I beamed jokingly.

There was a kennel in front of the Davies' home with half a dozen golden retriever puppies yipping at Chance and me the second we got out of his car.

"I hope you're not here for one of the dogs—they're all spoken for." A man, easily in his seventies, came around the side of the house, shovel in hand, trying to clear the driveway of the couple of inches that had fallen in the last hour or so of our trip. I was sure it was Wayne from his military crew cut and how his gait looked almost like a march.

"I'm Chance Harper, sir." Chance outstretched his hand to shake Wayne's. "This is Violet Price. We're both teachers at Montgomery."

Wayne shook my hand next.

The wary look in his eyes was hard to miss.

"We really appreciate you making time to meet with us," Chance added, following Wayne as he turned without a word to head back into the house.

"Not like you or my wife gave me much of a choice," Wayne huffed, holding the door open for both of us as we entered his home, whereupon we were immediately accosted by three gregarious full-sized retrievers, all fighting for our attention.

When Wayne bent to remove his boots in the entryway, we followed suit. He ushered us into a formal front living room, complete with floral frilled couches and matching honey-colored wood furniture pieces.

"The case hasn't been formally closed, so there isn't much I should be discussing," Wayne said stiffly.

Chance politely restated an abbreviated version of his connection to the case. He didn't reveal that he was related to Daniel, only that he and I had become interested in the case, and when we'd discovered the older missing students, we thought there might be a connection.

"All of this is off the record?" Wayne questioned.

"Of course," Chance replied.

"You're not recording some true crime podcast? Because you wouldn't be the first to come sniffing around this case for media coverage and lie about it."

Chance pulled out his wallet and handed Wayne his Montgomery faculty ID badge, giving me a look requesting that I do the same, which I did.

The confirmation seemed to finally satisfy Wayne. "What exactly do you want to know?"

"I was curious as to your lead suspects or theories on the case. I'm trying to rule out the potential for the same person to have been involved in all three disappearances. There are many tenured staff at Montgomery who were present during both incidents," Chance dove right in.

"The commonly accepted theory about the Marshall girls was that it was a kidnapping gone wrong," Wayne stated, but the tone of his voice indicated he wasn't so sure.

"Surely it wouldn't have been out of the realm of possibilities for children from wealthy families to be targets for ransom," Chance argued, likely to goad him into revealing his actual thoughts.

I had to wonder if Chance, being from a wealthy family himself, had ever had experience with something similar. Maybe I'd ask him about it later.

"The problem is that there was no evidence. And not just no evidence for the kidnapping theory, but no evidence period. It was as if the girls disappeared into thin air. And we combed those woods more thoroughly than I'd seen before, or have seen since," Wayne offered.

"What would you have expected to see if it was a botched kidnapping?" I asked, simply out of curiosity.

"Signs of a struggle, witnesses, any kind of trace evidence. But there was nothing."

"So they went with someone they knew?" Chance speculated.

"Or ran away and met their fate somewhere far from Montgomery," Wayne said, but it was clear he didn't believe that.

"Do you think someone at Montgomery was capable of hurting those girls?" Chance asked point-blank.

Wayne took a deep breath, then said, "There were plenty of people who were capable of hurting two naive young girls, but only one that had a reputation for it."

I blanched.

"Winston," Chance said solemnly.

Wayne's jaw clenched, all but confirming Chance's accusation. "If someone like that were involved, I would have to advise you to keep your distance," Wayne began, being very careful with what he said and precisely how he said it. "Someone like that might be slippery, dangerous, have friends in very high places, and would stop at nothing to keep their status. So they wouldn't blink at ruining the lives of two young teachers who were snooping around."

His warning was entirely sobering.

I felt Chance go rigid beside me.

"I'd warn you to stop digging, although I'm not sure it would do much good. It might already be too late, depending on how careful you've been so far." Wayne grimaced.

Chance took a beat, then stood, again extending his hand to Wayne to shake his. "Thank you for your time, sir. I appreciate your insight, and we will take your recommendations under advisement."

"I hope that you do," he said solemnly.

Chance and I silently made our way back to the car. We sat in the stillness of the snow continuing to fall around us as the car warmed up. Absently, Chance reached across the console again, seeking the comfort of my hand in his.

"What are we going to do?" I finally had the nerve to ask.

Chance shook his head, unsure. "Just get back to Montgomery. I need time to think." He sighed, his eyes meeting mine. "I think some Christmas movies and mac and cheese would be a perfect distraction."

I returned the smile. "Don't forget the sparkling cider," I added.

"The bottle has been chilling in my fridge for a week." Chance grinned, turning on the radio to have something to dull the alarm bells that were likely raging in his mind, just as they were in mine, due to the stark warning we'd just received.

We were halfway back to Montgomery when the snow began to intensify, and traffic came to a standstill. As if on cue, a news announcement interrupted the music. The interstate had just been closed, due to a large accident and impending blizzard.

"A blizzard!?" I looked at Chance wide-eyed. "You couldn't have checked the weather report before you abducted me from my bed?" I whined.

Chance slumped back in his seat. "Fuck."

29

SNOWED IN

I t took us two hours to get off the highway and another few to drive around looking for a place to stay overnight. We stopped at four hotels before we finally found one with an available room. And there was only one left: the honeymoon suite.

"This is a joke, right?" I hissed at Chance. "Did you orchestrate this whole thing? You knew about the blizzard, and the clerk is in on it because you already booked the room and gave her a twenty to pretend she's never talked to you before. Was everything with Wayne a setup too? I *knew* it was weird he'd agree to meet with you only on Christmas Eve." I pointed a finger at Chance's face in the hotel lobby.

Chance grabbed my finger and calmly lowered it. "She's just hangry," he told the wide-eyed hotel clerk.

"So you want the room?" she squeaked, her eyes darting back and forth between Chance and me.

"Obviously we want the room," I snapped.

"Do you have room service?" Chance asked.

"The kitchen had to close because of the storm—short-staffed. So just vending machines." The girl pointed to an alcove next to the check-in desk.

I thought I might cry.

"Just the room then." Chance slid his ID and a credit card across the counter.

"I'll pay you back," I mumbled, not sure how, but determined to do so anyway.

Chance placed his arm around my shoulder, pulling me into his side. "This is my fault. I'll take care of it. I'm sorry, Violet." He kissed the top of my head, and I let him.

There wasn't much to do to get settled in the spacious hotel room, as I hadn't expected Chance's surprise adventure to turn into an overnight trip.

Other than the size, the only thing that seemed to make it a honeymoon suite was the giant jacuzzi taking up half the bathroom. As would have been expected for a small hotel some ways off the interstate, much of the room was dated. The beige carpet had been vacuumed to oblivion, the remote sported duct tape on the back to keep the batteries in place, and the outlets near the bedside tables did not work.

But lucky for Chance and the hotel, I was far from picky. The sheets were clean (I could smell and feel the crisp remnants of bleach), the cable was working, and the water from the tap turned warm quickly enough. What more did you need from a quick overnight stop?

The door lock clicked, and a moment later Chance came in, his hands full. I hurried to help him with everything.

He had grabbed a spare gym bag, which included a change of clothes, from the trunk of his car. The front desk had toothbrushes and deodorant, and I had no idea how much money he'd spent on the mountain of food from the vending machines.

"It's not sparkling cider, but we could mix them together and try to pretend it tastes as good?" He held up two bottles of light beer in one hand and two bottles of apple juice in the other.

I couldn't help but laugh. It would probably taste disgusting, but his ingenuity impressed me.

"I'm sure nothing beats your mac and cheese, but the closest they had were a lot of cheese-flavored things." He pointed to the half a dozen bags of various chips, pretzels, and salty snacks.

"If we crunch up some chips and put them in with the ramen noodles"—he picked up the four Styrofoam cups of ramen noodles before setting them back down again—"it might be close enough?"

I stifled a laugh, amused by his effort and by just how far he was trying to stretch the vending machine food to fit within the parameters of my regular Christmas Eve activities. He was being so sweet, it continued to melt my resolve. "I'll probably just eat them separately though. I'm not a fan of soggy chips." I scooted to the edge of the bed, kneeling so we were almost at the same eye level.

"Right." He nodded. "They did, however, have hot chocolate packets. No milk, but we can use hot water from the coffee machine." He glanced over his shoulder to the small plastic machine sitting on top of the ancient mini fridge, which hummed so loudly you could hear it even when the heater was on.

"Come here." I crooked a finger at Chance.

He took a few paces forward to close the distance between us.

Once he was within reach, I wrapped my arms around his torso and leaned my head against his chest. "Thank you." I breathed him in. As usual, he smelled fresh and clean, but there was also the added scent of the snowfall from outside. It was heavenly.

He returned the embrace, resting his head on the top of mine. "I'm really sorry I ruined your Christmas Eve." His hand gently stroked up and down my back.

"You didn't ruin it," I sighed. "We'll just postpone everything until we can manage to get back." I looked up at him. "I'm just glad I'm not alone."

"Me too," Chance simpered. He traced the edge of my face with his finger, tucking my hair behind my ear, before leaning down to kiss me gently, just for a moment, then pulled back, not wanting to push me further than I was willing to go.

Although surprisingly, and maybe it was because we weren't at Montgomery, I found that I was willing to test those boundaries I had put up weeks ago.

"I'm sure we can find holiday movies on TV too," I added, trying to show him that I was calming down over the whole situation.

Chance smiled, opening one of the beers and taking a swig.

It had been dark for quite a while by the time we got settled. We ate cross-legged on the end of the bed, on top of the comforter, passing chip bags back and forth between each other. Chance had also procured an assortment of cookies from the vending machine. They tasted a little stale and definitely full of preservatives, but I didn't mind so much.

After the first movie, we were both starting to fade, so we decided to get ready for bed. Out of nowhere, the butterflies had returned in full force, considering there were two of us and only one bed.

"Do you have an extra shirt?" I worried my lip, nervously. I'd been in such a rush that morning, I hadn't put on anything underneath my hoodie, just my bra...which I also realized at that moment, I couldn't very well wear to bed.

"Catch." Chance tossed me a dark T-shirt across the bed.

"Thanks," I said before ducking into the bathroom. I tried not to look at myself in the large mirror, knowing whatever I found there, good, bad, or ugly, I'd pick it apart. The air in the hotel room was charged, as if it knew something was going to happen before we did, and I felt it too, that we were teetering on the edge of a precipice and that whatever happened that night, we'd pick which side we were going to land on.

When I walked out of the bathroom in nothing but Chance's shirt, which was at least long enough to hit my short frame at mid-thigh, covering a view of my underwear, Chance was on the far side of the bed, arranging some sort of makeshift bed on the floor.

"Chance…"

He looked up, gulping as he took me in from head to toe.

I immediately turned beet red. I didn't have to see myself to know. I could feel the heat pouring off me, under his scrutiny.

"You don't have to sleep on the floor," I said quietly, peeling back the covers on the side of the bed closer to me.

He seemed to mull over my words for a long moment, eyeing me cautiously, as if this was some sort of trap.

"Really?" he gave me one last out.

"Yeah."

Abandoning his nest, he grabbed the pillow he was planning on using and hopped up on the bed, a Cheshire grin adorning his stupid, handsome face.

"What?" I growled.

"I knew you wanted to cuddle. I said so this morning." He scooted under the covers, then flipped his light off, leaving the room in complete darkness, save for the sliver of light from the parking lot that streamed through a crack in the curtains.

I felt his warm hand reach out, pulling me against him. For a brief moment, it felt like an out-of-body experience, being surrounded by such warmth, feeling comfortable in his hold, and wanting to be held…only by Chance.

And then he had to go ruin it by continuing to joke around. "I thought you'd at least put up a fight," he murmured, his lips skimming the column of my neck, his breath hot on my skin.

I huffed in annoyance, which seemed to delight him. His lips took purchase around my pulse point, and my breath hitched at the sensation. Chance let one hand run down my side, only skimming the edge of my breast and finally coming to rest on my hip, which he used to pull me even closer at the same time that he pressed into me.

Feeling his erection between us, I couldn't help but let a soft moan escape as he continued his ministrations. "I'll kill you if you leave a mark," I muttered half-heartedly.

"Promises, promises." Chance laughed, sliding his hand back up, this time under the shirt I was wearing, splaying his searing palm over my rib cage, just shy of where I wanted him to touch me.

"Chance?"

"Hmm..."

My body was singing in his capable hands, and I didn't want to keep the boundaries up any longer. I wanted him, and I was sick of fighting it with everything inside me.

Why couldn't I let myself have this?

Why couldn't I let myself give in to him?

Would it really be so bad to let him in?

"Do you think...maybe because we're not at school...that their rules shouldn't count?" I whispered.

Chance froze.

I turned around, still half in his hold, to face him, even though I could barely make out the outline of his face in the dark. I reached out to him, cupping his face with my hand. "Just for one night? Maybe?" I faltered, still not sure what was going through his mind, without having the ability to analyze his expression.

"One night would never be enough for me, Violet," Chance finally spoke, his voice hesitant.

I closed my eyes, trying to figure out what he was trying to say and how to respond in a way that wouldn't make things worse somehow. "Maybe we could just start with tonight?" I offered.

I didn't want tonight to be the only night, but I didn't know how I'd feel when we got back to Montgomery. If my anxiety over what would come next hadn't been so overwhelming, I thought I might have given in to Chance a while ago.

"You're sure?" His voice came softly through the darkness. He was seemingly just as afraid as I was.

I thought about what to say, but decided it would be better if I showed him. I leaned forward, pressing my lips to his, continuing to lead the charge when he parted his lips to let me deepen the kiss.

He tasted minty from the toothpaste. His kisses were urgent and just as heated as the rest of my body felt. Our hands roamed each other freely, unburdened by what had stopped us before.

As our desperation for more increased, Chance pulled away to gently roll onto his back, bringing me along with him. My leg hitched over his thigh, in just the right position for me to grind against, if only he'd bend his knee just slightly to give me the perfect angle to pursue the high I was after...and then he did.

I moaned with the glorious friction created by the subtle movement.

"Fuck, Violet," he cursed into my mouth. "Keep doing that."

I felt Chance's fingers skating over the sensitive skin at my hip, just above my panties, and then he ran his fingers over the hem.

"Vi—can I—please?" His words were breathless as we continued to move together to chase our respective pleasure.

I tilted my hips up, silently granting him permission to touch me where I needed him most. His fingers tickled against my pussy before he skimmed them along the seam for only one pass before dipping them into the liquid heat I was sure he would find there.

"Baby, you're so wet for me," he groaned into my neck.

Wanting to touch him too, I let my hand graze his dick, over his boxers, feeling his muscles tighten as he drew in a sharp breath.

"I need to touch you first, or I'll get too distracted," Chance asserted, plunging two fingers inside of me, causing me to arch against him.

I felt myself speaking, but the words that came forth were nonsense—I was already so far gone.

"Have you been thinking about what it would be like for me to get you off?" he whispered, low and dirty.

I could only moan in response as he continued to drive me closer and closer to the edge.

"You're all I can think about," he confessed. "I dream of all the things I want to do to you." Chance paused, his motions ceasing.

I cried out in frustration.

Our eyes met, even in the dark. "You want me to do those things to you, don't you?"

"Please," I keened, seeking the pressure of his fingers, never so desperate for touch as I was in that moment with Chance.

"God, I love hearing you beg, Violet."

He circled my clit while I writhed against him, and all it took was for him to assert just the perfect amount of pressure with his thumb for me to spiral into the abyss, crying out as I shattered against him. He continued to use his fingers to help me prolong the sensation. As with everything else, Chance knew exactly what I needed at that moment.

I'd never come so quickly before, and it was the first time someone had gotten me off without me asking first. Chance had proven himself to be nothing if not a gentleman.

He had only just slipped his fingers from my panties when I made a move to pull his boxers down, freeing his hard cock from its confines. He released a low and heady groan as my hand encircled him at the base, gently running it up and down the length.

"You don't—have to," he choked out.

I had learned by now that Chance would always give me an out, but *he* should have learned by now that I wasn't going to take it. What he couldn't have predicted was when I moved down the bed slightly, making it easier for me to take him into my mouth.

"Oh fuck..." Chance grunted.

I didn't think I'd ever had the desire to give any of the guys I dated head, but there was something about the noises Chance made, how he had insisted on making me come first, and how sweet he had been for weeks, going out of his way to make me comfortable, but making sure I knew he was still very much interested.

I wanted Chance to feel good, and I wanted to be the one to do it.

What I couldn't fit in my mouth, I used my hand to stroke, occasionally grazing his balls, if only to hear the guttural grumble that would emit from Chance as a result. He muttered encouragingly, stroking his hand softly down my back, occasionally pausing when something I did felt particularly good.

Bobbing and sucking and swirling my tongue around the tip, I went back and forth, driving Chance into a frenzy. Eventually he was so incensed that he had to remove his hands from me entirely, clenching the sheets in his fists, trying to hold on for as long as he could.

"I'm going to come," Chance ground out, giving me enough time to pull back. I gentled my strokes as he spilled his release on his stomach, stilling only when his fingertips grazed my hand in a silent request to stop the motion.

We both sat there for a moment, panting and dazed. Already what we'd done felt surreal.

Chance reached out to me, coaxing me into another slow and sensual kiss. It was as if there were a million things we both wanted to say and think, but letting our lips do the talking was a much better option and seemed to say more than words ever could in that moment.

Chance's kiss reassured and calmed me, telling me that he was in this, that he was going to take care of me, and that I meant something to him.

God, I felt it.

He kissed me like I belonged to him and he'd fight to keep me. That was the kind of thing I'd been searching for my entire life.

And in my kiss, I let Chance take the lead, communicating that I was in this with him, and was fighting my instincts to pull away. I was fighting for him...for us. And I fought for his kisses and his adoration and his kindness. I needed him to understand that I saw him for who he was...who he truly was, on the inside, not the facade he'd been forced to hide behind under his father's watchful eye. I saw him and I wanted him, just as he was.

Pulling back, breathless, Chance said softly, "We should clean up."

I nodded, though I wasn't sure if he could see me, but he seemed to comprehend nonetheless. He made quick work of himself in the bathroom, leaving the light on for me when he returned.

Again I avoided looking at my reflection, unsure of what I would see there. But when I got back in bed, Chance tugged me closer, pulling me into his arms. His embrace, just like his heartbeat, was warm, strong, and steady.

"You are fucking everything," he breathed, combing his fingers through my hair, my head resting against his chest.

30

THE NEGATIVES

Chance Harper was staring at me.

To clarify further, he had been watching me as I slept.

"Ugh." I covered my face with my hands. "Why are you staring at me?" I grumbled.

Chance just chuckled, placing soft kisses down my forearms, probably because he couldn't reach my face.

"Still stalking me, I see." I tried to push him away, but that only made him grab me around my middle and pull me into his chest. "Once a creep, always a creep."

"You're just mad because you like it." Chance's morning voice was painfully husky—like I was ready to crawl back on top of him and show him some other tricks I had up my sleeve, husky.

I groaned, not wanting to admit it out loud.

Chance pried my hands from my face, needing to see me when he asked, "Any regrets?"

I sighed, "No."

"I'm glad you're so thrilled about that," he half chuckled, half winced.

"I don't regret anything," I stated more firmly.

"I sense a 'but.'" He used the pad of his thumb to gently run across the length of my bottom lip, causing heat to flare as all the details from the night before came pouring in, like gasoline on a fire.

But with the desire, also came the reality of what we'd done...what I'd done. Chance and I had passed the point of no return. There simply was no going back. Either we kept moving forward, or it was over, and I knew it couldn't be over. I was in too deep.

"Talk to me," Chance pleaded, his face crestfallen. "You're worrying me."

"It's not us." I stumbled to try and find the right words. I didn't want him to misunderstand. So I started there. "I'm processing everything. I don't regret last night. I promise. I don't regret you."

The corner of his mouth curved just enough that I thought he understood.

"I can't help but worry, but it's not that I worry about you." I swallowed. "I'm worried about getting caught. I'm worried about what happens when we go back to school. I'm worried about what you'll expect from me and how quickly, because things went really fast last night."

Chance's brow furrowed.

"I wasn't pressured—I wanted to," I stuttered. "I just—it wasn't planned. I didn't know that was going to happen, and I'm not upset that it did, but my brain needs to catch up."

Chance still looked tense.

I reached out, taking his closest hand in mine. Being so honest, so very vulnerable, had my nerves frayed, but I wasn't going to let a miscommunication set us off course. "You made me feel so good. I feel safe with you. And I want to do it again, but I'm just not sure when."

Those, it seemed, were the right words.

Chance's shoulders relaxed, and I cuddled into his chest. "I'm not pulling away," I told him. "I'm fighting so hard to work through my anxiety because this matters." I looked up at him, his blue-grey eyes still worried, but *for* me, not because of me. "Because *you* matter."

"Okay." Chance kissed my forehead. "Okay," he reassured himself just as much as he tried to reassure me.

Likely because it was Christmas day, the interstate was miraculously cleared and reopened much earlier than either Chance or I thought it would be.

Not wanting to delay my annual Christmas call to my mom, I got her on the line shortly after Chance got back on the highway. But as with most of our calls, it was short, and what was the word Chance had used, oh yes...perfunctory.

And after only a few minutes of surface-level pleasantries, the sound of Jake and Jenny's children in the background continued to pull my mom's attention from me. So I ended the call, with my usual promise to call her again soon, although we both knew that "soon" likely meant not for a long while.

The quick call left me feeling hollow. The reminder of so much loss front and center on a day that used to bring me so much joy always made the emptiness so much more tangible. Sensing my discomfort, Chance reached across the console, taking my hand in his, offering a reassuring squeeze, understanding that a physical tether was what I needed.

The rest of the drive back was quiet, yet stilted. I realized the closer we got to Montgomery, the more the tension seemed to increase.

It felt nice to think about who we could be...what we could be, together, without the shadow of Montgomery's outdated policy waging a silent war against us. I didn't know what we were doing 'exactly, but I think we both agreed we just wanted to do what felt natural. We didn't need labels or timelines or pressure. I just wanted to be close to Chance, whatever that looked like.

I meant what I'd said to him—that I was fighting the urge to run and hide, but not because he'd done anything wrong. Quite the opposite, it was because he was doing everything right. I'd had such awful luck with relationships, I was half convinced I'd mess it up...hell, I'd already complicated matters so thoroughly by playing hot and cold with Chance for as long as I did.

But I kept reminding myself to give Chance the benefit of the doubt. He wasn't Jake or Harry. He was Chance. He was kind, thoughtful, and careful with me. I had to trust him, and trust that he was going to do right by me, because if I couldn't do that, I'd drive a wedge so large between us that nobody would have any hope to bring the two sides back together.

When we were just twenty minutes out from Montgomery, perhaps sensing the discord roiling in me, Chance began to excitedly run through the list of traditions we had to accomplish by the end of the day, as if I wasn't the one who had shared them with him in the first place.

I thought it was so considerate of him to care so much about traditions he hadn't known existed until a month prior. Since he had disrupted my normal plans, it felt like he was on a mission to make sure I was thoroughly satisfied with this year's schedule of events.

I had only started the traditions to make myself feel less lonely and homesick on Christmas. The idea that, in a way, they could become his traditions too...ours really, made my chest and throat feel tight. I liked the thought that they could belong to both of us. And whether he cared about the activities themselves, or if he just cared by default because they were important to me, didn't matter.

What mattered was that we were going to find a way to make this work. I was bound and determined, whatever it took.

It felt odd returning to my room. It had been a little over twenty-four hours, but it felt like my entire world had shifted. Chance came over and set up his laptop in my room, helping me putter around to make the mac and cheese and whatever else I needed.

He later declared it was the best mac and cheese he'd ever had, and even though I doubted that, I believed that he meant it, which made me swell with pride.

The sparkling cider tasted even better than I remembered, and we set out more pastries to proof overnight to have something for the next morning, since the first batch I had set out for the previous morning had sat out for too long while we were away.

After dinner, we reconvened in the lounge. Chance brought up two mugs of hot chocolate (with milk, thank you very much), and settled on the window seat near the fire. Only the fire, Christmas tree, and string lights illuminated the room in a soft and ethereal glow.

Chance extended his hand with the second mug toward me. I took it, but set it on the study table. His brow furrowed in confusion.

I grabbed the stocking from the chair, where I had stashed it when I came up just before he arrived. "I got you something for Christmas. I thought I'd give it to you yesterday—"

"Don't worry, you gave me plenty yesterday." Chance chuckled, diffusing my self-doubt, as usual.

I swallowed hard, trying not to think about going down on him again, although I wouldn't have been opposed.

Stay focused, Violet.

I pulled the stocking out from behind my back and handed it to him. It was made from a red knit sweater material with a white felt letter "C" with red stitching attaching it to the red fabric beneath. It wasn't anything special, and didn't cost much, but it matched the one I had, already tacked to the mantle, with a white felt "V."

"Violet..." Chance simpered, smiling sweetly at the gift. "Thank you." He looked up at me. "Come over here, or I'll get up and drag you," he teased menacingly.

I stood my ground. "There's something else inside." I felt my stomach beginning to flip. I knew he'd be glad, but I wasn't sure if I had the nerve to remember everything I'd planned to say. I didn't want to leave anything out.

Chance pulled the negatives from inside the stocking. His lips parted, and he sighed in contentment. "You didn't have to do this." He knew exactly what they were.

I crossed the space to him, just wanting—maybe needing—to be closer to him. "You were right," I began. "The photos are beautiful. Even if their subject hadn't yet agreed to having them taken."

Chance laughed quietly, reaching out and taking my hand in his. His eyes flicked to mine, encouraging me to continue.

"I hated the thought of taking your art away from you. They belong to you. I would just ask that you refrain from distributing them amongst the students and faculty."

Chance laughed again. "You are so silly sometimes. You know I wouldn't do that."

I nodded. I knew it was an odd thing to worry about, but at least I had said it out loud, even if it was just to feel better myself. And then I said what I'd really been hesitant to offer. "But I'd be okay if you wanted to do a show. In fact, you should do a show. I want other people to see your art. You deserve that." I swallowed the lump in my throat.

Chance mulled over my words. "You really think they're good enough for an exhibition?"

I laughed through a sigh of relief. "Yes. They're more than good enough."

"If I had a show, would you come?" His eyes were lit up, knowing exactly what he was asking.

"Yes. Of course. I want to support you."

Chance opened his arms to me, wanting me to join him on the window seat. I darted back over to the table, grabbed my mug, and settled between his legs, my back to his front.

He buried his face in my hair, taking a deep breath in. "I think you're the only person I'd want to invite," he said sweetly before kissing just behind my ear.

"You wouldn't at least want your mom and sister to come?"

"They can if they want, but you're the only one who matters. You're the first person in a *very* long time who has encouraged me to pursue my photography," Chance admitted.

I half turned in his arms. The narrow bench made it more difficult. "You're a brilliant photographer. Don't you dare let anyone say otherwise," I told him firmly. I needed him to see, hear, and feel my conviction. I hated that those around him had let him down. He was just like our students. All he needed was one person to push him to try.

Chance's face softened, then, with a slow smile, he repeated words I'd said to him on the day we met: "I really want you to kiss me."

"I bet you do," I chided. Blushing, I leaned forward and kissed Chance sweetly.

"Thank you for believing in me," he whispered.

31

MISSED CALLS

Ever since the hotel, Chance and I had been in this awkward sort of limbo.

We were definitely more affectionate now than we had ever been before. Most days we'd cuddle on the couch in the lounge while he talked to me about his photography and showed me some of his favorite photos he had taken. Other times, his amused eyes would follow me as I paced back and forth in front of the fireplace as I ran through my lesson plans and lectures, before he'd eventually grab my hand and pull me to him, just to hold me for a moment and breathe me in.

He was always within reach, more often than not, somehow physically touching me, which I loved. However, there was still a chasm between us.

And each night, he'd wrap me up in a tight hug, kiss me soundly, surely knowing he was leaving me aching and wanting more. But then he'd leave for his own room, climbing back down the snow-covered fire escape, which I was certain was one screw away from disconnecting from the exterior wall and plunging him to his death, not that Chance would listen to me.

Even I couldn't quite figure out what I wanted. At some moments, I felt such relief that he was giving me space to process everything, just as I had asked. But at other times, I was desperate for his touch and longed for him to make a move. I wasn't sure when or what it would take for my inner turmoil to calm and for things to become more clear.

I felt fortunate that Chance seemed to read me better with every passing day. Whether I wanted him inside my head or not, it appeared as though he had already made himself quite comfortable, readying himself for the moment things changed. But I didn't want him to wait on me forever.

I was actively trying to work through my emotions to feel comfortable and confident enough to push through whatever was blocking me from letting go of the last bits of my anxiety and hesitation. I was close, but not quite there yet.

The day before New Year's Eve, Chance received a response from Bryce Osbourne, the previous year's student newspaper's editor-in-chief. Neither of us had been expecting a response over break, as Bryce had graduated the year before and was at college across the country.

"What does it say!?" I nudged Chance over on the couch, crowding into his personal space.

"Geez, give me a minute." He pulled the laptop between us and double-clicked on the email, which read:

Good afternoon Mr. Harper,
I'm sorry about what happened to Daniel, but I'm

glad to hear that you are still looking into his disappearance. I agree, he was far too driven and bright to have simply run away, as the police have concluded.

Unfortunately, Daniel was always rather secretive about his projects, not wanting to put anyone else at risk, and if I'm honest, I think he didn't trust that it would stay a secret long at Montgomery, so complete discretion was required.

What I do know about the exposé he was writing at the time of his disappearance was that he was investigating a matter that involved Headmaster Winston.

Daniel mentioned working with an inside source to gather evidence and testimony from witnesses. I remember him saying he believed what the source told him about the headmaster, but I got the sense he didn't trust them completely. When I asked for more information about the source's identity, he refused. I just wanted him to be safe, but he thought he was doing the right thing by protecting their identity. I guess I'll never know.

You also asked about where he saved his research. He had a bright orange external drive he always kept on him, which he used to store his files. He did have another backup somewhere, but I didn't even bother asking him where it was. He wouldn't have told me.

I wish there was more. I wish Daniel was still raising hell at Montgomery. Please keep me updated

on what you find, and if you have any other questions,
I would be glad to help.
Good luck,
Bryce

I released a loud sigh, and Chance leaned back into the couch. Both of us processed what we had just read.

"Daniel *was* investigating the headmaster," Chance said, vindication on his tongue.

"And it seemed he had an inside source with dirt to share, and maybe even other witnesses," I added.

"It gives Winston the motive we thought he was lacking," Chance thought aloud. "Do we know where he was when Daniel went missing?"

I swallowed. "He was here. I saw him. Most of the school saw him. He was busy with the rest of the admin staff preparing for the graduation ceremony."

"Winston has the trifecta. He had motive: Daniel was going to pin something big on him. He had opportunity: we know he was around the school the last day Daniel was seen. And I think he easily had the means. Winston would do anything to save his reputation—Wayne Davies said the same thing. If a student was going to take him down, I have no doubt he would have done something drastic to stop it from happening."

Chance laid out a good argument, and I didn't like Winston either, but I wasn't completely sold. I needed more proof. We needed the drive. "You don't think it's weird that Bryce said he didn't trust his source completely?"

"Maybe he was worried they'd change their mind or get scared and tell Winston what Daniel was doing?" Chance hypothesized.

"Without his files, we'll never know." I rested my chin in my palms.

Chance and I were silent for a while, both mentally reviewing what we knew so far. I was surprised when Chance next spoke.

"How much have you thought about what Davies said?" Chance asked out of the blue.

"I don't know. I mean, he didn't exactly tell us anything we didn't already know."

"Well, he said that the headmaster was his lead suspect," Chance stated.

I nodded, agreeing with him.

Chance ran his hands over his face, sighing in frustration. He looked down at the floor as he continued. "The thing is, I know in my heart that Daniel is gone. However horrible that is to say, I feel it in my gut."

He looked up at me, his blue-grey eyes glassy. "I still want to know what happened to him, but what if we push too hard and we get hurt like he did? I just don't know if this is worth it anymore."

I opened my mouth to argue that we needed to continue, but Chance's phone rang out for the umpteenth time that day.

He scowled at the caller, silenced the phone, and shoved it back in his pocket.

I cocked my head at him, waiting for an explanation. I'd already been more than patient.

"What?" he snapped.

"You know what. Who's been calling you nonstop all day?" I folded my arms over my chest, thinking it might make me look tougher than I felt.

Chance groaned, slumping back against the couch, running a nervous hand through his hair. "It's Amanda."

"Your sister?"

"Yeah."

"Well, what does she want? Why aren't you taking her call?"

I tried to reach into his pocket to grab his phone, but he caught my wrist before I got the chance.

"We said no secrets," I pouted.

Chance rolled his eyes, annoyed that he'd been bested.

I grinned at him, waiting for him to spill.

"Every year my parents host a big New Year's Eve party."

I waited for him to continue, but he did not. "And?"

"And Amanda wants me to go."

"Is it in Portland?" I asked, knowing that was where Chance's family home was, after all the stalking Jolene and I had done on Thomas Roberts while we had been trying to figure out who Chance really was.

Chance nodded, his face grim.

"But you don't want to go?" I inferred.

"I'd rather claw my eyes out," he deadpanned.

"But Amanda wants you to go?" He was not making this easy for me.

"She has a new boyfriend she wants me to meet." He shrugged. "I've been telling her I'm not going for weeks, but she won't take no for an answer."

"You should go. I thought you were on good terms with Amanda?" I was confused.

"I am. But she'll be there with her boyfriend, and then I'll be left on my own, surrounded by jackals." Chance sneered. "I'm telling you, these parties are *awful*. Everyone makes polite chatter with backhanded undertones. It's so fake—all pomp and circumstance. I hate it."

"But you love Amanda?" I knew the answer, but I asked anyway. Chance huffed but did not respond.

"She's your only sister. She wants your approval because your father is a dickhead. Maybe just go and suck it up for her," I reasoned.

"I can't stand to be in the same room as my dad after I learned what happened with Daniel and his mom. He doesn't even care that Daniel went missing. I can't see him." Chance gritted his teeth, as if the thought of seeing his father made him physically ill to even consider.

I took a beat. I hoped I wouldn't regret what I was about to offer. "I could go with you," I said softly.

"What?" Chance raised an eyebrow.

I sighed, knowing he'd heard me. He was just being difficult. "If you want, I'd go with you," I said more solidly.

The corners of his lips quirked. "Really? You would?"

I immediately grew suspicious. "Did you plan this? Is this some sort of elaborate ploy you've concocted with your sister?" I accused him.

Chance placed a hand over his heart, "Violet, darling, you wound me. You always think the worst of me."

His theatrics did not diffuse my cynicism. He hadn't outright denied the allegations. "If I find out this was all a ruse—and I *will* be asking your sister—I will make sure you regret it."

Chance knelt down on the carpet in front of me, which considering our difference in height, put him at eye level with me. He took my face into his palms and gave me a soft kiss.

"You already said you'd go. You can't back out now," he whispered, smiling sweetly.

32

LADY IN BLACK

I couldn't help but fidget nervously in the car, the entire three-hour drive to Portland.

Chance had asked me to pack an overnight bag, saying that we'd likely be staying with his parents, but that if anything went wrong, he'd be happy to abandon the party and find a hotel. We'd also timed our arrival much later in the evening to limit just how long we'd have to spend at his childhood home.

The problem was that I was fully unequipped and unprepared to meet his parents. Everything was still so new. I had no idea what we were to each other, and neither did Chance. Surely his parents would ask, and we would have no answer.

To further my impending mortification, I only owned the one black dress, which would likely make me look more akin to the waitstaff than the other guests, in their black-tie accouterments. This was a slow-motion disaster in the making and I was helpless to stop any of it.

"My sister can loan you a gown. She has plenty," Chance had offered.

I shook my head in refusal. He didn't know her measurements or mine. All women don't fit into the same clothes. Was he nuts?

"Then tell me what I can do to make you more comfortable. I don't want you to feel out of place. Although I'm sure nobody will say a word."

You could turn around.

I choked out a laugh. "Chance, we're showing up together. They'll be looking, and judging, and gossiping for weeks to come."

"None of them matter." Chance squeezed my hand. "Fuck 'em."

I sighed in exasperation. It wasn't as easy as that. I was allowing him to drive me into the lion's den. I was putting myself on display in front of the type of people who made me want to shrink and become invisible.

It wasn't that I cared about what they thought, exactly, it was that I didn't want to even be around them. I didn't want to risk my fragile and slowly burgeoning self-confidence, which Chance had been nurturing for weeks with small touches, soft smiles, and his quiet, but patient respect for my boundaries.

One snobby look and all of that work could be shattered in an instant. I didn't want it to happen like that, but I had to acknowledge that it would be a possibility.

Pulling into the long driveway, I could see the twinkling lights of the mansion in the distance. Avoiding the line for the valet, Chance pulled around back to the service entrance. It was where I belonged anyway.

"Violet." He grabbed both of my hands after parking and turning off the car. "Look at me," he commanded.

It was hard to ignore him when he used that voice. I felt my cheeks flush as I briefly wondered what it would be like if he used that voice on me in different, more intimate, circumstances.

He squeezed my hands, and I involuntarily met his gaze.

"You are the smartest person I know—"

I guffawed.

Chance clenched his jaw. "I don't care that you don't believe me. I know what I see in front of me. You are smart, beautiful, sexy, and you're *mine*." He emphasized the last word, his eyes searing into mine with dark intensity.

I swallowed the lump in my throat. I'd never had anyone lay such a claim on me before. I wasn't sure if I loved or hated the way it made my stomach flip to hear him say that. Maybe both.

"Whatever happens in there, whoever is beyond those doors, it doesn't matter—*they* don't matter. Only *we* matter. Do not let them rattle you. They don't hold a candle to you. None of them know shit about classical history, or care about the education of their children, other than the prestige of the school, and none of them believe in me like you do. So fuck 'em, right?"

He nodded toward me, encouraging me.

"Fuck 'em," I said in a small voice.

Chance shook his head, smirking. "Oh little muse, you can do so much better than that."

I bit my lip upon hearing his nickname for me again. "Fuck 'em," I said with a bit more force.

"Louder," he ordered.

"Fuck 'em!" I practically shouted in his face.

He grabbed my face, pulling me in for a bruising kiss. Showing me with his mouth and tongue how proud he was to call me his, proving that we could weather this storm.

I was finding it harder and harder to second-guess myself when Chance overwhelmed my senses and took control. Consequently, I was finding it easier and easier to let go when I was around him.

And it wasn't just my thoughts that were loosening, but as the days passed, the more I thought about what had happened in the hotel. How he'd touched me and how he'd made me practically combust. I wanted it to happen again. I *needed* it to happen again.

Everything he did got me worked up. I felt the liquid desire pooling at my core and had to stop myself from rolling my hips against nothing as the console separated me from Chance, and I wasn't about to crawl in his lap, parked in a car, behind his parents' mansion, where anyone could happen upon us.

Finding it hard to ignore the thought that had just occurred to me about being discovered by a wayward partygoer, I reluctantly parted from Chance.

If he was trying to distract me from my anxiety spiral over what was to come, damn it if it didn't work like a charm.

"Fuck 'em all," Chance panted, resting his forehead against mine, before placing a soft kiss on the tip of my nose.

I thought I knew what to expect when it came to Amanda because I had seen a few photos of her while stalking Chance, prior to our original confrontation and my discovery of his own stalking. But the young woman absolutely took my breath away.

Her blonde hair was expertly twisted into an updo with elegant curled tendrils framing her face. She was dripping with ruby jewelry, and I didn't even ask if they were real, too scared for her to confirm they were, let alone mention anything about how much they might have cost.

She was dressed in a striking red silk dress. And while the front appeared to be high-necked and modest, when she turned, she revealed a cowl back that swept dangerously low, skimming just the top of her rear. She was tall and wispy, and had the perfect figure to pull off such a stunning look.

Amanda met us at the back door and ushered us inside quickly, past some staff scurrying around. But everyone was so busy with their duties, they didn't spare us a glance.

"I'll bring her back to you soon," Amanda told Chance as she looped her arm through my elbow.

"Wait. What?" My head swung back and forth between Chance and Amanda, both sporting devilish smirks and the same mischievous blue-grey gaze.

"Chance said you needed a dress, silly." Amanda tugged me toward the back stairs.

"But you're so much taller than me," I argued. "Chance?" I called out to him to save me, but he only waved his fingers, smiling as he disappeared around the corner.

"I've got the perfect dress, and it will work just fine with your height," Amanda assured me as she dragged me up the stairs, which opened up into a wide and bright hallway with pristine marble floor tiles, immaculate large sideboards dotting the walls every so often, with massive flower arrangements taking up the entirety of the table tops, and chandeliers glittering above.

I wanted to put up more of a fight, truly I did, but I found myself surprisingly speechless as I stared at the ostentatious opulence surrounding me. I couldn't believe that my Chance had grown up here.

Whoa. Since when had he become my *Chance?*

"I'll be fine in what I'm wearing," I mumbled as Amanda pulled me into what I assumed was her bedroom, as I was finally able to see signs of an actual person inhabiting the space.

"Let me just show you what I have, and if you like it, great. If you don't, then you can go back downstairs," Amanda offered. "Chance mentioned you were worried, and I have so many gowns. Dad only lets me wear them once for appearance's sake. Normally I donate most at the end of the season, so you're not putting me out," she prattled as she walked into an enormous walk-in closet.

I didn't follow her. I was instead fixated on my scuffed and worn heels.

"Violet?" Amanda peeked out of the closet. "Come in here. Don't be scared. I don't bite." She smiled sweetly, and it reminded me of Chance a little too much. I thought maybe I should be afraid.

"This is the one I was thinking of." Amanda pulled a black velvet, off-the-shoulder, A-line gown from her rack, where dozens were hung. "It's tea-length on me, so it should go to the floor on you, and it has a lace-up corset in the back, so we should be able to make it fit snug. What are you...a C-cup?" She tilted her head, staring at my chest.

"On a good day." I frowned.

Amanda only giggled. "You'll have to forgo a bra, but I'm sure Chance won't mind."

"What if *I* mind?" I deadpanned.

Amanda laughed again, shaking her head, as if she had expected my attitude, and was amused that it was exactly as Chance had probably reported to her. "Strip, please," she commanded.

I swallowed hard, still staring at my shoes nervously.

"Are they uncomfortable?" She followed my gaze, misunderstanding my frustration.

"No, just—they're not nice enough for the dress," I admitted, feeling my cheeks flush in embarrassment.

"Nobody will notice, trust me. Besides, I think the dress will be long enough to cover them. I'm afraid we're different shoe sizes, although Mom might have some gifted shoes stowed away in some bedroom," Amanda offered.

"I'm fine," I said to reassure myself just as much to pacify Amanda.

Before I had the chance, she was tugging my dress roughly over my head. I cupped my hands over my breasts when she got to my bra clasp before I could get a word of protest out.

"So you and my brother, huh?" Amanda finally asked what I had been waiting for. And she was going to be the easiest conversation of the evening, so I needed to buck up quickly.

"I guess." I about smacked myself in the head when that was all I could muster.

Amanda smiled as she pooled the dress on the floor, making room in the middle for me to step through. "Just so you know, I don't think I've ever seen or heard him happier," she offered as she pulled the dress up, tucking the bodice under my fingers and making her way to the corset ties at the back. She was right, the dress just skimmed the floor on my petite frame.

"Has he mentioned Ashley?" Amanda's tone was suddenly wary.

"Was she the one who cheated on him?" I asked. Chance had never mentioned an ex by name, but I remembered him commiserating with me about how being cheated on was a special kind of torture.

"Yeah." Amanda scowled. "I wasn't sure if he'd get over what she did to him. I don't think he was in love with her at the end, but he never expected she would step out on him without having the decency to break things off."

"How long were they together?" I ran my fingers over the ruched velvet bodice that crisscrossed over my chest, showing off the perfect amount to make me feel feminine without being worried about being seen as too revealing by the likely conservative crowd that was milling about beneath us.

"Four years. But she cheated on him for half the time, so I don't even know if it counts." Amanda tugged on the corset strings, almost pulling me back with her. "All the while, she was trying to mold him into this perfect robot version of what she wanted in a husband. I never liked her."

"That must have been hard for both of you."

Amanda fastened the tie at the base of my spine, stepping around to give me a once-over. "You've met him. He doesn't always listen to reason."

I snorted a laugh. I'd pushed him away for months, and he kept pursuing me anyway. He was stubborn to a fault, but I found it difficult not to see that as an endearing quality in Chance.

"I like your hair and makeup. You have a very natural and elegant beauty, so I'm glad you didn't do anything too dramatic tonight." Amanda tucked a tendril of my light brown hair behind my ear.

I had only put on mascara and a rosy pink lip gloss that smelled like vanilla.

"There's something missing though." Amanda turned and walked to her dresser, returning a moment later with a small jewelry box.

"Oh no—I couldn't." I waved my hands. I'd fight her on this. I didn't want to wear anything expensive and risk losing it.

Amanda smiled conspiratorially. "Afraid you don't have a choice. Chance asked me to pick this up for you weeks ago." She opened the box to reveal a simple gold solitaire necklace.

Weeks ago...

I gulped. "I can't. It probably cost more than my student loan debt," I pleaded with her.

"It didn't cost anything." Amanda was already pulling the necklace from the box.

"What?"

"I got it from a security deposit box—it belonged to my grandmother." She looped the necklace around me, ignoring my jaw on the ground.

"That's worse!" I exclaimed, eyes wide. "That's *so much* worse, Amanda!"

She just laughed. Amanda was much too similar to her brother. They both seemed entirely too amused by making me uncomfortable.

Stepping back once more, Amanda appraised me. "I hate to admit it, but he does have excellent taste." She admired the necklace.

I felt like it was burning my skin. I was terrified I'd lose it. How could he trust me with a family heirloom like it was nothing!?

"Hmm..." Amanda hummed.

"No," I stated.

"You didn't even hear my idea!" she argued.

"It doesn't matter. Whatever it is, it's a no."

Amanda turned and rummaged around a drawer in her closet for a moment before returning victoriously with something small pinched between her fingers. Upon closer inspection, it appeared to be a vintage hairpin, adorned with mossy gemstones artfully scattered across the length of the pin.

"They're green sapphires," Amanda answered my unspoken question. Taking a front piece of my hair, she twisted it in her fingers and used the pin to secure it at the side of my head. "I won't be argued with; they match your eyes perfectly, and I've had the pin for ages and never worn it. Green isn't quite my shade. I'd much rather you have it."

When she was done, Amanda pushed me toward the full-size mirror mounted to the wall next to the large ornate door, where I got the first real look at myself. I felt the air leave my lungs in an audible *whoosh*.

How was it possible that in a matter of minutes and with three simple items, she had completely transformed me into a different being entirely? I felt like a stranger was staring back at me in my reflection, not the mousey and diminutive history teacher from Montgomery.

Sensing my awe at her work, Amanda smiled behind me. "Chance won't know what hit him."

I met her gaze in the mirror. "And what about your parents?" I asked nervously.

"You'll make a good first impression, but they'll know this is borrowed." She tugged on the dress. "Mom picks out all my gowns." Her tone was conciliatory. "But all that should matter is that you make Chance happy, and I know that you do."

I sighed. "I'm not sure that will be enough for them."

"Why do you say that?" Amanda's brow furrowed.

"Because Chance was never enough for them," I replied as if it was the most obvious thing.

Amanda's shoulders slumped. "I won't defend them, but I think they did the best they could. Some people just aren't cut out for parenthood."

I nodded, my eyes again falling to the floor.

"Do you love him?"

My eyes shot to Amanda's.

I was frozen.

She gave me a soft smile.

Love?

That was a big fucking word. It had already been such a battle to get as far as we had. That was a large enough step that I hadn't even fit *love* into the realm of possibilities. It was far too complicated to bring that into the picture so soon.

"But you'll take care of him?"

I nodded emphatically.

Her smile grew, and she slipped her hand in mine. "That's more than anyone's done for him before."

She opened the door, ushering me outside. Our heels clicked as we strode down the hall, going the opposite direction from the way we'd first come.

"You ready for this?" Amanda asked, just before we turned the corner.

"I have to be—for him."

As we began our slow descent of the grand staircase, all eyes in the room suddenly swinging to us, she squeezed my hand in solidarity and whispered, "I'm glad he found you."

33
COUNTDOWN

Halfway down the stairs, I spotted Chance, looking absolutely debonair in his suit. A lazy grin on his face, he only had eyes for me. And despite the stares I knew I was getting from the curious partygoers, Amanda was right: he was the only thing that mattered. For me, Chance was the only other person in the room.

He made his way through the crowd to meet us at the bottom of the stairs. It was only at the last step that I realized he was flanked by another handsome man, who promptly swept Amanda off her feet, twirling her around, and conveniently drawing the attention from us, allowing Chance and me to blend into the crowd of dancing pairs.

A string quartet played classical versions of pop songs that sounded vaguely familiar, but none that I could remember the lyrics for. Chance splayed his palm at the base of my spine, the heat of him searing through even the thickness of the velvet fabric. He used the other to draw one of my hands up, to trap it between us. I wrapped my free arm around his waist as we gently swayed to the beat, following the movement of those around us.

"You looked stunning before, but seeing you…" Chance drew back from me, making a show of looking at me from head to toe. "You take my breath away." He pulled me into him again.

"Thank you," I told him.

"It was Amanda's idea," he answered.

I glared up at him, not believing for a moment he wasn't at least partially responsible for my makeover.

"She asked what you were wearing, and I told her about how hot you look in your little black cocktail dress. I thought you would have been fine, but she assured me she could find something you'd like better." Chance's eyes twinkled as he smiled down at me. "I hope you like it better."

"I do, but I wasn't thanking you for the dress," I told him. I narrowed my gaze as he met my eyes. "Your heart was in the right place, Chance, but you know I cannot accept it."

His eyes flitted to the necklace at the hollow of my throat.

"Would you really deny my dead grandmother her dying wish?" He feigned hurt.

"Cut it out. Don't put the wishes of the dead on me. I can't go around wearing diamonds this big," I hissed under my breath.

"It's only two carats." He seemed genuinely confused by my refusal.

"Two!?" I sputtered.

He pulled me even closer. "It was rotting in a box at the bank. I wanted you to have it," Chance pleaded.

"I—" He seemed so genuinely hopeful. I wanted to tell him he had to put it back, but the words would not leave my mouth.

"What if I lose it?"

Chance leaned in and kissed my temple. "Don't worry, it's insured. But you won't lose it. It'll be alright."

"Chance..."

"It's okay. I can hang on to it for you. If you change your mind."

I swallowed the lump in my throat and looked away. How had I found myself so far gone that I could no longer refuse him, despite feeling itchy at the thought of the necklace? I hated that I couldn't just accept the gift. All I could think about was how much it was worth.

"I—It's okay," I mumbled. "I love it, I just..."

"I know." Chance craned his head down, resting his cheek against the side of my head. "I didn't quite think that through. My grandma died when me and Amanda were really young, but she left all her jewelry to Amanda, mostly to piss off my relatives, I think. From what I could tell, she was a very feisty woman and never let anyone tell her what to do. I think there are old articles about her in *Page Six*. She caused several scandals my aunts and uncles still bring up from time to time.

"After Thanksgiving, I found myself thinking of you, as I so often do, alone in my bedroom." Chance laughed darkly. "It occurred to me that she would have really loved you. And I think she would have thought we made a wonderful pair. So I asked Amanda if she wouldn't mind giving me the simple and modest necklace, for you."

We continued to sway to the music. I still felt many eyes on us, but Chance and I had somehow created our own little bubble that was only minutely penetrated by the sound of the string instruments.

Upon hearing his story, I decided it would not only be impolite to return the necklace, but rather impossible, given the thoughtfulness of the gesture, and the meaning behind the gift, as well as the involvement of his sister, who I already knew I adored.

"But if you don't want it—"

"I want it." I stared up at him petulantly.

Chance smirked down at me. "Oh little muse, if you had any idea what you do to me when you look at me like that."

My cheeks heated at the implication.

Chance glanced over my shoulder, his body going rigid.

I turned in his arms to see what had caused such a tense reaction, only to recognize a tall older gentleman, who was the spitting image of Chance, although his features were distinctly colder, striding toward us: his father.

Immediately my protective instincts took over. That man had traumatized Chance and had made him feel less than for his entire life. I didn't want Chance to have to interact with him if he didn't want to, and clearly his body language was screaming that he wanted to be anywhere other than under the gaze of his father.

On top of all that, I wasn't sure how I'd react to meeting the infamous Thomas Roberts. I wasn't sure I'd be able to hold back from telling him what I really thought of him and his treatment of Chance growing up. What if I blurted out that he didn't deserve to have such a kind, thoughtful and creative son, who shaped his own destiny, in spite of what he had been put through? I didn't trust that I could play the polite, obedient, and charming girlfriend.

Girlfriend!?

"Let's get some air," I said quickly.

Chance's body was tense as he escorted me off the dance floor, through the areas where servers were working, and toward the back of the house, where he ushered me into a glass atrium, lit with dozens of strings of fairy lights. It was like something out of a movie.

The buzz of the crowd and the faint music of the string instruments could just barely be heard through the open door. Chance's father, it seemed, had not followed us.

Although the atrium was enclosed, the lack of insulation still left the room much more frigid in the winter cold. Without having to say a word, Chance removed his suit coat and slung it around my shoulders, before leading me to a comfortable padded bench facing toward the darkness of the backyard. Even with the string lights, I could just make out the constellations dotting the skies on such a clear night.

"Do you think the dress is okay?" I asked, still needing reassurance that I hadn't made a fool out of myself and him as a result.

Chance held my hand as I tucked the dress under me to sit without tripping over the skit.

His eyes widened at the question. "Okay?" He chuckled.

I followed him as he sat down next to me, wrapping an arm around me to pull me into his side. "I didn't think it was possible that I'd like looking at you in anything more than those skin-tight cat burglar pants of yours, but you've outdone yourself tonight."

"You mean Amanda outdid herself," I corrected him.

He narrowed his gaze at me. "No. This dress is all you. Black and dark, but soft to the touch." Chance ran his fingertip along the hem resting just below my collarbone. "My muse, always wanting to hide in the darkness and pretending you aren't as tenderhearted as I know you to be."

Chance leaned his cheek against the top of my head. "I think that's why I was so drawn to photographing you. It was in the moments when you thought nobody was watching that I began to see the real you. The one you don't just hide from everyone else, but the one you try to hide from yourself. The Violet who cares about others. The Violet who cares what others think of her—hating that their opinions matter so much, but not sure how to get out of your head to move beyond the need to please them."

I flinched at his unfortunately accurate assessment.

"I know, sweetheart." He ran his hand up and down my shoulder. "I won't tell anyone."

It'll be our secret.

How was it that despite what both of us had been through in our lives, how our parents had failed us so spectacularly, that we had still managed to find each other? It occurred to me then that it was rather miraculous, in fact. And we'd both fought, in our own ways, for each other.

It felt inevitable in some way, that our paths were always meant to cross, that Chance and I were always meant to form a connection, that we needed each other to fill in the gaps that the other lacked. There was a certainty...a finality in how far we had come.

"There's something I've been meaning to mention to you," Chance said cautiously.

My heart fluttered. If he was about to say what I thought he was about to say, I wasn't sure I was ready—I didn't know if I could say it back.

I glanced up at him. His blue-grey eyes met mine, in turmoil. Inside, the party guests began to chant, counting down together, toward the new year.

Ten.

"I think we need to stop looking into Daniel's disappearance."

Nine.

My mouth popped open. That wasn't what I had been expecting. "What?" I squawked.

Eight.

"I just think it's time."

Seven.

"Bullshit." I reeled back. Where on earth was this coming from? "Tell me why. The real reason," I demanded, glaring at him.

Six.

We had set off on this path, and I intended to follow through. We had made such progress, and sure we were in a bit of a lull, but things could turn around at any moment. It wasn't like Chance to quit like this—not so suddenly. There had to be a reason.

Five.

Chance sighed, his shoulders falling, knowing he had no other option but to tell me the truth. "Daniel is gone," he said mournfully. "But you are still here. I can't lose you too."

Four.

"Why would you lose me?" I shook my head.

Three.

"What the detective said—he's right. We're in over our heads. If anything happened to you, I could never forgive myself." He paused. "I would *never* get over you. You are the only thing that matters to me."

Two.

I swallowed the lump in my throat. His declarations sat low and heavy in my body, transforming me into a new version of myself. A Violet that didn't want to be in the dark, if it meant I wasn't by his side, even if he stood in the light.

I tried to push the doubt away—I shouldn't have needed confirmation again, but I needed it, one last time. "Why would you put me over him? He's your family." I turned toward the open doorway, gesturing to the house. "What could I possibly have to offer someone like you?"

One.

"Everything," Chance growled, growing angry. "You are *everything*, Violet. Everything I've ever wanted and everything I'll ever need. You call me on my shit, you back me up, even when you don't want or mean to. You don't judge me for who I want to be, and you like me for exactly who I am today." He took both my hands in his, his eyes boring into mine, so I would finally get the point, as he ground out, "You. Are. Everything."

Happy New Year!

I pulled at him, my lips crashing into his, desperate and needy to feel his skin against mine.

He had it so wrong.

He was everything.

Nobody had ever sacrificed for me the way Chance had. The fact that he was willing to abandon the search for Daniel made my chest ache with longing for him. I hadn't realized a gesture of that magnitude would be what was required to bring down the remnants of the walls around my heart.

Chance had put me first, when nobody had ever done that before. I was besotted with him.

I couldn't get close enough to him on that stupid, narrow bench. Understanding my need, Chance pulled back. "Upstairs?" he panted.

I could only nod, my lips already swollen from his bruising kiss.

34

NO GOING BACK

With my hand in his, he led me through the hallways, avoiding partygoers and staff alike, up a different back staircase, spilling out into the same wide hallway where Amanda had taken me earlier in the evening. But Chance led me to a different door.

Beyond the threshold, the room was distinctly masculine, awash in variations of greys across each surface, the obvious elegant touches of his mother still visible. While Chance made haste to lock the door behind us, it struck me that the room was completely void of anything that seemed particular to Chance. Sadly, not a single photograph was in sight. Not one with him in it, or one he had taken.

"Rather depressing, I know." He came up behind me, coiling his arms around my waist and pulling my back to his clearly aroused front.

"Where is your photography?" I craned my head to look at him.

Chance chuckled. "It wasn't considered a worthwhile pursuit, and my work was therefore ineligible from sullying the walls."

But Amanda had things hung up that were personal to her and didn't match the fancy veneer of the mansion. Maybe Chance didn't want the reminder of how his life was being decided for him.

"How long is this going to take to get off?" Chance impatiently tugged at the strings of the corseted back of the dress, having already undone the bow Amanda had so neatly tied.

"Just loosen them; you don't have to unlace the entire thing," I advised him over my shoulder.

I could feel the heat rolling off him as he tugged and pulled at the strings. I held the bodice against my front and stopped him when I sensed it was loose enough. Stepping out of my heels and kicking them to the side, I turned around to face Chance.

Slowly, I stepped backward toward the bed. "There's no chance your parents are going to barge in here?" I questioned, just to be sure.

Chance shook his head slowly, his eyes hooded, focused on me and my retreating form. "You better not be running from me now." He began to stalk toward me, unbuttoning his shirt as he progressed.

"Nowhere to go." I shrugged, letting the dress drop to the floor, exposing me completely, save for my black lace panties and the gifted necklace.

Chance froze, his gaze instantly heated, and his jaw slackened while he slowly drank me in from head to toe.

"I think I'm done running," I told him, hopping up on the bed, already feeling entirely aroused just from the way Chance's eyes had darkened.

"Don't say things you don't mean, little muse," he threatened, as he continued undressing, slowly making his way to the bed.

"I wouldn't dare," I teased.

"Take your panties off. I want to see all of you," Chance commanded.

"You do it," I challenged, feeling a wave of desire course through me. It had never felt like this before. I'd never been with anyone that had driven me so crazy with lust.

Chance shook his head, glowering at me as he crawled up onto the bed, making his way to me as I leaned against the headboard, waiting for him. I no longer thought I was imagining the fact that he was clearly turned on when I sassed him. I'd have to file that away for later.

He dragged the fabric down my legs at a torturous pace, delighting when he could see I was growing impatient and already wet for him. Chance kissed and sucked his way back up to my mouth, paying special attention to my breasts, laving the flat of his tongue against my nipples.

Leaning on his elbow to make sure his weight did not shift on top of me, he used his leg to force mine open while he explored my mouth, occasionally taking breaks to nip and suck on other sensitive areas nearby. His hand reached down my body, finding my center. I bucked against him when he found my clit.

When I tried to reach to pull his boxers down, he practically pulled away. "You first. I'll wait my turn," he said into my mouth, continuing his stroking a moment later.

Any noise I made incensed him. His eyes would dart to mine, his trademark smirk would deepen, and I could only writhe on the precipice of both pleasure and agony.

All previous sexual partners paled in comparison to how Chance made my body sing for him. Just like he could read me like a book, he always seemed to know exactly what I needed, often before even I did. Sometimes that worked to my advantage; other times, when he was feeling naughty, it worked against me.

"Fuck, Chance..." I cursed, arching into his hand, begging for more friction. "Please let me come," I keened.

"I do love it when you say 'please.'" He smiled against my lips, finally providing enough pressure in just the right area for me to combust. He continued to stroke me, but at a much slower pace and with a lighter touch, so I could ride out my orgasm as long as possible.

I groaned in pleasure as he moved over me, slipping his boxers off, his erect cock bobbing against his stomach. Using one hand to stroke himself, he made use of the other to gently position my legs around him, right where he wanted them.

Lowering himself to close the distance between us, he used his hands to massage my breasts while continuing to kiss me so deeply I was barely able to keep track of anything other than the embers of my previous arousal slowly catching once more.

His hips began to move, his cock slipping through my arousal. It was easily the most sensual thing I'd ever been a part of. I thought I might combust if he didn't fuck me already. I'd never been so needy for a man before.

I groaned in frustration, moving my hips to try to chase the feeling of him against me, when all I wanted was him inside me.

Chance paused, making eye contact with me as he asked, "You're sure? There's no going back after."

But I didn't need a warning. I was already too far gone. I had been, I realized, for quite some time.

"I never want to go back," I stated resolutely, before reaching down to grab his cock and place it at my entrance.

Chance jumped at my sudden movement, but a moment later, he could only laugh at my impudence. "So desperate to be filled?" He placed his hand on top of mine, silently requesting I let go.

Reluctantly, I released him, but before I could start arguing with him, he began to slide into me. A low moan sounded from me as I arched into the pressure, my body stretching deliciously around him.

"Geez, Vi..." He groaned into my neck, once fully seated. "I just need a minute. You're so fucking tight, and it's been a while, and I just..."

I skimmed my fingers down the corded muscles of his arms, giving him the time he needed to adjust to the feeling. Then, so slowly I almost didn't realize it at first, he began to move. Alternating between searing kisses and burying his face into my neck, sucking at my pulse point, his hips pumped in and out of me in the most glorious rhythm, working me up into a steady fury.

I hadn't had sex that was so intimate before. Chance was right there with me, every second. His eyes would flit to mine, checking in every so often as he rolled his hips against me. Groans of encouragement would result in deeper kisses and faster momentum. Panting and teetering on the edge, Chance pulled away from my mouth.

Afraid he would separate himself from me, I locked my legs around his hips, pulling him deeper than he'd been before.

Chance moaned into my neck, but his hips moved faster then. He was chasing his release, the same as me. I'd mentioned being on birth control before, and we'd both tested negative for anything. I'd told him that when we were ready, I was okay if he came inside me. Now that he was inside me, I wanted it more than I thought I would. I hadn't let anyone before.

"Please, Chance..." I whispered.

His eyes met mine, dark and focused, as he reached a hand between us and used his fingers to take me over the edge again. I cried out, overwhelmed with the sensation of how it felt to come with him inside. The way my body convulsed around his cock dragged Chance into his own climax. He continued to pump into me until we were both completely sated and spent.

"You're mine now, Violet," Chance grumbled, pulling my naked body into his. "You can't take it back."

"I won't," I whispered, drifting off quickly. "But you were mine first," I argued.

Chance could only laugh in agreement.

35

AN AWKWARD INTRODUCTION

Waking up tangled in Chance's arms the next morning almost made having to get up so early bearable. A round of sleepy morning sex couldn't be helped, once Chance stirred.

Lying next to him, I found it hard to believe how far we'd come. It had taken me months to get past my initial feelings of embarrassment at how we'd met and to push through a lot of my own shit to feel worthy of Chance and to be open to the idea that maybe I was deserving of being wanted by someone like him.

"Turn your brain off, muse..." Chance trailed soft, wet kisses along my collarbone. "Or would you prefer I do it for you?" The gleam in his eyes turned devilish.

I pushed him away, with laughter on my tongue. Not to be outmaneuvered, he trapped me in his arms quickly enough. "You wanna get out of here before we run into my parents?" he asked while nipping at my ear.

"Yes." I nodded emphatically.

We'd been lucky to avoid them the night before and had only narrowly missed Thomas Roberts, who had thankfully allowed our retreat to the atrium.

"Promise me you won't get all weird again when we're back at Montgomery." Chance hadn't yet released me.

"I promise." I turned in his arms to face him. "But we need to be careful. I know everyone says that rule isn't enforced, but I can't risk it."

"I'll do anything and everything to keep this"—he gestured between us— "a secret. You don't have to worry." He kissed the tip of my nose for good measure.

"Ugh," Chance groaned, "you brought the pants?"

I had just exited the bathroom after having changed into the spare clothes he had told me to bring. I thought he might enjoy seeing me wear the cat burglar leggings again. I couldn't have been more pleased at his reaction.

He lifted me into his arms. I instinctively wrapped my legs around his hips, before he dumped me on the bed. "We're never getting out of here." Chance leaned down to kiss me thoroughly, still occupying the space between my legs.

"I want coffee," I moaned through his kisses.

"In a minute."

"You're messing up my makeup."

"You're not wearing any."

"Chance!" I shoved him away. My lips were still bruised from the night before, and I was sore all over. Not that I would have really minded having him again, but I was itching to get out of the house. I felt as though I was an intruder. I'd never been in a house as nice as his, and even breathing made me worried I might break something worth more than my life.

Chance reached a hand out to me and helped me off the bed. He glanced over at his desk. I had neatly laid Amanda's dress over the back of the chair. "You're not going to take it with you?"

"It doesn't belong to me."

"I'm sure she said you could have it," Chance argued. "She usually only wears nice dresses once and then donates them. You *should* have it." He walked over and ran his fingers over the bodice.

I shook my head. Even though Amanda had offered it to me, it didn't feel right to take it. It would just sit in my closet, gathering dust and making me sad I'd never have an occasion to wear it again. "I don't make it a habit of attending operas or galas," I told Chance.

"Let's bring it with us," he pleaded, taking the dress from the chair. "You can wear it to my first photography exhibition," Chance suggested.

My eyes met his. I could tell he'd been thinking about what I had said on Christmas when I'd returned the negatives to him. The thought of being able to see his work on display made my chest tight. I wanted that so badly for him. And the dress would look nice at an event like that... "Okay."

Chance beamed at me, picking up the backpack, where we had both stowed our spare clothes, and slinging it over his shoulder before folding the dress over his forearm.

"Ready?" He reached for me with his free hand after opening the door to the hallway, and likely shattering the little bubble we'd been inhabiting since first stepping foot in there. Chance led me down the hallway, protectively winding his unencumbered arm around my waist, tucking me into his side.

"Coffee?" I whispered, looking up at him through my lashes.

"Should be some in the kitchen."

But that wasn't the only thing we found when we arrived.

"Violet!" Amanda barreled toward me. "Everyone was talking about how gorgeous you looked in the dress last night!"

I could feel my cheeks heat as her words sunk in. Chance dropped the backpack and the dress onto a chair and went about fixing us coffee.

"Did they?" I gave a nervous laugh.

"From the moment you arrived, they were whispering about the mystery woman that had taken Chance off the market." Amanda gossiped. "The prevailing theory is that you're a French heiress!"

"What?" I spluttered.

"I *know*! I told you, you looked so sophisticated in that dress. It was made for you." Amanda glanced at the heap of black velvet. "I'm happy it found a new home. It looked miles better on you."

I choked a laugh at the thought that I would look better in anything than Amanda.

"Stop pestering her," Chance snapped at his sister.

"Pestering who?"

The room fell silent, for Cynthia Roberts had just crossed the threshold. And I was wearing ten-dollar Walmart leggings and a ratty old university hoodie. I heard myself gulp when her blue-grey eyes met mine.

"Well, hello," she purred, eyeing me from head to toe. I remembered Chance telling me how his mother loved children's charities, and how he had gone to her to help him convince his father to aid Daniel. I knew I shouldn't be frightened of her, but she was his mother...how could I not be?

"It's nice to meet you, Mrs. Roberts." I robotically extended my hand to shake hers. "I'm Violet."

"Don't be silly." Her once composed face broke into a soft smile that was identical to Chance's. "Call me Cindy." She wrapped her arms around me in a tight hug.

It was the hug only a mother could give. I felt a pang of guilt, thinking about my own mom. I couldn't remember the last time I had hugged her.

Pulling back, she examined me again. "I'm surprised you don't have a French accent, if rumors are to be believed." Cindy laughed, making her way over to Chance, where she ruffled his hair and kissed him on the cheek. "You might have introduced me to your friend before last night, dear," she chided.

"Girlfriend," Chance corrected her.

My face grew impossibly redder. We hadn't had that discussion. But I supposed labels weren't really important. What mattered was that we were together and that there was no one else. That was enough.

Cindy raised a brow, leaning against the kitchen counter, not willing to let Chance get away with such a bold statement so easily.

"The first girl you bring home in—what? Seven years? And that's all I get?"

"You wouldn't have gotten anything if Violet didn't need coffee." He smiled at his mother, clearly trying to egg her on.

Folding her arms across her chest, she glanced over his shoulder at me. "I hope he's nicer to you than he is with me."

Amanda giggled at the counter, enjoying the entertainment.

"Well, now you've met her." Chance moved around his mom to grab two travel mugs from the cabinet.

"Chance..." His mother's tone softened as she reached out to place a hand on his shoulder. "Is there any way you'd consider calling your father?"

Chance froze. "Why?" His tone was clipped.

Cindy gave Chance a long, hard look. "You're his son. He misses you."

Chance laughed while he poured coffee into the mugs, shaking his head, as if her response was meant to have been a joke. "He doesn't miss me. He misses having a son on a leash to parade around at parties for his business associates. He misses having a male heir he can tell them will be taking over operations when he's gone, so they'll invest more money with him. He misses not having to lie on the golf course when someone asks if his family is well, because he has no idea where I am, let alone how I'm doing."

Cindy bristled. She appeared to have known she'd be in for a fight, but I don't think that she'd expected him to clap back so sharply. "Well, think about it," she suggested warily.

"Think about it?" Chance paused, tipping his chin down to look his mother in the eyes. "Does he think about Daniel? Does he think about anyone but himself?"

"That's enough." She pursed her lips, seemingly aware of how this must look to the interloper who was standing in their kitchen with hair that looked like she'd been freshly fucked and sneakers that had a hole in the sole.

Chance poured a fair amount of sugar into one of the mugs before tightening the lids securely. "We have to get on the road." He handed me the mugs, and I made a note of which one held my precious sweetener.

Grabbing the backpack and dress in one hand, he placed the other at the small of my back, pressing firmly to steer me outside into the cold.

"It was nice to meet you!" I called out. "Thank you for the dress, Amanda!"

Chance was quiet for quite a while, fuming as he drove.

Occasionally I would hand him his coffee, so he didn't have to look down to reach between the console for it. It wasn't until we were almost halfway back to Montgomery that he finally broke his silence.

"I'm sorry."

I turned to face him. I didn't know what he was apologizing for.

"I know you're upset."

"No, I'm not."

Chance's brow furrowed. "You aren't?"

"Why would I be upset?" I asked, bewildered.

"Because I didn't properly introduce you to my parents. Because I called you my girlfriend without asking. Because I didn't think my mother would be down there, so I didn't prep you beforehand. Because I picked a fight with her," he rambled, stopping only when I began to laugh.

When the furrow in his brow deepened, it only made me laugh harder.

"I'm confused," he finally said, taking a moment to stare at me.

"I'm not mad at you." I grabbed his hand across the console, so he could feel the words. "I don't care about any of that. Sure, I probably would have dressed a little differently, but I'm just glad it wasn't your dad who strolled through. I'm not strong enough to pull you off him."

Chance visibly relaxed.

"Did you think I was angry the whole ride?" I used my thumb to rub circles in his palm. "I was only giving you time to think and calm down."

"So we're okay?"

"We're better than okay." I smiled at him, glad to have cleared up the misunderstanding so easily.

"But you still seem stressed. If it's not me, then what?"

I sighed. I hadn't realized it was so obvious. No wonder he was worried. "Just school," I began. "I'm nervous about the kids coming back, and not being able to be like this with you all the time. How am I supposed to hide the way you make me feel?"

A lazy grin spread along Chance's face. "How do I make you feel?"

Oh, so we're playing that game?

"C'mon." I gave him a playful nudge.

"Won't you tell me anyway?"

I rolled my eyes, feeling a blush creep up my neck to my cheeks. "Just butterflies. All the time. And really fucking good orgasms. But don't go getting an out-of-control ego about it." I pointed my finger at him.

"Too late." He shook his head, still grinning. "Never letting that go. Ever."

I grumbled.

"I'm glad you came with me. I think it's the only Roberts party I've ever been to that I actually enjoyed."

"You only liked it because of what happened after the party." I snorted a laugh.

Chance merely shrugged in agreement before moving on. "At school, maybe we can come up with a signal, so we know we're okay, even though we need to keep things private?" he offered, maneuvering back to the original topic at hand.

"What kind of signal?"

"Maybe you can touch your necklace?" He glanced over at it. "Which I know you won't be taking off, because my feelings would be terribly, terribly, terribly hurt. And my grandmother would probably be spinning in her grave—"

"Alright, alright," I gave in. Because he *was* right. I had planned on taking it off and squirreling it away the second we got back, too terrified to go around wearing something so valuable. "But you don't have a necklace."

"I'll just put my hand over my heart. That's where you live now anyway." He gave me a cheesy wink, and I shoved him again.

"I'm going to have to lie to Jolene," I said soberly. "I'm still worried about putting her in danger. If we were to be discovered, I wouldn't want her to get in trouble for knowing. If I keep it from her, I'll feel like an asshole, but at least she'll have plausible deniability."

"I know it doesn't feel right." He squeezed my hand. "She'd do the same thing, to keep you safe."

"I just—this big thing has happened, and I—I wish I could share it with her. I wish I could tell her how my world has completely shifted on its axis." I slumped against the seat. "I know you're right. But it hurts all the same."

"It won't always be this way. We're dropping the Daniel stuff, so you won't have to worry about hiding that from her. And maybe we can talk to the headmaster and see if we can get an exception to be together or something."

That wasn't a terrible idea. If it had been long enough for the administration to take it seriously, and they could see that it was a real relationship, maybe they would be willing to be more open-minded.

"I'd like that." I smiled up at Chance.

36

THE MISSING DRIVE

For two whole weeks, Chance and I had the campus practically to ourselves. Not that anyone would have known, as we pretty much lived in my bed. The proverbial glass having been shattered, we couldn't quite manage to keep our hands off each other.

On the last evening before school was meant to resume, Chance had insisted on one last sleepover, despite my protests and the fact that I was feeling woefully behind on my prep work for the new semester. But he was terribly difficult to argue with, so I hadn't.

Chance's face was between my legs and had been for a while. If I didn't know any better, I would have thought he enjoyed edging me just as much as he enjoyed getting me off.

He had also taken it as a personal challenge to elicit noises from me while we were messing around or having sex, as I had told him that we needed to be more careful and quiet once the rest of the faculty returned.

"But the noises you make are my favorite," he'd complained. "I'll just try harder then."

"You're taking too long on purpose," I groaned when he decreased his tongue's pressure on my clit, just as my legs began to shake, a sure sign that I was on the crest of another release.

"I wouldn't dream of it." He pressed a wet kiss to the inside of my thigh.

Suddenly, there was a knock on my door. We both froze.

Chance looked up at me, wordlessly asking if I was expecting anyone to drop by unannounced. Seeing as it was eleven forty-two on a Sunday night, I most definitely was not.

"Get back to your room," I hissed, careening off the bed, searching for my shirt amongst the pile of discarded clothing on the floor.

"Just a minute!" I called out to whoever was waiting in the hallway.

"I wasn't finished," he argued in hushed tones as he danced back into his pants.

"Neither was I." I glared at him, the space between my legs wet and throbbing.

Once adequately dressed, and hoping that Chance was already on his way down the fire escape, I opened the door a crack.

"Isabelle?" I asked, puzzled as to why Claire DeLongpre's roommate and best friend was at my door.

"Hey, Miss Price." She shuffled nervously from foot to foot, clearly freezing in her pajamas, with a peacoat thrown over the top that appeared to offer her little warmth. Her dark hair was parted in the middle with two neat French braids on either side.

It was clear from her skittish behavior, she was well aware of how much trouble she could get into for breaking the dorm curfew, as well as being seen in the faculty housing across campus. "Umm, do you know where Mr. Harper is?" Her teeth practically chattered as she spoke. Whatever she needed, she didn't trust me with it.

"Why do you need Mr. Harper?" I asked softly, taking a step into the hall.

"I—" She glanced back down the hall, perhaps worried that another faculty member would suddenly appear, then pulled a bulky padded envelope from the inside of her coat. "I was rearranging the furniture in my room—they never reassigned someone after Claire—" She paused, her eyes glassy. "She liked it a certain way, but I was just trying something different."

Isabelle glanced down at the bubble mailer. "This was taped under her bed." She still kept the envelope clutched tightly in her hand.

"Why do you need to give it to Mr. Harper?" I looked down at the envelope and back up to her.

"It has his name on it." She flipped the parcel, revealing what I assumed was Daniel's boyish scrawl across the front that said, *If found, return to Chance Harper.* "He didn't answer his door." She looked over to Chance's apartment door, feet away from mine.

"I can give it to Mr. Harper if you—"

"No." She shook her head emphatically. "I'd like to give it to him myself. Do you know when he'll be back?"

"He's probably just asleep," I told her. "Let's try his door again." I closed my door behind me and moved down to his, knocking sharply three times. "Mr. Harper, it's Miss Price."

I heard some shuffling behind the door, and a moment later, he answered. The clever bastard had thrown on pajamas and messed up his hair, his room dark behind him, making it appear as though he had just woken up. What a show he was putting on. I was delighted at the thought of giving him shit for it later.

"What's going on?" he asked groggily, eyeing Isabelle curiously peeking out from behind me.

I rolled my eyes at his theatrics—now he was overdoing it. I repeated to Chance what Isabelle had told me, and stepped aside to let her speak to him.

"I know about Daniel..." she said in a low voice, glancing at me sideways, still unsure if I could be trusted.

"What did Claire tell you?" Chance asked, his voice lacking the faux-tired tone he'd sported only a moment prior. "It's okay." He motioned to me, indicating Isabelle could speak freely.

"I was the only one who knew she was dating Daniel. She didn't think her parents would approve, and she was worried if they caught wind of it, they'd pull her out of Montgomery. I guess they were hoping they could use her as some sort of bargaining chip to form an alliance with one of her dad's business partners, as if she was nothing but a means to an end." Isabelle twisted one of her braids between her fingers.

"Claire told me you were trying to help her find out what happened to him. After what happened to her..." Isabelle paused to compose herself, her voice growing weak, still grieving the loss of her friend. "I recognized his handwriting. He used to give me notes in Chem to give to her in Math." She reluctantly handed the envelope to Chance.

"Thank you, Isabelle." Chance smiled kindly at her. "If this is what I think it is, you have no idea how much this will help."

The girl paused in the doorway, clearly wanting to ask something else. Chance and I waited patiently to give her the opportunity.

She looked up, meeting Chance's eyes. "Someone pushed her, didn't they?"

Chance's shoulders fell. "I'm not sure," he replied truthfully.

"But you think it's possible?" It felt like Isabelle needed some sort of confirmation.

"Yes." Chance winced.

"And if they did—could it have been because of that?" She nodded at the envelope.

"I don't know, Isabelle." Chance's voice was calming.

She raised her chin in defiance and said plainly, "If you find out who hurt them, make sure they pay for it."

His eyebrow raised, clearly impressed by her tenacity.

"I will."

"Did you tell anyone about what you found? Or that you were coming here?" I asked.

Isabelle shook her head. "I knew it was important," she replied, referring to the drive. "I'm not sure how I'll get back without getting caught, but I was worried if I gave it to you at school, someone would see me."

"You did the right thing," Chance reassured her. "I need you to promise this will stay a secret between the three of us."

She nodded, sensing the gravity of the situation.

"I'll walk you back," I offered. "I can distract the dorm monitor while you slip back in." It would be far less conspicuous for me to strike up a conversation with whoever was on duty, than it would be for Chance. And if something went wrong, at least it would be a female teacher bringing Isabelle back, not a man.

After grabbing my coat, Isabelle and I made quick work of sneaking her back in. The dorm monitor was dead asleep at her post. I waved goodbye to her and quickly made my way back to the carriage house in the frigid cold, thinking of how sad Isabelle had looked. I knew it wasn't quite the same, but I had grieved for my lost friendship with Jenny, and even though she was still alive, it had been traumatic nonetheless.

I had a lot of empathy for what Isabelle was going through. Losing Claire was going to affect her for the rest of her life, and if she had been, as we suspected, pushed down the stairs, the circumstances that had led to her death were that much more tragic.

I let out a small yelp when the door to the carriage house swung out before I could grab the handle. Chance was inside, and it appeared as though he'd kept an eye on me while I'd made the quick journey across campus.

"You scared me." I placed my hand over my heart.

"I'm sorry. I was worried about you." He grabbed my freezing hand, warming it with his as we ascended the three staircases back to our rooms on the fourth floor. For once, ignoring the ceremony of sneaking around, Chance simply followed me back into my room after he stopped by his, to grab the envelope and his laptop.

"It's *the* drive. I already looked," he confessed the moment the door closed. "But it's not the orange one Bryce mentioned. It's the secret backup he kept."

"Do you think it will help?" I shrugged out of my coat, hanging it on the rack by the door, and making my way to stoke the fire to warm up more.

"I think it could crack this whole thing wide open."

37
HIDDEN FILES

I think perhaps there was a brief moment where Chance and I considered not going through the drive. He had told me he wanted to be done with it, that he was worried for both of our safety. But that was before we were handed what could likely be a smoking gun.

And so, before he could ask, before it became something we needed to discuss, I assured him that I was all in. We'd be as careful as possible, but we had to at least try. And I was glad that I did, because the shit that was on that drive was toe-curling, motive-making, and I was certain it would lead us to some sort of conclusion.

Like accessing Daniel's laptop, due to the sheer amount of data, and because of the lack of time, due to our full-time jobs as teachers, it took us weeks to comb through and make some sort of sense of everything we found.

Daniel had been working on multiple stories, and while he seemed to try to keep his files organized, I thought he might have only done so in batches, so all the most recent files were dumped in one area, which made things significantly more difficult for us to wade through.

"Can we go through what we've found so far?" I asked, tucked under Chance's arm, with my laptop warming my legs. "It's been a minute since we've regrouped."

"We're only sorting through his work on the two relevant cases, right?" Chance confirmed.

Because, like us, Daniel had uncovered the original missing students, and had also suspected them going missing was somehow linked to the headmaster, who he had been investigating for grooming underage girls at Montgomery for decades.

"Yes," I confirmed.

"We don't have as much on the missing girls. From the file dates, it looks like he only started working on that a few months before he went missing himself," Chance surmised.

"Do you think he could have gotten access to the same file we found in the headmaster's office?" I asked.

"If his source works or worked at the school, which is what I'd guess, then I think it's definitely possible."

"Is there anything about the missing girls that Daniel had that we haven't discovered ourselves?"

"Just his notes, which give a little bit of insight into his personal thoughts about everything. He was clearly disgusted by Winston, but I think he may have been a little too earnest to pin the case from the nineties on him without enough proof. It would certainly make the more recent story that much more splashy."

I thought it noble of Chance to try and be as objective as possible when it came to the case. I had come to the same conclusion about Daniel seeming a little too overzealous about the potential connection in his notes, without much else to go on, other than Winston's pattern of abuse.

"But the grooming is a different story. He had written testimonials from eleven women, including his source," I noted.

"But all of those testimonials are anonymous. Do you think he could have gotten traction without at least one name? Would any career journalist or major publication have wanted to pick up Daniel's reporting without at least one name?"

"I don't know." I frowned. "What do you make of the source?" Daniel had recorded written transcripts of all their meetings. It was possible he had audio files, but we couldn't locate them on the drive. However, the witness statements came via email, so assuming they were real, they would likely be of more interest to the authorities.

"I can see why he felt wary of her. He seemed intimidated by her. And she did bring him all the other witnesses, who seem to have panned out. He was a teenager, so I could see him feeling out of his depth," Chance commented.

"She got more aggressive as he continued to work with him. It felt like she was anxious for the article to be published, and she didn't understand why it was taking him so long to write it, but from my point of view, he was trying to cover his bases, doing his due diligence, like any reputable reporter should. You can't go accusing old white men in high-ranking positions of such heinous crimes without proper evidence."

"From reading the transcripts, do you think she could have hurt him?"

"No." I shook my head. "She reads as skittish. She was probably putting a great deal on the line coming forward and was trying to prepare herself for the fallout. There was enough specific information about how Winston groomed her that he probably would know who she was. I'd be scared too. She never threatened Daniel. Did you read it differently?"

"I agree with you. She was agitated, but without knowing who she is, I don't think I could say whether she was capable of hurting him or not. But according to the transcripts alone, I suppose it never gets that serious."

"And the other statements, you think they're real?" I asked. Since they had come through emails, I supposed that anyone could have made new accounts and sent their stories in to Daniel. But that would have been an awful lot of trouble to go through to bring down Winston, and would have quickly unraveled the entire case, if they had been fake.

"They read like different people for sure." Chance seemed certain. "I look out for this kind of thing when I'm correcting papers by students to make sure they aren't paying someone to write their homework for them. These are all quite distinctive voices, with specific choices in wording. Some have more limited vocabularies than others, and differences in punctuation, style, flow, and phrasing." He leaned back into the couch. "If someone faked these, they did a damn good job of it. I think they're legitimate."

"Which means Winston is a fucking predator," I spit, unable to hold the disgust from my voice. "We need to figure this out and do something fast, so we can turn this over to the school or authorities or someone who will keep him from being around these girls."

"Do you think he's still pulling this shit?"

"I don't know." I stared at the fire, trying to stop my heart from hurting at the idea of him luring young girls into his web. "The source seemed to think it had stopped, but with men like that, you just never know. Sometimes it's a mental compulsion."

Chance narrowed his gaze at his screen. "Something's not right here."

I peered over his shoulder. "What?"

"It says the total files on the drive here." He pointed to the screen. "But if I highlight all the folders and look at the properties, there are over a hundred more files listed in total."

"That's...weird." I hadn't seen something like that before.

Chance yawned and closed his laptop. "I can't see straight. I've been staring at this thing too long."

I closed mine in agreement. "Yours or mine?"

"Yours." He gave me a peck on the lips before standing, his hand extended to help me up.

"Hidden files!" I shouted, scrambling up the trapdoor stairs into the lounge, knowing that Chance was already up there waiting for me, as I had volunteered to grab dinner from the kitchen that evening.

"What?" Chance came around the study table to take the food containers from me.

"I ran into Milton on my way to the dining hall—I asked him about the file number discrepancy, and he said they were probably hidden files."

The food forgotten, I loomed behind Chance as he did an internet search, quickly finding directions for how to locate the files. A few clicks later, and boom, we were staring at the interview audio files and some photos.

"The transcripts," I breathed.

Chance hit play on one of them, and Daniel's voice could be heard through the laptop speaker.

"When did the grooming start?" Daniel asked. His voice sounded even younger than I remembered, but he was confident. My heart broke hearing him.

"It's hard to tell." The source's voice was distinctly female, but it sounded as though she was using some sort of voice filter to modify it so it would be unrecognizable. "I went to Montgomery for four years, and he was always very nice to me, but it wasn't until I was a sophomore that he started asking me to help him in his office, and then maybe a couple months after that was when he started touching me."

I had to pause the audio, not wanting to hear more. I'd already read the transcript. I knew what was coming next. My stomach was churning. Hearing her recount it made it feel so much more real, so much more disturbing, and so much more heart-wrenching.

"The source is definitely female, but her voice sounded strange, kind of like auto-tuned. They must have had these interviews over the phone or internet," I suspected. "What's that?" I pointed to a single video file at the bottom of the folder. Curiously, it was dated right before Daniel went missing.

Chance double-clicked on the video and it began to play immediately. The footage was so dark, it was hard to see anything. Chance stopped the video and tried to brighten his screen, but it didn't help much.

"I'll turn off the other lights," I told him, already on my way around the room. The fire couldn't be helped; the lounge would be freezing without it.

"I think it'll work!" Chance shouted across the room when I flipped the last switch off.

The video was still dark and very grainy, so fine details couldn't be made out, but it appeared the video had been taken inside. Frankly, the room looked like something out of a horror movie. Dust and cobwebs coated much of the expansive space, the windows were covered by tattered, thick, heavy drapes, and everything else was in ruin.

I noticed a kitchen area in one corner, with cabinetry and vintage appliances, tarnished and dusty with age. Perhaps he had discovered an old residence on campus, hidden in the woods?

But there was something oddly familiar about the room, though it could have been anywhere on campus. There were plenty of un-explored and decrepit nooks and crannies around, long abandoned by past inhabitants. My lounge was a perfect example of how easily things were abandoned and quickly forgotten.

Because of the date of the video file, which was a few weeks before Daniel's disappearance, I assumed it had to have been on campus, but I supposed we couldn't be sure who had filmed the video.

"Oh shit!" Daniel's voice came out of the video suddenly, startling both Chance and me. Then the camera started shaking violently, as if he was desperately scrambling to get as far from whatever had spooked him as possible. In the last few seconds of the video, the camera was a blur, jostling around as he ran, the sound of his panting breath the only audio, and then the video stopped abruptly.

Before Daniel shouted, there had only been sounds of muffled movement and Daniel's soft breathing. Both of us were trying to catch our own breaths from the accidental jump scare.

Something was bothering me about the video. "Can you rewind, frame by frame?"

"I think so." Chance tried pressing the arrow key, and sure enough, it worked.

"I want to see if he got on camera whatever scared him."

Leaning forward to get a better look, Chance clicked back through the video at my instruction. There was a single frame, while the camera was swinging from one side of the room to the other, the split second before Daniel's frantic escape, that was clear enough for us to see what had frightened him.

"No way..." Chance breathed.

Partially hidden under a dusty tarp was what looked like the mummified skeletons of two girls, their hair still framing their skulls.

Daniel had discovered Faith and Hope Marshall.

38

THE OTHER SIDE

It was exactly one week later when I realized where Daniel had discovered the bodies.

I had fallen asleep on Chance in the lounge. We'd been debating all week whether or not we should turn over the drive to the police. It had all of Daniel's evidence against the headmaster on it, and if that didn't make them take his disappearance more seriously, I didn't know what else would.

The problem was that both Chance and I were worried about being implicated in Daniel's case, as we'd been trying to go around solving it ourselves and perhaps committing some crimes, like breaking and entering, in the process, which we didn't think the police would take too kindly to.

There was also a high probability that our relationship would be exposed as a result, and depending on the outcome of whatever investigation or investigations, plural, they needed to conduct, and how much traction they gained in the media, there was no way the administration wouldn't come down hard on us—if not for the relationship, certainly all of our amateur sleuthing.

We both agreed that if we could find the place where the bodies were located, we could tip off the police, maybe even anonymously, and watch from the sidelines as things unfolded. We even talked about mailing the hard drive to the police if we failed to make any more progress on our own.

Winston needed to be punished for what he'd done. I was reasonably sure he wasn't still hurting girls, but I couldn't be one hundred percent sure. It wasn't worth the risk for the lifetime of trauma he could cause even a single one.

But that evening, dozing in Chance's lap after reviewing the video for what seemed like the millionth time, I dreamt I was in the room. Everything was static around me, as if I was in a single frame of the video, rather than the room itself.

There was no sound. There was no movement. And even though it was just a dream, it gave me the perfect opportunity to examine all the little details that had been so difficult to discern in the grainy, dim video.

And it was then that I noticed the wallpaper and the wainscoting. Eerily familiar because I'd seen them before. I'd spent hours gazing at them, in the cozy light, from the couch in the lounge.

Awaking with a start, I frightened Chance, who had himself dozed off.

"What!? Are you okay?" he stuttered.

"It's the other side!" I jumped up from the couch a bit too quickly, needing to steady myself on the armrest to wait for the dizziness to subside. "They're on the other side of the lounge!" I pointed toward the bookshelves.

"The wallpaper—wainscoting—" I babbled. "We couldn't tell they were bay windows because of the curtains."

"What?" Chance was reasonably confused.

"How do we get over there?" I pointed at the bookcases again.

Chance shook his head. "I don't know. You said you can't find the original staircase."

"C'mon." I grabbed his hand and pulled him toward the trapdoor ladder in my bathroom.

"Where are we going?"

"We're breaking into the room across the hall from my apartment." The first year I had been alone on the fourth floor. I'd chosen my room because it had the best view and the best light out of the four rooms on the fourth floor.

I wasn't sure what made Chance choose his, or if perhaps it had been assigned, but I knew nobody had occupied either of the rooms on the opposite side of our floor, though I'd been told they had been renovated at the same time as all the others and were ready for occupancy.

"Violet, it's got a deadbolt," he argued from behind me as I marched across the hall. "We're going to need a crowbar or something, unless you happen to be skilled at lock picking."

"Fuck," I growled, staring at the door. He was right. I reached down to jiggle the doorknob, only to find that the door wasn't locked at all.

Chance's wide eyes met mine.

"Wipe the handle off with your sweater." He pointed to the door-knob. "We can't leave evidence. If there are bodies up there—" He looked up at the ceiling. "Stay outside. I'll go up to look," he decided.

"Like hell," I snapped.

"Violet—"

"I'm not letting you go up there alone. So fuck off with the machismo!" I half shouted. For all we knew, the killer was squatting up there. There was no way I was going to let him march off into danger without any backup.

Chance huffed, but didn't argue. "No prints." Chance pulled his sleeves over his hands.

"No prints," I confirmed, doing the same.

Slowly and cautiously, he entered the room first, with me right behind. He flipped the light switch on inside the door, bathing the room in a bright glow from the one overhead fixture in the middle of the room.

The room had the same layout as Chance's apartment, which was a mirror image of my own. Although the room was empty, making the space feel quite cavernous, it had an odd sour smell that seemed to permeate the walls.

"Hello?" Chance called out, grabbing my hand to comfort me, or himself, or maybe both.

We stayed quiet for a moment; the only noise we could hear was that of our breath. Everything in the room was still and silent. Satisfied that we were alone, we made our way to the bathroom, and sure enough, just like in my room, there was a trapdoor in the ceiling. Except the cord had been cut, and all that remained was a frayed nub.

"Wait here," I told Chance before marching back over to my apartment, returning a moment later with the fire poker and a chair, handing them both to Chance.

Without needing an explanation, he crawled up on the chair and used the poker to dig into the wood of the trapdoor, in order to carefully pry it open, gently releasing the folded stairs to the ground.

Instantly the sour smell became more noticeable. Taking out his cell phone, Chance turned on the flashlight before he began his ascent with me right on his heels. He took only a few steps up the ladder, and the moment he got a look into the attic space, he practically fell backwards.

"Are you okay?" I stumbled back, helping him stay on his feet. "What did you see? What's up there?"

His blue-grey eyes had never been more fearful than when he looked over to me and said one word: "The bodies."

39

RANSACKED

The weeks following our discovery of the bodies were sheer chaos.

Chance had been the one to call the police and explained that he had smelled something off and had gone looking for the cause of the odor, discovering the unlocked door, the trapdoor to the attic space, and subsequently, the bodies of Daniel and the girls.

They'd all been bludgeoned to death, and the bloodstains present suggested that it had likely happened up there. While the girls' remains were all but mummified after being hidden up there for almost thirty years, I had wondered why I hadn't smelled Daniel's body, and was too scared to bring it up to Chance, who had enough to deal with between all the police interviews and his grief.

However, one afternoon I heard some forensics investigators talking in the hallway outside my room while they were on a break, and they said that there was an ancient chest freezer in the kitchen area I'd seen in the video, that was miraculously still running after all these years.

"They just don't make 'em like that anymore," one of them had commented.

Whoever killed Daniel had placed his body inside the freezer, which was why nothing had seemed amiss throughout the summer. The fact that he had been so close, the whole time, was heartbreaking.

The police had located and opened up the elusive stairwell I'd long suspected had to be around. The entrance had been plastered over at the top of the stairs and looked like any other wall. I never would have found it. But in order to remove the chest freezer and a lot of other evidence, they'd gotten permission from the school to open it up.

Chance had to come clean about his connection to Daniel to the police, and even admitted that he'd pursued the teaching position at Montgomery to poke around, but had no luck. What he hadn't told the police was that I'd been there with him.

I hated having to lie, but the police didn't have any reason to believe I hadn't been grading papers alone in my room. And if we had told them we had been investigating together, it only would have had the wrong people asking the right questions, leading to reprimand, at best, or being let go, at worst.

Chance and I hadn't needed to worry about figuring out how to get Daniel's external hard drive, with all of his evidence and reporting work, to the police. The bright orange drive Bryce had mentioned had been found in the room, inside his backpack, completely unharmed. I guessed that whoever had hurt him, had no idea what it was, or that he had been carrying it on him.

I'd had to keep my distance from Chance for over a week while the police worked in the cordoned-off areas. Chance and I were allowed to stay in our apartments after the police searched them.

I hated that I couldn't be with Chance while he grieved, knowing for certain that Daniel was gone. When he'd told me before that he had felt it in his gut, I'd wanted to argue with him. Oddly, I was glad that I hadn't. He seemed to be taking things in stride. Perhaps feeling for months that Daniel was already gone had allowed him time to process and sit with his grief, so receiving confirmation was merely the conclusion he'd been awaiting.

The school was in disarray as they pulled anyone and everyone who had known Daniel in for interviews. Any faculty or staff that had been working at Montgomery at the time of the Marshall disappearances were interviewed for hours, asking what they remembered of the event.

Students were being unenrolled from the school left and right. What parent in their right mind wouldn't be terrified their child might not be the next victim of someone who was still on the loose?

Jolene had been inundated with calls from the press asking for comments from the headmaster and interviews with the faculty and staff. She couldn't disconnect the phone, but it wouldn't stop ringing, poor thing.

But perhaps the worst part was that the police had ransacked my lounge.

They'd torn apart everything, pulling books off shelves and leaving them in haphazard stacks, turning the gaming tables on their sides to search underneath. If the baby grand hadn't been so heavy,

I suspected they might have done the same to it. There was a layer of fingerprint dust over every surface that the police just left, without cleaning up.

Jolene had even mentioned she had heard rumblings that the administration was considering building a public entrance to the lounge for the other faculty in the carriage house to use. The news sent me into an absolute spiral, although she couldn't find anything official that had been filed, or any review meetings scheduled.

After they'd cleared out the bodies and were satisfied with their search of the lounge, they had cleared me to use the space again, but the first night I'd gone back up there, even with Chance, who'd come to check in, not wanting to stay too long and garner any suspicion, I'd taken one look around the mess and started to cry.

Chance held me while I tried to come to terms with the idea that my secret and sacred place—our place—had been turned upside down by strangers. It was all too much. Daniel was gone, and there was nothing either of us could do about it.

The invasion was just one more thing on a long list that left me feeling violated and frustrated. I knew they were doing their jobs, although if they had done a better job of it the first time, maybe this wouldn't have happened. Still I didn't think it was necessary for them to trash the place. It would take me ages to reorganize the shelves.

"I'll help you. It'll be okay," Chance comforted me.

But I wasn't comforted. I was forced to sleep alone in my bed, unable to be with Chance. He'd stolen my heart, and I didn't feel right without it or him by my side. But until the police left for good and some of the commotion died down, it wouldn't be safe for us to sleep in the same room, like we had been since winter break.

I hadn't realized how quickly I'd gotten used to having Chance around all the time. I felt more content when I was near him. Things with Chance were just easy. I felt silly for having fought my feelings for so long.

We supported each other in a way that I didn't think I'd ever felt with a partner. The fact that we were both teachers also made me feel understood like never before. Maybe I should have been more open to making friends with the other faculty sooner, and I wouldn't have felt so alone.

When we felt safe enough to start sharing a bed again, I found myself dreading the mornings more than I ever had before I'd met him. And that was saying a lot, because I had never been a morning person and had feared the rising sun more than most. All I wanted was to feel safe and warm in his arms.

Instead we had to go about our lives at school as if we didn't know one another more than colleagues. But every time we passed in the hall or glanced at each other across the crowded dining hall, or in the great room, watching over the students, on cue, I would clasp my necklace in my hand, and he would place his over his heart, making eye contact, if it wasn't conspicuous, but often averting our gazes from each other entirely. It was torture. Until we could be reunited in the comfort and quiet of my room.

"Are you okay?" Chance asked me softly late one night, over a month after our grisly discovery, both of us on the verge of sleep.

"As good as I can be." I sighed, snuggling into his side. "You don't have to worry about me."

"I'll always worry about the girl that I love," he murmured, falling into slumber a moment later, his even breaths giving him away.

All I could do was stare up at him in the dark. It had been a slip of the tongue, but I'd heard him. He'd said it. My heart hammered in my chest, and I felt tears welling in my eyes.

But it was the last moment of peace I'd have for a while.

Because the next morning, Headmaster Winston was found dead.

40

THE CONFESSION

Chance and I were awoken by shrill police sirens.

Haphazardly pulling on clothes, I stopped Chance. "We can't go out there together."

His shoulders fell, but he knew I was right.

"I'll go ask what happened. Just give it a few minutes before you come down," I instructed.

"Nobody would believe that you'd wake up earlier than me, let alone be able to get ready faster," he argued half-heartedly.

I rolled my eyes before slamming the apartment door behind me.

Down on the front lawn, students, faculty, and staff were starting to wander out and congregate, wondering what could have possibly happened now. Some of the staff were trying to corral the students back into the dorms, but were less than successful with the worried and curious teenagers.

I clocked Jolene's car in the staff lot. I knew if I could find her, she'd know what was going on.

I'd felt increasingly guilty for pulling away from Jolene, but the more things had progressed with Chance, and certainly when the shit had hit the fan with the police, it had been easier to avoid her, rather than lie to her. There was a huge part of my life that I couldn't share with her, and just because it was to keep her safe didn't make me feel that much better about it.

It didn't take me long to find Jolene. Her despairing wails coming from the entrance hall, carried through the air like a portent of death.

The police officers surrounding her, attempting to calm her, almost stopped me, until her face lifted and her gaze met mine. "Violet!" she cried, pushing past them to run to me. Her face was red and blotchy from crying. Her sky-blue sweater sported fluffy clouds, with sun rays poking out of one side and a rainbow sprouting from the other. It couldn't have been more contradictory to her mood.

I soothed her hair as she cried on my shoulder, looking around to the police officers for some kind of clue as to what had happened, but they were useless.

"He's dead," she moaned, clutching onto me tighter.

"Who's dead?" I asked softly, not wanting to upset her further, but wanting to understand.

"The headmaster." She sobbed. "He—he shot himself."

My eyes widened, searching the police officers for confirmation. I found only pursed lips and averted gazes, which told me enough.

"I'm so sorry, Jolene," I soothed her back and let her continue to cry.

"I found him in his office. There was—it was everywhere."

"It's okay. Everything's going to be okay."

I soothed her like that for a while, until the police felt comfortable interrupting to ask her for a statement.

"I'll wait for you," I told her, when she was hesitant to leave. "I'll find some tissues."

She nodded, sniffling, and followed the officers outside.

While searching for tissues, I couldn't help but overhear a couple of the officers talking. "Can't believe the old asshole took the easy way out after what he did," one said.

"At least he had the decency to leave a suicide note confessing to all of it. Too bad he didn't explain how he killed the girls they found last month, but at least the families will get closure."

A suicide note?

Something about that didn't feel quite right to me. Winston was so prideful, I wouldn't have thought he would end his life, but if he felt the police had enough on him to make an arrest, I suppose he'd be capable of anything. After the grooming allegations, which were already causing quite the stir, though nothing had been substantiated, maybe the thought of a trial and prison sentence felt inevitable.

The suicide note, on the other hand...I wasn't so sure about.

If Winston really had killed himself, he would have known that it would have pointed to his guilt, but I couldn't see him having the kindness to offer the closure the officers spoke of to the girls he had abused, to Chance, or the Marshall family. If anything, I could see him denying things until the very end and deciding to take matters into his own hands, versus letting a court of strangers decide his fate.

It wasn't until much later that I was able to find Chance and tell him about everything. He'd discovered the reason for the police presence on his own, but he'd known better than to seek me out.

"He confessed?" Chance's brow furrowed as he paced around my room. We'd been in the lounge less and less; it hadn't provided the same sense of safety and privacy that it had once offered.

"I know. I was surprised too."

"The Winston I know wouldn't have confessed. He would have refuted everything. But I also never thought he'd take such drastic action to end things." Chance leaned against the window, peering out into the darkness of the courtyard.

"Jolene told me the police have been by to talk to him a lot in the last week. If he thought they were close to arresting him—I mean, what he did to all those girls—Daniel had all the evidence on his drive. The police had been served everything on a silver platter. They would only need to substantiate it." I thought aloud. "I could see him deciding to end things instead of living the rest of his life in prison, labeled a predator."

Chance nodded. "You're right. But the confession still feels wrong. He was a prick. He wouldn't have cared about any of those girls, or Daniel. We never could figure out a motive or opportunity for the Marshalls. And nothing about Claire...Maybe we were wrong and it really was an accident..."

"So let's say he didn't leave the note or kill himself, or both. What happened then? He's been our primary suspect this whole time, even though we couldn't figure out how he'd managed to kill the Marshall girls while he was on a plane." We were clearly still missing pieces. Or maybe we had all the information we needed, but we couldn't see clearly.

"If there's somebody else involved, they've been completely off our radar." Chance sat down on the edge of the bed. "Can we make a list of all the faculty and staff that have been here for everything?"

"It'll be a long list." I sighed.

Two weeks later and we still hadn't gotten anywhere.

Although the Portland Press Herald had somehow gotten ahold of Winston's confession and published it.

All of it's true. The girls, the Marshall twins, and the young reporter. I have no other recourse. I'm so sorry to those I have hurt. This world will be better off without me in it. I'm sorry, Janice. You didn't deserve any of this. None of them did.

The words felt hollow, rather than vindicating. The fact that he hadn't even mentioned Daniel by name got under Chance's skin. He hadn't named a single person other than his wife. After reading the note, I felt more confident than ever that it wasn't right.

He wasn't sorry. I didn't believe him.

Chance had taken leave to attend Daniel's funeral, after the body was finally returned to his family. I'd wanted to go, to be there with him, knowing he'd have to face his father, who would likely mourn in front of the media, though Chance would know it was a ruse.

But it was because of the media that I couldn't go. The events at Montgomery had become national news since Winston's death. Dozens of true crime podcasts and documentaries were no doubt being written as I lay in my bed alone, awaiting Chance's return.

The one saving grace was that there was only a week until spring break. Before everything had spiraled, I would have begged Chance to stay at Montgomery with me, holed up in the lounge and in bed. But with all the pressure of external forces bearing down on us, the idea of going somewhere, just the two of us, felt like a much-needed reprieve.

So when Amanda had called to offer us her penthouse apartment in New York for the week, as she would be conveniently vacationing in Europe at the same time, I'd put aside my initial reaction to decline any extravagance.

"Think of it as a gift," she had stated her case before I could dissent. "And if you can't accept it, then it's a gift for my brother, and you're simply his plus-one."

Hard to argue with that. So I hadn't.

While Chance was away, I found myself spending more time with Jolene. It felt too lonely in my room without him.

Jolene had been more reserved since finding the headmaster. I couldn't blame her. It would traumatize anyone. I think she was also having a hard time coming to terms with everything that was emerging about the headmaster. She hadn't exactly liked him, but she had worked for him for so long, it would have been hard not to have some sort of feelings or connection to him.

Over lunch one day, Jolene seemed ready to talk about everything that had happened, and I was glad to be the shoulder that she could lean on.

"I didn't want to see it for a long time." Jolene picked at her food. "But I think maybe I knew something was wrong. Of course I'd heard rumors, and when he was younger, he was good-looking and charismatic.

"He liked having student aides when I first started, but they never did much around here. He hadn't asked for one for a while though." Her gaze was clouded, focused over my shoulder, as if recalling a distant memory. "But now all these little things make sense. Now I see him for who he was and what he was doing.

"When the police started coming by more often, I knew something was up, and he did too. Lots of frantic phone calls to all of his buddies to see if someone could pull strings to get him out of it. But it was too big, it was over their heads, the papers had already latched on. I guess he only saw one way out." She paused and looked at me, observing me for a moment as she prepared to say what came next. "Does it make me a bad person if I'm glad that he's gone?"

I shook my head. "No. It doesn't."

We both ate in silence for a while.

There was a moment, before the headmaster had died, that I wondered if Jolene had perhaps been Daniel's source. She had the means and the connections to have gotten him in touch with past students.

But talking to her about what had happened, I felt she was being honest about not knowing. And Jolene had always worn her heart on her sleeve. I liked to think I would have known if something was going on with her. Sure, everyone had their secrets, but Jolene was such an open book. I no longer thought it a possibility.

"I'm still sorry you had to find him like that."

She smiled up at me, the sequin flowers on her sweater twinkling with her movement, reflecting the overhead lighting.

Unable to help myself I said, "I'm still confused about how he was connected to the bodies they found in the carriage house."

"I figured they were also his victims." Jolene shrugged. "They probably threatened to expose him and he thought it would be worth the risk to shut them up. Just like Daniel."

I swallowed the knot in my throat. I wanted to mention that he had been out of the country when the girls had gone missing, but I wasn't supposed to know that, as it had come from the police file we'd stolen from the headmaster's office.

"How has Headmistress Jones been treating you?" I switched topics. The former deputy headmistress, Marilyn Jones, had easily slid into position as the interim lead for the school. In an effort to assure parents and donors, she had begun to crack down hard on any infractions and was tightening up the ranks across the board, looking for any areas where Winston had been lax.

Jones had always struck me as a practical leader. If she could stop the enrollment from hemorrhaging, I was sure she'd be offered the position permanently. I thought maybe with someone like her in leadership, we'd start to see positive changes around Montgomery. At the very least, a little bit more gender diversity, or diversity in general, and less tolerance for the boy's club mentality that had tainted Montgomery for its entire existence.

There was a lot of work to do, but she didn't strike me as someone who would be afraid of work. On the contrary, she seemed like someone who would embrace it, and usher Montgomery into the next phase of prosperity.

"She's great." Jolene beamed. "She doesn't make me stay late. I guess it could be a Department of Labor violation, and she doesn't want to take any chances."

"That's good." I smiled.

"I like that she follows the rules," Jolene offered. "She's predictable. I don't have to guess around her. And she's nicer to me than Winston was. She doesn't curse at me, or admonish me in front of people."

"I'm sorry you had to put up with that." I frowned. While I'd often witnessed Winston's poor treatment of Jolene in the time I'd been at Montgomery, she'd always seemed to let it roll right off of her. If I'd known it had bothered her, I would have tried to say or do something about it.

"It's okay. It's over now."

41

WHEN YOU'RE READY

"**C**hance!" I squealed, launching myself at him.

He'd been gone a little less than a week to attend Daniel's funeral, which had been long delayed due to the autopsy, and I'd been going out of my mind. Texting just wasn't the same.

"Hello, muse," he simpered, gathering me into his arms for an epic kiss, kicking the door behind him, to close us off from the outside world. "I missed you," he panted between kisses, coming at me until the backs of my knees hit the bed. I sat down, allowing him to occupy the space between my legs, pulling his face down to meet mine.

"You're wearing too many clothes," I pouted, tugging at his coat, which he quickly shed.

"You're the one wearing too many clothes." He pulled my shirt over my head, exposing my torso. Looming over me, as I lay back onto the bed, my legs dangling off the edge, he was still between them. Annoyingly he still hadn't removed more than his coat. He slowed his pace, kissing me long and hard, while his hand explored my exposed flesh.

"I don't want it slow," I whined as he took a nipple into his mouth; his eyes darted up to mine. "You were gone so long."

Smiling, he released me, stripping faster than I'd ever seen him capable of before, while I wiggled out of my pajama bottoms.

His hands were on me a moment later. "Of course you're already wet for me." Chance groaned, slipping a finger inside me easily. After a couple months, he knew exactly what buttons to push to get me going, and the only thing I loved as much as the noises he made during sex were the dirty words he used while working me up.

"How much did you miss me?" He sucked on the juncture of my neck and shoulder as he used his fingers to stroke me, building my climax bit by bit.

"So much..." I keened.

"Did you think of me when you touched yourself?"

He applied just the right amount of pressure to my clit to force me to arch against his hand.

"Yes!" I cried out, chasing the oncoming release.

"But nothing's as good as when I'm inside? Is it?" He circled my clit, not giving me enough friction to tip over the edge.

I shook my head back and forth. "No—it's never as good..."

I gasped when he pulled his fingers away. "Chance..." I whined.

"Relax," he cooed, and I felt the tip of his cock pressing against my entrance. "I'm giving you what you want."

I released a long and low groan as he slipped inside, wrapping my legs around his hips to pull him in deeper.

Words were forgotten then, as he rocked in and out of me, eventually his fingers returning to finish what they'd started. As requested, Chance moved at a quick and brutal pace. I soaked up every thrust, relishing in the mutual need we had developed for one another.

And when I came, he followed shortly thereafter.

I'd given in to Chance entirely, and had somehow, never felt more free. We worked together seamlessly, and we supported and saw the best in each other. Things that would have caused fights with past partners were easily overlooked. Matters that had been misunderstood were quickly resolved because we wanted things to work and were intent on giving each other the benefit of the doubt.

For so long I had wallowed in the betrayals of the past, and I'd let them define me. But now, I couldn't find it in myself to regret anything that had happened, because it led me to Chance. It had all been worth it to be with him, to feel that we belonged to each other. It surprised me how much the simple idea that one person having my back could uplift me to such great heights.

"Remind me again what our plans are exactly for next week?" I asked Chance, cuddled up next to him, after another round in the shower.

"Plans?" He lifted an eyebrow. "I plan to keep you in bed for seven days straight."

"Awfully ambitious and a tad presumptuous of you," I scoffed.

"If you're challenging me, I think you know you'll lose." He chuckled.

"I've never been to New York. I don't want to stay inside the whole time."

"What do you want to do or see? Make a list, and we'll go." He kissed the top of my head. "Whatever you want, I'll make it happen."

I'd never been able to travel before. I'd often thought about what it would be like, but I'd never really given myself permission to dream about what I would actually do.

"Talk to me." Chance was concerned over my silence, knowing how much I liked to spiral when left to my own devices.

"I've never really traveled before, other than just to move for school or work. I don't think I know how to travel," I admitted, drawing shapes on Chance's chest with my fingertip.

"There's not much to it—don't stress too much." He pulled me in closer to comfort me. "When you think of New York, what comes to mind?"

"Well, all the big stuff, but I don't like crowds, so I don't think I'd really like them in real life. Maybe we could go to a museum?"

"I know the perfect one." He began to comb his fingers through my hair. "What else?"

"Good food?"

"Tons of good food in New York. We'll get you sorted there."

"Something scenic, like Central Park?"

"See, you're not so bad at this." He smiled. "Do you think I could take some photographs of you, while we're there?"

I glanced up at him. He hadn't asked to take any photos of me since I'd discovered the first set. Errantly I thought, if the police found the negatives I'd returned to him while searching his room, nothing had come of it.

"If I'm supposed to be putting together a show, I'll need more work to display."

"You don't have any other photos you've taken before?" It wasn't that I didn't want him to take pictures of me, but there would always be a shy part of me, where self-doubt festered.

"I do, but for my first exhibition, I'd like to share my muse with the world." His face was hesitant. I realized Chance was nervous.

"Can I have final approval?" I bargained.

A giant grin split Chance's face. "Of course."

"Okay," I agreed, burying my face against him to hide the blush on my cheeks. But I was sure Chance already knew... He always knew.

"I love you, Violet," Chance breathed.

I peered up at him.

Had I heard him right?

No, I knew I had.

I wanted to say it back, but the words got caught in my throat. The last two times I'd given them to a partner, everything had gone to shit. I knew it wouldn't be like that with Chance, but I was still paralyzed with fear.

Sensing my panic, Chance smiled sweetly, tucking my hair behind my ear. "Only when you're ready, and not a moment before."

I relaxed in his hold.

Soon, I thought.

But only a few days later, everything came crashing down around me.

42

EXPOSED

"Miss Price?" A student aide from the administrative offices interrupted my last class on Friday afternoon.

"Can I help you?" I replied, slightly irritated that whatever it was couldn't have waited twenty more minutes for class to have been dismissed for break. My stomach flipped as the urgency of the matter sunk in. I hoped everything and everyone was okay. I'd been through enough in the last two months.

"The headmistress needs to see you right away," the timid young boy said.

I sighed, looking at those remaining in class, who hadn't already left early for luxurious vacations on their parents' dimes. Their attention was on me, eagerly awaiting what they knew was coming next. "You're dismissed." I waved a hand in defeat. "But don't get me in trouble for letting you leave early," I warned them.

Nervously, I made my way down to the basement offices. The familiar chill from the eerie space crawled up my spine. The closer I got, the more anxiety began to tear at me, piece by piece.

When I made it far enough down the steps to see the front desk, it only made matters worse. Jolene's face was long and drawn. Even the cheerful, smiling chipmunk on her sweater looked apologetic for whatever was waiting for me.

My heart dropped.

Something was very wrong. Had they found someone else? Was Chance okay? I hadn't told him that I loved him, even though I knew I did. I just hadn't been able to say the stupid words. Would I regret being frozen with the vestigial fear of past relationships, if something had happened to him?

"Jolene?" I asked worriedly, approaching her desk. "What's going on?"

"I—I don't know." She shook her head. But I think she did know. I think she was too afraid to tell me. "The headmistress is expecting you." She turned to look down the hall. When her gaze returned to mine, it was nothing if not ominous.

I wasn't sure why Jones was the one who needed to speak with me. I hoped I wasn't in trouble. I'd never had the misfortune to have crossed her in the past, and had no plans to do so in the future, especially not with her recent crackdown on rules and procedures at Montgomery across the board.

Maybe they'd finally come to their senses and realized that my teaching was subpar and they'd found a replacement for the remainder of the school year that had more tenure, a degree from a more elite university, or a more prestigious background?

Each step I took toward her office was a battle. Every fiber in my being was telling me to bolt in the opposite direction, to race across the lawn and hide in my room until Chance found me.

I was halfway down the hall when I heard Chance shouting. I was both relieved he was okay and concerned with the anger in his tone. What could she have told him that would have caused him to yell at the headmistress like that?

The answer struck me like a lightning bolt, and I had to lean against the wall to stop my knees from buckling.

She knew about us.

This was it.

This was the end.

"You can't be serious," Chance scoffed.

"I assure you, Mr. Harper, I'm dead serious," she hissed.

"Look lady, you obviously have no idea who I am—my name's not Chance Harper. It's Alexander Roberts, as in, the son of esteemed alumnus and billionaire, Thomas Roberts." He chuckled menacingly.

The sound resulted in a cold sweat breaking across my brow. Chance may have been behind that door, but whoever was speaking to Marilyn Jones wasn't the Chance I knew.

"I was bored, so I came here for shits and giggles to get my father off my back. He wanted me to find a purpose in life. And I found one. There's nothing to do around here, so what could be more fun than seducing and bedding unassuming women?"

My head began to spin; the only thing I could hear for a moment was the blood rushing through my ears.

He was lying.

He had to be.

Because if he meant it—if this had all been a joke to him...

"Excuse me!?" The headmistress balked.

"Oh, get over yourself, Marilyn." He snorted.

"You're telling me that you put that young woman's career at stake for another notch on your bedpost?" She was incredulous. "You're disgusting."

"Like I said, I was bored," he replied nonchalantly.

"Get OUT!" she shouted. "You're fired. Effective IMMEDIATE-LY. Get out of my office. Pack your things. I want you off this campus NOW! I don't care who your father is!" She slammed her fist on something hard enough to rattle the doorframe.

Suddenly the door flew open and Chance skulked out, followed by the seething headmistress.

"Chance?" My voice quivered, betraying my dread.

Cold and vacant blue-grey eyes, which matched his father's demeanor so precisely, met mine. "Sorry, Violet." He shrugged impishly.

"Enough, Mr. Harper." The headmistress shoved him past me. "In my office, Miss Price," she barked at me.

"Chance!" I called out after him. I couldn't believe what he'd said to her. He'd told me he loved me. We'd spent nights tangled up in each other. He'd been so open about his family, and I with my upbringing. This couldn't be happening.

He turned slightly, before the headmistress shoved him around the corner and out of my sight. But for a split second, I could have sworn I saw his hand placed over his heart. Had I only seen what I wanted to see, stuck in some sort of delusional state? Or had he really done it to show me I shouldn't believe what I'd heard—the way he'd looked at me, like I was nothing?

"Jolene, have him escorted back to the carriage house right now—he's not to speak with anyone."

I heard a flurry of activity as Jolene went into action to call the security guard on duty to come to the admin offices.

"And you," the headmistress spat. "You should be ashamed of yourself." She was out of my sight, but I was sure she was addressing Chance.

A moment later she appeared at the end of the hallway, stalking angrily toward me. "I told you to get in my office."

Still in a daze, I numbly entered the room, shaking as I sat down on the chair opposite her desk.

It was still warm.

Chance had only been there moments earlier.

Was this some sort of nightmare?

"I'm sure by now you know why I called you in here." She rounded her desk, taking a seat herself.

I nodded slowly, too embarrassed to make eye contact with the intimidating woman.

"Judging by your reaction, I'm guessing he was telling the truth."

I looked up at her, knowing my face was flushed and feeling tears threatening to spill down my cheeks.

"He took advantage of you?" she questioned in a softer tone, perhaps just then realizing how frightened I was.

I nodded again.

If Chance meant what he'd said, he'd done so much more than taken advantage of me...he'd ruined me.

"How—how did you find out?" I whispered, my eyes back on the carpet.

"These arrived today. They were sent to me and a few board members." She slid printed photos across the desk. They had been taken in the lounge. Chance and I were in various states of undress, and thankfully, neither of us were fully exposed in the images, but it was blatantly obvious we were having sex.

I shuddered at the thought of someone being in the room, taking those during our most intimate moments. And it could have been anyone, since the police and everyone else on staff at Montgomery knew about the lounge.

I was mortified.

"I'm sorry," I whispered. "I'm so sorry." I tried to stand to leave, knowing I'd surely be dismissed, and frankly, I thought I might throw up and didn't want to do so in front of her.

"Where are you going?" she snapped.

I looked up at her. "I know I broke the rules. You don't have to fire me. I'll go quietly." I was already ashamed enough. I just needed her to let me leave with the single shred of dignity I had left.

"Sit down," she commanded.

I obeyed.

"He seduced you?"

"I—" It wasn't quite so simple, but I knew what she wanted to hear, and I didn't want her to yell at me or admonish me further. "Yes." My eyes were firmly trained on the floor.

"You like teaching?"

I glanced up at her, nodding more slowly that time. What was she getting at?

"You like teaching...at Montgomery?"

I met her gaze more firmly, nodding a final time.

"You're on probation from now until the end of the following school year. Any indiscretion, no matter how small, and you're gone. Do you understand?"

"Yes," I breathed, in shock that she wasn't going to fire me.

"I sent him to pack his things. You are not to go near the carriage house until he's gone." She held eye contact with me so I understood her stern instructions.

"Okay." I swallowed. I needed to see him. I had to ask him myself if what he'd said was true. If it wasn't, we'd find a way to be together, but if it was...

"You can go."

I rose from the chair once more. "Thank you, Headmistress," I replied softly before staggering down the hallway.

43

LITTLE COMFORT

"Violet! What happened!?" Jolene ran out from behind her desk, almost knocking me over to embrace me.

"He's leaving—but I have to talk to him," I mumbled.

Jolene pulled back from me. "How long were you seeing him?"

"Since Christmas—or Thanksgiving—I'm not sure." I looked over her shoulder to the stairs. I'd still have time to catch him. But if Jones found out...I'd be done at Montgomery.

Jolene guided me over to the couches in the lobby area. "Violet, why didn't you tell me?" she scolded. "I'm your best friend. I could have warned you that he'd do something like this."

I looked up at her with glassy eyes. "I thought I was protecting you. I didn't want you to get in trouble for knowing. I didn't want you to have to lie about it." I shook my head. "It made sense at the time." But what I really meant was that Chance had made sense when he'd persuaded me to keep her in the dark about everything.

"It's my fault." She rubbed my back to calm me. "I should have known something was going on with you. You've been so distant, and I thought you needed your space. Now I know he was keeping you away from me."

"It wasn't like that…"

But maybe it was…

"Violet, if he really cared about you, he wouldn't have isolated you from your friends."

"He didn't—" I paused, trying to sort through the chaos in my mind. Had he isolated me? It didn't feel like that. He'd encouraged me to make friends with the other teachers. He'd changed how I'd thought about things.

"You're better off without him." She smiled encouragingly.

"I need to talk to him." I pulled out my phone to text him.

I had to know.

Either way.

I had to.

"Violet, I heard the headmistress. She'll fire you," Jolene hissed, grabbing the phone from me. "Why are you defending him? I heard some of what he said. It was awful."

"I love him," I choked out, quickly wiping away tears I hadn't meant to shed, and grabbing my phone back from her.

"No, Violet. You just thought you did. He tricked you. You heard him." She grabbed my shoulders, trying to talk sense into me.

But I wasn't ready to hear any of it yet. Not until I knew for certain. I tried to replay the moment he'd turned the corner. Had he really given me our signal?

"I have to go." I got up, shrugging out of Jolene's grip.

"Go where!?" Jolene was frantic. "Violet, I need you. You can't get fired!"

"I just need some air." I couldn't take a deep breath, not in the musty basement. It felt like the decrepit walls were closing in on me.

"I'll go with you," Jolene offered, following me as I made my way to the stairs.

"No." I shook my head, extending my arm, gesturing to her to stop. "I just need to be alone."

"Promise me you won't go back to your room before he leaves. She'll find out. Then you'll be gone too." Her voice began to quaver. She'd lost so much. Her world was falling apart, just as much as mine was.

"I won't." I sighed. As much as I needed to see him, I knew it would be a death sentence. But if I could just get him to call or text me, then I could figure things out.

But luck wasn't on my side that day. I think it had completely turned its back on me. Calling Chance's phone, it didn't even ring, as if it had been turned off. I tried texting, but it didn't show as delivered, which was unusual.

And then I realized that the phones he and I used were issued by the school. Another perk of the job. It seemed his had already been deactivated. I had no way of getting ahold of him after he left campus, but I couldn't approach him.

I wasn't sure how, but I ended up outside the kitchen. Pushing through the doors, I found it blissfully deserted. Hidden behind a countertop, I sunk to the ground and began to cry, too overwhelmed to do anything else.

How could I have been so foolish to have fallen for Chance? If what he'd said was real, if everything wasn't some terrible nightmare...I'd never get over Chance Harper...I'd never get over what he'd done to me.

I replayed all the things he'd told me over the last few months. All the quiet, sweet words of adoration and devotion. He'd told me he'd loved me only a few days earlier.

How could this have happened?

The bell rang, signaling the end of classes for the day. Spring break had officially begun. Twenty minutes ago, I had been oblivious, teaching in my classroom. Twenty minutes was all it had taken for my life to be upended.

I didn't want to move, so I just stayed there, on the floor, for god knows how long. But just when I was considering going back downstairs to find Jolene, somebody else found me.

"Oh, kiddo...I heard what happened." Chef Lenny gingerly sat down next to me.

"News travels that fast?" I felt embarrassment coursing through me. It was silly of me to think everyone would know immediately. I'd be a laughingstock. Maybe I would have been better off if I'd been fired. At least I could have had a fresh start somewhere else.

"It's Montgomery." Lenny sighed.

"Is he gone?" I whispered, terrified of whatever answer I'd get.

"Yeah. Left about an hour ago."

I couldn't believe I'd been sitting alone in the dark for that long.

"He's probably halfway to Portland by now."

The thought of him being so physically far from me sent me into a fresh wave of tears.

Lenny wrapped me up in a tight hug. "It's going to be okay." He spoke softly, making me wish I'd had a grandparent growing up. If they were anything like him, I think I could have used one.

"You didn't hear what he said. It was awful," I sobbed.

Lenny pulled back. "You didn't believe any of it? Did you?" He was surprised.

"I don't know what to believe." I used the back of my hand to wipe my tears away.

"He fell on his sword for you, surely." Lenny was adamant. "I've seen how the two of you speak of one another when the other isn't looking. He can't fake that shit with someone like me."

"I'd never seen him look at me so coldly before...like I was nothing." I swallowed the lump in my throat. "Jolene said he was isolating me from others."

"Don't listen to Jolene." He scoffed, "That girl's a busybody—has been since she was a student here."

"I didn't know she was an alumna..." I sniffed. "How'd she afford it?" I could have sworn she'd said she had gone to high school in Florida, that she'd grown up there. But Lenny had an excellent memory. Why wouldn't Jolene have told me if it was true?

"Scholarship, probably." He shrugged. "Have you talked to Chance? To clear things up?"

I shook my head. "They turned his phone off, and the headmistress forbade me from seeing him before he left. I've already lost him and made a complete fool of myself—I didn't want to get fired on top of it." I brought my palms to my face. I was exhausted. "I can't believe she let me stay..."

Lenny snorted.

"What?"

"She was one of the headmaster's many affairs. A woman scorned...well, you know the rest." He sighed. "She's been in your shoes. That's probably why you're still here. And because you have more allies at Montgomery than you realize."

I choked back a sob. Chance had said the same thing to me once.

"You really think I'm wrong—that he still..." I couldn't even speculate aloud. My heart wouldn't let me go down that path.

"Nobody can fake the way he looks at you." Lenny gave me a poignant stare.

I wanted to believe him, so badly. "I hope you're right."

"C'mon." He grasped the edge of the counter to help himself to his feet, then extended his hand to me. "I'll walk you back to the carriage house."

44

LINE OF SIGHT

I stared at my half-packed suitcase and disheveled bed sheets. Only that morning, I'd made love to Chance in that bed, but it felt like a lifetime away. I couldn't make sense of anything.

Even being in my room, knowing Chance wasn't next door, or up in the lounge, or even nearby on campus, filled me with an aching dread.

How had things gone so wrong?

Without a way to get ahold of Chance, I had no hope of sorting through the mess.

But I had one mission left in me.

Grabbing my phone, I headed for the bathroom. I needed to figure out where those photos had been taken in the lounge.

I stood behind the study table, trying to recall the framing. It had to have been from behind the couch, or the shots would have been much more graphic.

I remembered Chance prattling on about techniques he used to define his style as a photographer. One of the things he had mentioned was the line of sight. Similar to how he'd line up his shots while playing pool, there had to be a direct line of sight connecting the photographer to their view of us on the couch.

Following the imaginary line, I found myself in front of one of the bookshelves along the shared wall between the lounge and the other side of the attic space. Crouching, I tried to see at what point my vision was cut off from view by the gaming tables, and when it was too high to mimic the photos I'd seen in the headmistress's office.

Narrowing the area of search, I stared at the target area, then spun around slowly, trying to look for something I'd missed. I was certain if someone had been up in the lounge, we would have heard or seen them. Yes, we had been distracted, but I had been in Chance's lap, facing directly toward the camera, for heaven's sake.

I turned back toward the bookshelf.

"Could they have shot through the wall?" I asked aloud to nobody in particular.

I walked closer to the shelves. When the police had searched the lounge, they hadn't displaced all the books, just enough of them to aggravate me and necessitate two weekends' worth of reorganization.

Going shelf by shelf in the area of interest, it didn't take long for me to find an odd gap in the books, which I'd never noticed. One book was wedged at an angle in the gap, covering a small hole that had been cut into the drywall and through the bookshelf itself.

"You've got to be fucking kidding me." I reeled back, staring at the gap in disbelief.

The hole was just big enough for a charging cable, which could have been plugged in on the other side. The photos the headmistress had shown me had been grainy, and I wondered if they were from a webcam, or even a small spy cam, that could explain the low resolution images. Whatever had been used to take the photos was long gone, but the evidence of its existence remained.

How long had it been there? How long had someone been spying on us?

A wave of disgust and the thick feeling of being violated coursed through me. I could only hope that photos were the only evidence of our affair. I couldn't handle the thought of a video existing on the internet of Chance and me together like that.

I was a teacher. If it was out there, I knew it was only a matter of time before a student found it. The photos were bad enough. They would, without a doubt, make the rounds within the board. I'd have to worry about that later.

Circling back to the bookcase, I pulled my phone out of my pocket and turned on the flashlight. My heart began to beat out of my chest as I peered through the small hole. I'd only viewed the room on the other side while watching Daniel's video, as Chance had refused to let me see what was up there after his discovery, both to save me the trauma and to make sure I didn't inadvertently leave any evidence.

Why would he have protected you if you had meant nothing to him?

After the police presence left, I didn't dare cross the caution tape that was still up, blocking the door. I was pretty sure the investigation had been closed, but nobody had bothered to come back and take down the tape.

The room was dark, even with my flashlight. I couldn't make out much through such a small hole, even with a bit of dim moonlight filtering through the dirty glass of the windows, as the police hadn't closed the curtains before they'd left.

I pulled back, leaning against the pool table as I ran through what I knew.

After we'd discovered the bodies, it hadn't taken long for the whole school to be made aware not just of the scene, but of the lounge's existence. So it could have been anyone who snuck in and took the photos.

But then I remembered something from the photos. The Christmas tree had still been up. Only Chance and I had taken it down the weekend after school was back in session after winter break, which would have been mid-January. And that was *before* we'd discovered the bodies.

Whoever had taken those photos had known about the lounge *before*. Which meant they had known about the bodies.

"The killer took the photos..." I choked. "But the photos arrived today..." And I hadn't seen any postage on the envelope under the photos on the headmistress's desk.

Looking around the lounge, I felt suddenly exposed. Whoever had killed Daniel, at the very least, was still around, and they could have been watching me at that very moment.

With shaky legs, I bolted down the stairs, barricading the door to the bathroom with my desk, as the wardrobe had been too heavy for me to push by myself.

Huffing with the exertion, I tried to remember who had known about the lounge before the police. But other than Chance and Lenny, the only person I'd told was...

"Jolene..." I whispered.

And then everything began to click into place. Pieces of the puzzle that had always been there suddenly fit together where they hadn't before.

She'd known about the lounge.

She'd known Chance was really Alexander Roberts.

She had lied to me about attending Montgomery, and given her age, she would have attended the school around the time the Marshall twins had gone missing.

I recalled our conversation after the headmaster had died. I'd thought she might have been Daniel's source, and perhaps she had been, but she'd seen and heard everything that had gone on in the admin offices. She'd had access to everything and everyone.

She'd found both Claire and the headmaster.

She could have easily pushed Claire, and deduced she was working with Chance based on what I had told her.

As for the headmaster, she'd been perfecting his handwriting for the better part of twenty years to take care of his correspondence because he was too lazy to do all the paperwork himself. Whether she'd been the one to pull the trigger or not, I was positive she'd forged the note and left it behind to cover up everything else.

I didn't know her motive for the twins or Daniel, but if she'd known about the bodies, she'd had to have been involved. It was all too much when you put it together.

I needed help, and I didn't know who I could trust. A thought occurred to me then. I whipped out my laptop, remembering that Chance had emailed me before, from his personal address.

I let out a cry of relief when I located it, writing a quick reply:

> *I don't care if this was all a joke to you, please come back to Montgomery to pick me up. I think Jolene killed Daniel. I don't know who else I can trust. Help me!*

45

STOLEN LIVES

The campus was deserted.

It seemed everyone had left already, which would make my task much simpler.

I knew it was a risk to leave the relative safety of my room, but what other choice did I have? I could have called a taxi to come pick me up so I wasn't alone, but where would I go? And I had no way of knowing if Chance would see the email I'd sent, let alone actually come to get me.

The sound of the snow crunching beneath my feet echoed across the courtyard, bouncing off the dormant trees of the surrounding woods. The otherwise palpable silence was unnerving, and I felt foolish for not having grabbed my coat, even for the short trek to the main building.

The door lurched open after I scanned my badge to release the lock. I tried to close it as quietly as possible, in case there was someone skulking around. However the old hinges made a high-pitched creaking noise that reverberated down the entire entrance hall.

Only the after-hours lighting was on, illuminating the entrance in a dirty yellow sheen. I took out my cell phone, turning on the flashlight and shining it down the stairs, into the dark maw that awaited me below.

It occurred to me that it had only been a few hours since Chance had left. His path out of the main building for the last time would have crossed where I then stood. I still felt like maybe I was in a dream, or rather, a nightmare.

I shook my head. I couldn't let thoughts of Chance derail me. I needed to keep tabs on my surroundings, listening for signs of anyone approaching. I held my flashlight up, my hand trembling as I descended the stairs, making sure to use my free hand to trail along the stone walls to keep my balance.

The only other time I'd been in the admin offices this late at night had been with Chance. I didn't remember it feeling quite so foreboding with him goofing around next to me. But it didn't matter anymore. He was gone, and I was on this mission on my own.

Gulping as I made it to the bottom of the stairs, I tried not to think about the fact that nobody was around to help me. If something happened to me, down in that awful basement, nobody would hear me scream; nobody would even find my body until people started to return from break in a week.

"Geez, Violet," I scolded myself.

Sneaking down into the admin offices, I wasn't exactly sure what I was looking for, but I knew I was missing a final piece. I was having a hard time reconciling that my docile, cat-loving, sweater-making friend, Jolene, could have done anything so heinous.

Whether it was to find something that would disprove my theory, or a motive so strong that it would finally allow me to accept what

I knew was likely true, I had to keep looking. And the records room was as good of a place to start as any.

What Lenny had said wasn't sitting right with me. He had such conviction that she'd attended Montgomery. He had no reason to lie. But if I could verify his memory with something solid like a yearbook, then I could figure out how to move forward.

The door to the records room opened with an easy click, using Jolene's hidden set of keys. I propped the regular stone against the door to stop it from shutting, praying I wouldn't be locked inside. I decided to keep using my flashlight instead of turning on the overhead lights, too scared to make my presence that much more obvious than it already was.

The girls had gone missing in spring of 1992, so that was the first yearbook I pulled. I knew Jolene was in her forties, so the timeline roughly lined up. I found the headshots of the two girls, side by side in the section for the juniors. I'd seen the photos before, while Chance and I had investigated.

Leaning against a storage rack, I slowly made my way through the other student photos, until I found her.

I stared at the photo in shock. But there she was, on the second-to-last page of sophomores. Jolene Reynolds.

She was a natural brunette, so it took me a minute to reconcile what I was seeing without the bleach-blonde hair I had always associated with her, but despite the addition of a few wrinkles and a bit more makeup than her younger self, she hadn't changed much.

Her hair was still frizzy, just darker, her cheeks still round and ruddy, and she even wore what looked like a hand-knit sweater, although it didn't feature one of her elaborate designs.

Flipping between the pages, studying the photos of the three girls, I noticed something rather peculiar...the three of them bore an uncanny resemblance to one another. They had the same nose and mouth, and the same big eyes, albeit different colors, and the same hair color, but the twins' had pin-straight texture.

Suddenly the lights in the room flipped on, temporarily blinding me.

"You just couldn't leave well enough alone," Jolene said from the door.

I dropped the yearbook and my phone in fright.

"Jolene!" I gave a nervous laugh that I hoped hadn't given me away. "You scared the shit out of me."

Looking at her then, the hard set of her mouth, and her eyes narrowed in on me, I knew it was her. I knew she'd hurt Daniel and I knew she'd hurt those girls. But I still didn't know why. If I could play dumb long enough, perhaps I'd get the chance to find out before I could manage to get away, or before I became her next victim.

"I'm so embarrassed—I was trying to find that photo of Chance from high school," I lied, angling my body so she couldn't see the cover of the yearbook I'd been looking at. "I thought you were going to Florida for spring break, to visit your family."

"I've never been to Florida," she replied flatly.

"Isn't that where your mom—"

"I never knew my mom." She tried to get a look at the yearbook on the floor, but when she couldn't, she reached out to snatch it from me. Her nostrils flared as she read the year. "I thought we were best friends. And for what? Some lying, piece-of-shit rich dick? Are you really that desperate? I never thought you'd turn on me." Jolene glared.

"Turn on you?"

"Quit playing dumb. I'm not as stupid as you and everyone else around here think," she snarled. "I know you figured it out."

Seeing no point in keeping up the charade any longer, I decided to switch tactics. "I don't think you're dumb, Jolene," I said softly. "Whatever happened, I'm sure you had a good reason."

"I did have a good reason," she agreed. "They deserved to die after what they did."

"What did they do, Jolene?" I kept my voice even and calm, despite the panic racing through me.

"They stole my life!" she cried. "They're my half-sisters. Their father got my mother pregnant and just left her. But she didn't want me either, so she dropped me off at a hospital and ran."

"I'm so sorry."

"I don't know how he found out who I was, but one day, I got pulled out of my foster home and enrolled at Montgomery. I didn't know why until good old Chuck let it slip. Faith and Hope knew who I was, and they bullied me relentlessly at school. One day, I'd had enough. I was surprised how easy it was and by how quiet they were when it was done."

I held back a grimace at her almost gleeful recollection of killing her sisters. I'd never heard Jolene call the headmaster by his first name. My stomach roiled at the implication. "You were one of Winston's victims," I guessed.

"He's such a letch...well, he *was* a letch." She smiled, perhaps thinking of his demise.

"Did he really kill himself?"

"Yes, after I convinced him that I'd heard the police would be showing up with a warrant for his arrest and that they had solid evidence that would put him in jail for a long time."

"But you wrote the suicide note."

"I had to. You and your stupid boyfriend wouldn't stop digging. I figured you'd take the win and let it go."

"Did he know you hurt the girls?"

"He helped me cover it up from the very beginning. But I knew all of his secrets too, so I wasn't worried about him telling anyone, until you found my sisters." She smoothed out the sequins on her sweater.

"Why did you hurt Daniel? He was like you. Discarded by his family, just trying to survive. He was going to help you expose the headmaster, wasn't he?"

"He was helping Marilyn expose the headmaster. But if Chuck didn't have any secrets left to hide, then I'd lose my leverage for him to keep mine." She leaned against the doorframe. "And when he found Faith and Hope, I had no choice."

"And Claire?" I dared to ask.

Jolene cocked her head, "Violet, you know you're the one at fault there. It might as well have been you who pushed her. It didn't take me long to realize Chance was the person you were protecting, and I'd been watching Daniel for a while before I got rid of him, so I knew he was dating Claire. So if Chance was talking to her, it wouldn't bode well for me."

"Claire and Daniel were innocent." I shook my head. Who was she? How had this monster been right under my nose the whole time?

"Claire is one less rich brat on this planet, and Daniel was collateral damage. I hadn't expected a long-lost relative to show up and ruin everything, taking you away from me in the process. You should know, I took a lot of pleasure in exposing Chance Harper for the prick that he is to both you and the headmistress."

"He didn't take me away from you," I argued. "I'm right here—I'm still your friend. I'll keep your secrets. We can go back to how things used to be, now that he's gone." It was a long shot, but one of the few remaining cards I had to play.

Jolene uncharacteristically rolled her eyes. "Please," she scoffed. "It's obvious you're still holding a torch for that asshole. I hope he was worth it. I can see now you were never really my friend."

"That's not true!"

"It *IS* true!" she cried. "And you're going to wish you hadn't come back. But at least it will give me the chance to get rid of him for good. I don't think it will be too hard to frame him for your murder."

My eyes widened, and my stomach dropped.

The overhead light glinted off something metallic in her hand...a knife.

"Jolene, you don't have to do this." I put my hands up in front of me, only able to take two steps back before I hit a shelf, stopping me.

I had nowhere to go. She had me trapped.

"I don't think he'd fare too well in prison, do you?" She half-laughed as she paced toward me.

As if on cue, Chance's tall frame appeared in the doorway.

I gasped, surprised by his sudden appearance.

Jolene foolishly turned to see what had startled me, which gave Chance the perfect opportunity to shove Jolene hard, forcing her to stumble backward, deeper into the room, where she fell, tripping over her feet.

With one hand, Chance yanked me out of the room, and with the other, he pushed the door so forcefully it slammed closed, taking the heavy stone door stopper with it, locking the stone and Jolene in the records room.

"You okay?" he panted, hands braced on his knees, his gaze turned up to look at me.

"You came back..." I muttered.

Without another word, Chance pulled me into a crushing hug. "You better not have believed a single word I said down here," he growled. "I told Jones exactly what she wanted to hear. I was trying to save your job." He released me tentatively, looking me up and down. "Of course I fucking came back for you. I love you, Violet."

Tears spilled down my cheeks.

"Muse." He used his fingers to wipe them away. "I gave you the signal. I thought you saw. I thought you understood."

"They disconnected your phone..." I hiccupped through tears. "I wasn't sure."

"I'm sorry." He hugged me again. "I'm so sorry."

Jolene banged against the door, startling both of us. "Let me out!"

"Fuck!" Chance hissed. He let me go for a moment to turn on the lights in the main room. "Oh shit—I forgot." He pulled a different phone from his pocket. "Did you get all of that, Wayne?"

"Squad cars are en route." The voice of Wayne Davies came through the speaker. "Keep me on the line until they arrive, son."

"Yes, sir," Chance replied into the phone before turning to me to explain himself. "When I was packing, I realized that Jolene was the one who took the pictures—she knew everything; she knew about me and about the lounge. I figured she had taken the pictures and sent them to try to discredit me and run me out, or, best-case, both of us. I was scared to tell you, but I suspected she might be Daniel's source—"

"It was Marilyn," I interrupted.

A look of fascination crossed his face.

"I figured it out too. I found where she got the photos in the lounge."

"If I thought she would hurt you, I never would have left." He cupped my face in his palms. "You know that, right?"

I nodded, blinking back more tears.

"I drove straight to the police station, but they called the headmistress to try and verify some of what I was saying, and she told them I was a disgruntled employee and not to listen to anything I said.

"So I called Wayne, and he helped me figure out a plan while he tried to go through back channels to get someone to take me seriously. I parked my car outside the gates and walked through the woods. I saw you go into the building, and I followed, but hung back when Jolene found you first."

"You've been here the whole time?" I slumped against Jolene's desk. The distant sound of sirens helped to slow my hammering heart.

"I was trying to get evidence. Wayne heard everything. When Jolene made her move, so did I."

"I really thought I'd never see you again."

"I'm so sorry." Chance stepped forward, gathering me into his arms again and pressing my face against his chest. The warmth of his body soothed me as much as his embrace. "I fucking love you. I'd do anything for you."

"I love you too." I sniffled.

"I know."

I looked up at Chance, confused.

"You talk in your sleep. You said it weeks ago." He smirked.

EPILOGUE

"**W**hen was the last time you spoke to your mother?"

"Last weekend actually." I folded my hands into my lap, trying to get comfortable on the big couch in my therapist's office.

Dr. Short was a friendly-looking older woman, maybe in her late sixties. Chance had helped me find someone who was covered under the school's health plan, and after everything I'd been through, they had been more than willing to make sure I was able to see someone who could help me process everything, rather than sue them.

"How did that go?"

"Good." I met her gaze. "It's not as awkward as it used to be. I suppose I wish the circumstances were different, but a part of me is glad she has Jake and Jenny and their kids. I was never going to be able to give her what they do, so I'm lucky that she has a support system that can give her what she needs. I still don't feel a strong connection with her, or a desire to have her be a bigger part of my life, but I'm just not as angry."

"Hmm." Dr. Short liked to hum when she found something particularly interesting.

"I find these days I'm less angry in general."

"How's that?"

"Well, being that close to death makes one reevaluate things." I chuckled.

Dr. Short smiled, but she didn't comment.

"I realized after everything calmed down that I had been holding on to so much anger, for some things that had happened decades ago...things that couldn't be changed. And it wasn't serving a purpose for me to internalize all of those emotions." I looked out the window onto the main street of the town closest to Montgomery.

"I think I've needed to let go for a while. I need to move past all the resentment in order to step forward with my future." I paused, processing my thoughts. "I think it was Chance who made me realize how bad things had gotten. Because having a single person in my corner has changed everything. And if I hadn't fought so hard to push past my fear of betrayal and failure, things I was hanging on to from past relationships, I would have lost him. Facing that fear and making the choice to try anyway gave me everything. So I'm committed to doing that more."

"That's quite profound, Violet." Dr. Short smiled gently. "And things are still going well with Chance?"

I nodded, cheeks flushing at the memory of how deeply he'd kissed me in the car when he'd dropped me off for my appointment. I could see his car from the window. Knowing he was nearby made me feel a calmness I found hard to describe.

"We're moving in together," I told her. I wasn't sure why, but I'd been nervous to share the news with her.

She raised a brow, but remained silent, allowing me to continue.

"We could have stayed at Montgomery. Like I told you, the headmistress was willing to make an exception as long as we were discreet on campus. And we will be at school. I'm even helping the headmistress to update the code of conduct to be more gender-inclusive. A part of me will always love my time living on campus, but there were a lot of bad memories too, and it was hard to feel safe in the faculty dorms after everything that happened."

"It sounds like you've given this a lot of thought."

I nodded. "Neither of us took the decision lightly. We'll get a small stipend from the school for living expenses. I was able to refinance my student loans to lower the payment, and I got the courage to talk to my mom about the mortgage, and she agreed she'd be okay if I sent less home. She actually said I didn't have to send anything because she's been working for the last couple years, but I can't help it. It feels like the right thing to do."

"And how are you feeling about the move?"

"Excited." I smiled. "When I lived with Harry, everything belonged to him. I always felt like a visitor, and he never did anything to make me feel welcome. But it's like I'm building a life with Chance. He cares what I think. He puts me first." I paused, blinking back tears that had come out of nowhere. "He loves me."

Dr. Short was unable to hold back her own watery smile.

"Are you taking any steps to feel safe in your new environment?"

"Chance has been doing research for weeks to make sure we have the best security system, and Jolene is behind bars and not going anywhere anytime soon. Plus, I think having a fresh space that we can make our own will make it feel safer too." I leaned back into the couch. "I still have nightmares sometimes, but Chance helps me calm down."

She nodded, seemingly pleased with my response, and made notes on her steno pad. "And when are you moving in?"

"In a few weeks."

"Do you anticipate any challenges or stressors?"

"I think money will be tight for a bit, while we get what we need. I know Chance wants to just pay for everything, but I need to feel like I'm contributing equally, and although he only wants to help, he understands. He respects me and my decisions." I sighed in contentment.

"I'm sure we'll disagree on things, but we practically live together now. I don't know the last time he was in his room for anything other than to grab a change of clothes. I think we're both so motivated to make things work because of the deep connection we have with one another that we don't let little things get in the way." I shrugged.

I felt like perhaps I sounded naive, but having experienced a lot of adversity in past relationships, I could feel the difference with Chance and me every day, with every breath, with every word.

"Unfortunately, that's our time today, Violet." Dr. Short smiled kindly, unfolding her legs.

"I won't be here next week," I reminded her. "I'll be out of town for Chance's photography show."

"That's right." She smiled brightly as she walked me to the door. "Please pass along my congratulations."

"I will." I gave her a small wave. "Thank you."

"Can you help me with the corset?" I glanced over my shoulder at Chance, whose gaze was dangerously dark.

Per his request, I was wearing the dress his sister had given me for New Year's for his debut photography exhibition. Somehow brand-new and brand-name heels had miraculously arrived at our hotel room the day we checked in. Chance and his sister claimed to be innocent, but I knew better.

"I'll help you out of it." He smirked.

"I already gave in to you in the shower."

"But it's my big day."

"You've been using that for the last week." I laughed. "Please," I pouted. "I can't do the laces by myself."

"Fine," he huffed, getting up from the hotel bed. His hands went around my waist, and his chin rested on my shoulder. "We've got time," he purred.

"No, we do not," I replied sternly, but couldn't help but lace my fingers through his, imperceptibly leaning back into him.

"You're going to be the end of me, Violet." He placed a soft kiss behind my ear before pulling away to start tying the strings.

"Are you nervous?" I asked, probably because I definitely was. Sure, he had taken all the photographs, but it was my face that was going to be plastered all over, just like in his stalker darkroom.

"No. You'll be there. That's all I need."

I thought I might melt.

He tugged the strings. "Tell me when they're tight enough."

"One more time."

Following my instructions, he pulled once more, then tied a bow at the base of my spine. "Give me a twirl," he directed, taking my hand in his and lifting it above my head to keep me steady while I gave him a three-hundred-sixty-degree view of the dress.

"Stunning, as usual." He cupped my cheeks, tipping his face down to kiss me sweetly.

"Thank you, Chance." I smiled up at him through my lashes, the words coming out heavy, more than just gratitude for tying the dress in them.

We'd been lucky that the gallery that had agreed to host Chance's show had sent a car for us. I was sure that word had gotten out that Chance was related to the Roberts, likely due to his family being on the guest list, so they'd gone all-out to invite the who's who of the tristate area.

Walking into the gallery was surreal. Seeing so many versions of my face staring back at me was indescribable, albeit slightly unnerving.

Applause broke out amongst the crowd when we made it into the main room. The gallery owner piped up, "Our artist, Chance Harper, and his muse, Violet Price."

I felt my heart flutter in my chest, never having received such a reception before, and never having willingly been the center of attention at such a large gathering.

Chance tightened his grip around my waist, pulling me into his side. "They all recognize beauty when they see it," he whispered into my ear.

I could only blush in response.

While we made the rounds, Chance was so naturally charismatic that he found connections with everyone he spoke to, always checking in to make sure I was comfortable.

About halfway through the exhibition, a slight hush fell over the crowd as the Roberts arrived. Amanda, once again, looked stunning, wearing a chic black jumpsuit that made her look a million miles tall. Cindy and Thomas, arm in arm, looked an elegant coupling as they strode through, in Amanda's wake, while she winked and waved to acquaintances in the crowd.

"You did so good, big brother!" Amanda gave him a tight hug. "And Violet." She stepped back to admire me. "What a muse you are." She waved to someone over my shoulder. "I'll be back. Careful with Mom and Dad."

And not a moment later, Chance's parents came up to greet him.

"It's really something, Chance." His mother smiled, placing a reassuring hand on his arm. "I'll just be a moment, I need to go say hello to Mrs. Weathers." She excused herself, leaving Chance and me with his stone-faced father.

"I'm sorry about Daniel," Thomas said out of the blue.

"You're only saying that because mom told you to," Chance bristled.

"I'm saying it because it's the truth."

An awkward silence cut between them.

But Thomas wasn't ready to walk away. He looked around, at all the people, at the gorgeous photography Chance had created, and then turned his gaze back to Chance.

"I'm impressed."

Chance raised an eyebrow. "Didn't think anyone would turn up?"

"No, son." Thomas looked Chance in the eye. "I'm just impressed."

Chance's lips parted, clearly taken aback by the compliment.

"Do you take commissions?" Chance's mom returned, looping her hand through his elbow on the opposite side from me, unaware of the moment she'd walked into. "I'd love for you to take some photos for the charities I run, sweetheart."

"I'd love to," he agreed, still a bit shell-shocked by his exchange with his father.

"In case I forgot to tell you, I'm so proud of you." I snuggled into Chance's side. The evening had been exhausting, but never too exhausting not to enjoy each other for a little while.

Chance gave me a dreamy smile, still drifting in post-coital satisfaction. "I am nothing without my muse."

"Your father seemed to be proud of you too," I stated, curious of his response.

his response.

Chance's gaze softened into one of contemplation. "Figured hell would have frozen over first, but here we are."

Placing a soft kiss on his chest, I murmured, "Here we are. Putting our demons behind us, and starting anew...together."

"Always."

THANK YOU

Thank you for reading The Other Side!

If you enjoyed the book, it would mean the world to me if you would consider leaving a rating or review on Amazon, Goodreads, or the platform of your choice.

ACKNOWLEDGEMENTS

I wrote the first draft of this book over ten years ago. And it had a lot of firsts for me. It was the book that garnered me my first NaNoWriMo win, it was my first attempt at writing a proper murder mystery, and it was the first time I connected so fiercely to my characters that ten years later, I still thought of them fondly, and knew that Violet and Chance's story needed to find a way into the world.

When I was writing the first version, I had been out in Los Angeles for a couple years, after moving away from everything and everyone I knew in the Midwest. I was struggling, both financially and mentally. I was drowning in student debt, eating ramen noodles or toast for meals, and barely scraping by at a terrible job. Writing was my escape. Violet was a conduit of my experiences and frustration, and Chance was a wish...a hope, I had that men who saw you for who you were, flaws and all, and wanted you anyway, were out there.

Writing the first iteration of this book was cathartic at the time, and revising it a decade later and seeing how far I've come has also been a catharsis of a different type. It has been a reminder to acknowledge my accomplishments, to appreciate the small victories, and to embrace my creativity. It is also a reminder that things will get better. And they have.

I would be remiss not to mention and thank the lovely people that contributed to making this book possible, and allowing me to pursue my lifelong dream to become a published author.

Thank you to my friends, family, and coworkers, whose continued support has been such a blessing. The love you showed when I published my debut blew me away. Of course I knew you'd be there cheering me on, but having so many people express such genuine excitement for me was absolutely magical.

To the wonderful creatives who have contributed their expertise, creativity, and feedback to make The Other Side what it turned into, I am indebted to you.

Heather, LL, Ashley, and Kristin, my first readers and hype squad, I wouldn't have had the courage or motivation to keep pushing through this story without your encouragement and kind words. Reading your feedback gives me the strength to work through the imposter syndrome and self doubt.

Sam and Emarie, my editing team, I'm not sure what I'd do without you granting me permission to use em-dashes, and sending me giddy comments over Jolene's sweaters.

Rachel, you brought this book to life with your gorgeous graphic design on this cover. All the design work you did for this book has made it so much more real. I wouldn't have believed you if you showed me the cover ten years ago and told me it would be mine.

Sarah, Tiffany, and Mason, you've helped me connect with readers through the content you created, and the help you provided in growing my brand and my website, and I am eternally grateful for everything you've done.

Additional thanks are also owed to Karina, my lovely map designer, as well as my Saturday writing group and Monday night yoga crew, who give me consistency and community.

And speaking of community, to the wonderful people I've connected with on Instagram, I firmly believe I never would have published if I hadn't found other indie authors who were open and willing to share their stories and experiences, as well as the kind readers who have supported not just my writing, but also other indie authors. I hope you know how much of a difference you've made in the lives of those who choose to take on self publishing.

Finally, and perhaps most importantly, I would like to thank **you** for reading this book. Authors are nothing without their readers, and it has been a pleasure connecting with others who have resonated with something I've written, no matter how big or small. It means a lot to me.

Thank you for reading The Other Side and joining me on this continued journey of self publishing and self actualization. I can't wait to see you again in the next one!

ABOUT THE AUTHOR

AJ Wynn is a Southern California-based author who works in marketing professionally, but whose true passion lies in writing. Weaving captivating stories with romance, mystery, fantasy, and much more allows AJ to express her creativity and serves as a canvas for her boundless imagination. When not immersed in the world of words, AJ is an avid reader, book dragon, and interior decorating enthusiast. Her favorite cozy days are accompanied by a fresh cup of coffee and her faithful canine sidekick.

Stay up to date with AJ Wynn's latest releases by subscribing to her newsletter at AJWynn.com or following her on social media @AJWynnWrites.